Syd P

The Killing Ground

(A Foxx Files Thriller)

To my love, for believing in me even more than I do myself.

ACKNOWLEDGMENTS

The idea of this book sat tucked away in the recesses of my mind for some time before I actually put it to words. I was nervous about writing and publishing a mystery, as it is so very different from my first books. Finally, after months of thought and deliberation, followed by more months of research, I started to write and at times, scared myself a little bit. But I came out on the other side quite alive and armed with a tale that started out as nothing more than a crazy dream and ended up as more than I could have imagined.

I would like to thank Sarah for giving me the courage to move forward with this story, despite my "twisted" nature and for encouraging me to make this a series. I don't normally do sequels, I couldn't do the characters justice in a subsequent book. But this story just felt right, and I knew that there was much more story to be told than made it into this book.

A special thanks to Krista, for reading and saying, whether it's true or not, that every new book is my best one yet. I wouldn't have started this journey without your support.

To Terry, for believing in me from the start and for being my reading guinea pig and for letting me ask her if this story has already been told.

To Karen, for assuring me that I had made the bad guy just twisted enough to be believable. Your opinion and your friendship mean the world to me.

To Nanc, for allowing me to send her a sneak peak and schooling me on my pronouns, repeated words and not cutting out the most important scenes.

To Penelope, I would love to share a byline with you anytime, grasshopper.

"There will be killing till the score is paid."
--Homer, *The Odyssey*

Prologue

Icy pellets of windblown rain ticked against the awning, whipped around by the swirling November winds. The woman pulled the collar of her thin raincoat up around her face in a futile attempt to block the onslaught of cold wind. She hadn't expected the drop in temperatures this early in the season, and her regular evening walk from the office to the house she shared with her wife no longer held its normal appeal. She cast a desperate look at her phone. *Call ended.* She swore silently. According to the sterile voice on the phone, the wait for a cab was just under ninety minutes. She shoved the phone back into her pocket and cinched the tie of her coat as tightly as she could, but couldn't quite close the gap entirely. She mentally chided herself for the weight gain since last year. Throwing back her shoulders and burrowing her chin into her chest, she took a tentative step into the icy rain. She knew that she could either wait for the cab, or if she hurried, she could be thirty minutes into a hot bubble bath before the cab even hit the spot where she huddled away from the cold.

Normally, she enjoyed watching the storefronts and buildings as she passed them, but tonight her eyes focused on the ground as the lines disappeared beneath the rapid staccato of her clicking heals. The wind whistled around her, and she cursed her decision to wear a skirt today instead of her standard business slacks. *Damn board meeting!*

She tugged her coat up against her neck, unsuccessfully trying to burrow deeper into the flimsy layer of protection, almost convincing herself that she wasn't completely frozen through. She shivered involuntarily, her body's response to winter's first bite, and for an eerie moment, she imagined that it wasn't the cold that chilled her to the bone. She shook the feeling, convinced her own imagination and proclivity for scary movies were playing with her mind. Still she looked around her, even allowing a brief glance behind her, and seeing no one, she smiled at her foolishness.

A quick glance at her surroundings told her she was less than five minutes from home, and she breathed a small sigh of relief. She sped up imperceptibly—the cold biting at her bare skin with unforgiving fierceness. A cold gust whipped around her, and the faint shuffle behind her was lost in the night. She felt cold penetrate her spine, and she held her breath in expectation. She thought to look around her, but once again berated herself for imagining things.

It was at the exact moment, as she expelled a long breath of relief, that she felt an evil chill start deep within in her. She turned around, the fear so real she knew that her mind was not imagining it. She didn't have to see anything to know that the darkness she felt was very real, and if her senses were right, it was extremely close. In her head, she screamed, but her throat failed to respond, and her silence was lost in the night. She stood rooted to the spot, willing her legs to run, but fear froze her. She watched helplessly as the darkness approached her, evil shining in his black eyes. She finally picked her feet up and managed only a small stumble, her body pitching backwards to the ground below. She felt her body hit the hard pavement. She could feel a crack in her elbow, but felt no pain. Her only thought was the ominous presence that hovered over her.

Images flashed in front of her, her childhood, her lover, pictures that normally made her smile, but tonight in the brief seconds that they flashed before her, felt like sharp knives piercing her heart. She had heard that when a person is close to death, she sees her life flash before her eyes. Days, months, years all condensed into milliseconds. Her whole life reduced to this…a mere blink of the eye.

She felt him grab her arm roughly and jerk her up, dragging her into the dark alley, out of the reach of the lights and prying eyes. He pushed her to the ground and slammed his knee into her back; her rounded stomach smashed into the cold concrete under their combined weight. Her cry of agony disappeared into the night. Her fear grew as she felt him press the cold steel of an unseen knife into the side of her throat, and she knew that her life and her unborn child's life hung in the balance.

 She winced, the pain of the concrete pushing against her distended belly. She tried to turn her body to alleviate the pain, but the knee pushed harder into the small of her back, and the knife at her throat cut deeper. She could feel the warm trickle of her blood rolling down her neck and imagined she could hear it as it hit the pavement. She wavered between clarity and passing out, the oxygen levels severely restricted by the heavy weight atop her. She didn't move her head for fear the knife would cut deeper, but she blinked rapidly and took several deep breaths, or at least as deep as she could take given her circumstances.

Shortness of breath was standard with pregnancy she had been told, and the truth was she was probably used to it. However, nothing could have prepared her for this. She tried again to gulp in precious breaths, increasingly aware of the fact that she was slowly suffocating. He changed positions, lying prone on top of her. She swallowed bile, even as he pinned her down with his weight, and she felt his hard cock pressing against her buttocks. If her God was merciful, he would let her pass out long before her assailant did what she knew he planned.

"You fucking bitch." He said in a loathsome voice. "Did you really think you were special?"

She didn't answer, couldn't answer. God, she didn't want to be special. She didn't want to be the one he had chosen. She couldn't even fathom why she had been picked. She felt, rather than saw, the knife being pulled away from her neck, and she breathed a premature sigh of relief.

"You fucking women, always trying to play God." He pulled her skirt up with rough hands, exposing her to the cold

11

air. He cut the thin material of her hose and panties away, divesting her of the final barrier. "If you want a child, you need one of these."

The cold air hit her squarely, and the scream that she uttered when he entered her forcefully, ripping away her remaining dignity, died in the hand that covered her mouth. Ripples of pain tore through her like broken shards of glass, and she felt her stomach heave. She vomited into his hand. Her head snapped violently when he punched the side of her face as punishment. She felt herself slipping into black murkiness, and with one last thought of her lover and her unborn child, she closed her eyes for the final time.

Chapter 1

Jordan groaned loudly at the interruption and reluctantly pulled her mouth away from the soft lips beneath hers. She had ignored the first six calls, but she recognized Matt Riley's ring tone and figured it had to be important to bother her at two o'clock in the morning, or at least it had better be important or someone was going to pay. She grabbed her phone off the nightstand and flipped it open disgustedly, her voice a low growl. "Gray."

A soft chuckle was followed by her partner's voice. "Gray, it's Matt. Catch you at a bad time?"

Jordan rolled her eyes. "You always do, Matty." She turned back to the naked body beside her and made lazy circles in her soft curls, still wet from arousal. She slid her fingers lower and couldn't swallow a groan when she felt wetness envelope her fingers.

"Fuck, Gray." Matt said with a louder chuckle. "You get laid more than anyone I know. Least that explains the Houdini act on the phone calls."

"Did you call to tell me that?" Jordan asked sarcastically. "Or is there a good reason you've been blowing up my phone all night?" Her fingers continued to stroke and the woman beside her moved against her, barely audible purrs escaping from her lips.

"Mitchell wants us…now."

"Shit!" Jordan swore emphatically. Susan was not the person whose calls you wanted to ignore. Matt's emphasis on now made the hairs stand up on the back of Jordan's neck. She sat up quickly, pulling her hand away, her focus on the conversation. If the FBI Assistant Director in Charge wanted to see them at two o'clock in the morning, Jordan would bet money it was something big. "It can't wait until morning?"

"Negative." Matt responded, a note of irritation barely evident in his voice. He didn't like getting called in the middle of the night any more than Jordan did. As Special Agents with the Chicago division of the FBI, they were used to working odd hours, but the late-night call from their boss was something new. "I'm supposed to track you down and get us both to headquarters pronto."

Pronto meant yesterday, as far as Susan Mitchell was concerned. Jordan and Matt had learned early on not to cross her when she asked for something, which so far hadn't been very often. Jordan swiveled around and rested her feet on the floor, ignoring the groans of protest behind her. "I'll meet you there in fifteen."

"Don't be late." Matt cautioned, knowing his partner's weakness for naked women and her proclivity for tardiness.

"Worry about yourself, Matty." Jordan ended the call before Matt could respond and stood up slowly. Her earlier arousal was doused minutes before, and the hand that snaked around her naked body did little more than irritate her. She shoved it away forcefully. "I gotta go."

Minutes later, Jordan stepped out of her 370Z, the only other luxury she had allowed herself besides numerous encounters with beautiful women. She liked her cars as much as she liked her women, fast and dangerous. She glanced across the parking lot, noting that Matt's car was already here parked close to Assistant Director Mitchell's car. Shit! She figured he had probably called her from the parking lot anyway.

Jordan swiped her entry card and waited for the clearance check then pulled the heavy door open with a resigned sigh. The hairs on the back of her neck stood up again, and for the second time in only minutes, she felt an ominous chill course through her body. Jordan wouldn't say she had a sixth sense, but years on the street had made her wary and had given her an uncanny ability to read a situation well before she found out what was actually going on. If she respected that instinct now, she would readily admit that what was going on at the moment was bad. Her suspicions were confirmed when she stepped into Susan Mitchell's office and saw her red—rimmed eyes. She acknowledged her partner with a cursory nod then sat down across from her boss. "Assistant Director Mitchell."

"Gray." Susan said quietly. "I'm sorry to call you in so late, but this couldn't wait." Susan's voice quivered uncharacteristically, and she cleared her throat several times before continuing. "It's Julie. She's…" Susan broke off abruptly, unable to continue.

"Oh, fuck." Jordan murmured quietly. She and Susan weren't exactly close, but they had formed a bond when they found out that both of them were lesbians. Julie Keppler was Susan's partner. Julie was pregnant with their first baby, and Jordan's immediate thought was that something had happened to the baby. On second thought, she knew it couldn't be that or Susan would not have called her and especially not Matt into the office at this late hour. Her stomach wrenched violently when she realized with sick dread that whatever Susan was about to say was far worse.

Susan's eyes locked on hers, and Jordan could see the hurt evident in them. "Julie is in the ICU at Mercy."

"Oh, my God!" Matt leaned forward in his chair. "What happened?"

"Julie was attacked tonight." Susan held a closed fist to her mouth and swallowed audibly. She raised apologetic eyes. "I'm sorry. I'm not usually such a mess."

Jordan leaned forward, reached across the desk and put her hand on Susan's arm. "Don't tell us you're sorry. You have every right to be upset. We're here for you."

"I know. Fuck, this is difficult. You know it is never this hard when it's someone else. You know you learn how to disassociate yourself, but this, Julie. I don't know how to disconnect." Susan offered quietly, brushing away tears that welled anew in her swollen eyes. "Julie was attacked and raped."

Jordan sank back in her chair. Suddenly, the feeling of Julie's vulnerability slammed into her chest. "The baby?" She asked in a raspy voice.

Susan shook her head, unable to form the words.

Jordan stood up and went around the desk and against every rule of protocol, pulled Susan into her arms and hugged her fiercely. She waited while the tears fell and waited quietly, not offering empty words that everything would be all right, when right now nothing was okay. Everything was wrong.

Jordan waited and when Susan finally pulled away, her eyes were once again professionally guarded. She sat down and knew this time when she spoke, there would be no tears.

"Julie was attacked this evening." Susan's voice was even and monotone, belying her upset emotions, and her face was a carefully guarded mask devoid of any grief. "She was raped. Fortunately, someone happened by before her assailant could kill her. She's lost a lot of blood. It's not looking good. The baby…our baby…" Susan stopped again, the pain evident in her voice. Jordan knew she was close to falling apart. However, after a moment, Susan continued gravely. "Right now we don't know anything. If she…*when* she wakes up, I want you to take her statement."

Jordan's brow furrowed in confusion. "This isn't exactly our jurisdiction. Chicago Investigative Services should be working the attack. You know how uptight they get when we play in their backyard."

Susan pursed her lips. "This isn't an official investigation. I'm asking you to work this on your own time." She held up her hand to prevent protest. "I know it's not ideal, but from what I gathered from our contact at the CIS, we're looking at a serial killer. A killer they have not made any headway in apprehending. I don't want this to get shelved. I want Julie's attacker caught, and I need you guys to help…in an unofficial capacity."

Jordan's mind was working overtime. She stole a sideways glance at Matt. They had worked *off the record* cases before, even worked with the CIS in the past, but this time it was personal, and she wondered if Susan would keep an objective mind. They were bound to step on toes, and she wondered just how far they would have to push.

Susan handed Jordan a card. "This is the detective who is working point on this case. I want you both to make nice with the detective and glean whatever information you can get in addition to taking Julie's statement." Her fists clenched and the vein in her temple throbbed wildly, the only two signs that she was handling this in anything less than a professional capacity. "I need you two on this."

Jordan caught Matt's eye and she nodded slightly, sending him a silent message. *What the fuck is she getting us involved in?* She turned back to Susan, meeting her expectant eyes. "We'll find him." She hoped her words sounded more convincing to her boss than they did to her own ears.

"So what are you thinking?" Matt asked as he held the door for Jordan.

"I think we just got thrown into the lion's den." She ran a hand through her unruly brown hair and expelled a breath. "I've never seen Susan that out of control. This one isn't going to get swept under the rug."

Matt stared off somewhere in the night sky. He shoved his hands wordlessly into his pockets, waiting for Jordan to take the lead as she always did.

"I say we pay this detective a little surprise visit first thing in the morning." The corner of her lip curled up into the semblance of a wicked grin. "I want to catch her off guard. She's more likely to let something slip if she isn't expecting us."

Matt smiled. In the five years he and Jordan had worked together, he had grown to appreciate her sixth sense. It had helped them out of more than one tight spot, and he wasn't about to start doubting it now. If Jordan wanted to make an early morning visit, then he was all for it. Besides, from the sound of things, they were going to need every advantage available.

Chapter 2

Jordan pushed a hand through her dark hair, trying to brush it out of her blue eyes. She was weeks past needing a haircut, which only added to her street hardened look. She flicked her eyes to her wrist, noting that Matt was his typical ten minutes late. Per Assistant Director Mitchell, she and Matt were getting an early start on last night's case. She pulled Detective Rebecca Foxx's card out of her leather jacket and fingered the plain type. She wasn't sure what kind of woman she expected Detective Foxx to be, but she was pretty damn sure she wasn't going to like the FBI's intrusion into her case.

She shoved the card back in her pocket and let out a loud breath. "Fuck, Matty, where are you?"

As if hearing her sharp words, he came tearing into the parking lot, bringing his car to a screeching halt beside Jordan. He exited the car with a sheepish grin. "Sorry, Jordie. I was getting fuel." He handed her a cup of coffee and loped around to the other side of her Nissan. "Come on, we're late."

Jordan grunted loudly, stifling her biting reply. They rode in silence to the Area 5 on Grand. The Chicago Detective Division, or CDD, was located in Area 5 of the Chicago grid. Grand Central, as dubbed by its location on Grand, covered all of northwest side of the City. It was part of the Bureau of Investigative Services or BIS. Detective Foxx worked in the Detective Division. The CDD handled the criminal investigations for crimes such as murder, rape or those related to narcotics, gangs or organized crime.

Jordan pulled into a freight zone on Racine Street and stuck an FBI parking tag in her window. She caught Matt looking at her comically. "What?" She asked innocently.

He rolled his eyes. "Nothing."

Her only response was a smirk. Hell, Jordan knew if they couldn't use their position with the FBI for something as harmless as parking in a freight zone, she knew there was no chance the FBI's name would carry much weight with the Chicago Police Department either.

Jordan wasn't sure what she expected to find when they walked into the precinct, but none of the Barney Fife misconceptions existed here. She glanced quickly around a small waiting area then focused her attention on the officer who occupied a small corner of the room. Jordan knew the CDD would resent their intrusion. She cast a smile in his direction, hoping that the smallest civility would work to smooth over their involvement. "I'm Special Agent Gray, and this is Special Agent Riley with the FBI." They flashed their badges briefly, more in a show of attempted camaraderie than necessity, as the FBI's jurisdiction outweighed the CDD's territory. "We'd like to speak with Detective Foxx."

Had Jordan not been paying rapt attention to his response in an effort to gauge the request, she might have missed the almost imperceptible rise in his eyebrow. She decided to attribute it to the FBI's surprise visit and not as his opinion of Detective Foxx. She would wait and make her own opinion. She knew all too well that while women had made it a long way in a man's world, yet they continued to struggle with narrow—minded assholes that still felt a woman's place was at home. Perhaps Detective Foxx had bucked the system and the opinion that her fellow detectives and officers shared was that of a woman who was more forthright than she should be—a bitch to put it simply. Whatever the case, she would make that determination herself, and not based on the candid response of a youthful desk jockey.

"I'll see if she's in yet." He picked up the phone and dialed slowly. Jordan shot Matt a sideways glance and stifled a chuckle. She stole a glance at his badge and smirked. Officer Jackson was showing his ass. He wanted to let the FBI know who was in charge here. After a short, hushed conversation, he hung up the phone and sighed loudly. "You'll have to wait, Detective Foxx is tied up. She's really not sure how long she'll be." He nodded at two chairs nearby. You're free to wait…if you want."

Jordan caught Matt's eye again and nodded silently. They read his signal loud and clear. The CDD was not bowing down to the Feds. That was okay with Jordan. She had an immense reserve of patience when the situation called for it and today, the situation demanded it. If Susan Mitchell wanted their help finding Julie's attacker, no amount of snubbing from Chicago's finest was going to deter them. They sat down and waited, eyeing the invisible battle line that was slowly being drawn in the sand.

"Agent Gray." Jordan's head came up, and she focused on the woman who had just called her name. She made a show of checking her watch, letting Detective Foxx know right away that the thirty—five minutes they had waited was unacceptable, but she stopped short of letting the irritation show in her features. "*Special* Agent." Jordan's emphasis on Special was her way of setting the tone for this meeting.

Matt stood up beside her and smiled easily. "Special Agent Riley. Thank you for agreeing to see us, Detective Foxx." He offered his hand and Detective Foxx took it begrudgingly. This was their thing. Jordan played the bad cop to Matt's good cop. So far it had worked, but one look at Detective Foxx's face let them know immediately that whatever game they played, they would lose.

"Against my better judgment." She led them to her small office. From her glass office, she could see every desk in the house and Jordan could tell from the looks of the officers occupying those desks, Detective Foxx was not well liked. Respected, feared maybe, but not liked, and certainly not a woman that appreciated the FBI stepping over any lines. Jordan liked that about her. She understood that and in the few moments it took them to get settled, she studied Rebecca Foxx. The first thing a person would notice was her red hair, fiery would describe it well. Look away too quickly and they would miss the emerald-green eyes that Jordan thought might be beautiful if they ever smiled. She was thin, slightly shorter than Jordan's five foot eight frame, but underneath her shapeless jacket, she looked lean and defined. The lines around those green eyes spoke volumes. This was a woman who had lived a lot of years in what Jordan guessed was sandwiched into about thirty years. If she was ever outside of the sallow white lights, and she smiled, Jordan decided she would be a beautiful woman.

As if sensing she was being watched, Detective Foxx looked up from the pad she was scribbling on and met Jordan's inquisitive eyes. For a brief moment, a look of understanding passed between them. She leaned back in her chair and regarded the Agents thoughtfully. "I wouldn't have even allowed you to stay, but when you look in the eyes of someone's whose whole life has just been shattered, you figure that if ever there were a time to let the Feds come sniffing around in our investigation, this may be the time."

Jordan shifted imperceptibly and she saw Matt's leg jump. Detective Foxx's statement caught them completely off guard. They had assumed that getting the CDD to give them anything would be a fight. She opened her mouth to speak, but stopped when a hand was held up.

"This is still our case, but even I know, the FBI has resources at its disposal that we just don't have. You would have to live in a cave to not know that funding for the city police departments is way down and we just don't have the manpower to cover a case like this." She sat up quickly. "Don't misunderstand me. I'm not handing this case over, and *when* it's solved, the Feds don't take credit, but you will have the full cooperation of the CDD."

Jordan breathed a sigh of relief. "I'm glad to hear that, Detective Foxx."

Detective Foxx took a moment to study Jordan. "Just so we understand each other, I'm doing this because my number one focus is catching the son of a bitch that attacked Julie Keppler and killed those other women."

Jordan's temperature climbed a notch. She resented the fact that Detective Foxx had to clarify the reason they were all there. This wasn't an exercise in pissing off the CDD. Jordan could not care less about jurisdiction. She wanted the asshole just as much as Detective Foxx did, probably more.

Matt turned, sensing her agitation. "Detective Foxx, I think you will find that is our goal as well, and we have no plans to take the investigation away from the CDD. We are merely offering the FBI's resources, as you call them and asking for some shared information in return."

Jordan hid a smile. Good old Matty, always riding in on his white horse as the good cop. She watched Detective Foxx's face for a sign that she wasn't immune to his charm and good looks. She spotted nothing.

"I have no doubt, *Special* Agent Riley, that you have every intention of manhandling this case." She mustered a fake smile, turning Matt's political correctness right back on him. "Rest assured, that would hinder the successfulness of this joint investigation."

Jordan gave her a mental tick mark. Detective Foxx was all for a joint investigation, as long as she controlled the information being shared with the FBI. That, and Matty's normal charms didn't affect her in the least. "Detective Foxx, I give you my word that the FBI's involvement is under the radar. You won't see the normal bullying tactics. We can't risk the public knowing that we have an interest in this case. And believe me when I tell you, we are just as interested in catching the UNSUB, so whatever assistance we can provide each other will be handled with professional courtesy."

Detective Foxx studied Jordan's face a few moments longer, weighing her words. Naturally wary, she was trying to put the common good ahead of her natural instincts to protect her turf.

Finally, she decided she could take her at her word, but she left no doubt as to the consequences if the FBI pushed her too hard. "I hope I don't regret this, *Special* Agent Gray. Nothing shuts the CDD up faster than hearing that information pertinent to an investigation has been leaked."

Jordan nodded. "Understood." Jordan hated this political BS, but in this case, it was necessary. What she really wanted to do was flash her badge and tell Detective Foxx to go fuck herself, or at the very least, Jordan could take care of that. Without the glare, she would probably register on Jordan's radar anyway. *Maybe when this is over, I can show her who is boss.* But instead, she was here playing nicey nice and her badge meant nothing.

Jordan hid a smirk. She'd had a weakness for redheads. There was a definite air about Detective Foxx. Maybe she would try a different tactic. She always got more Intel from someone when their badge was on her nightstand. She leaned forward and licked her lips, her blue eyes holding Detective Foxx's emerald-green ones. "So now that we got that all straightened out, what do you have for us?"

Matt watched Jordan out of the corner of his eye and swallowed a laugh. Whatever she saw in the Detective, he didn't share her opinion. Although she had ignored him completely, so maybe she was a lesbian. It surprised him to see her roll her eyes in reply to Jordan's subtle advances.

"Let me guess Agent Gray, this is the part where I'm supposed to swoon because you are so handsome and give up my hand in this case?" Rebecca leveled her gaze at Jordan. "Let me let you in on a little secret. I didn't get where I am today by getting weak in the knees every time some badge with a power trip batted their eyes at me. You can put your dick back in your pants."

Matt snickered, and Jordan rewarded him with a glare. He suddenly realized that maybe he did have a shot with the lovely Detective Foxx. "Sorry." He muttered under his breath, all the while trying to mask the smirk on his face.

Jordan felt the heat rise in her face. It had been a long time since someone put her in her place like that. Properly chastised, Jordan dropped her eyes playing the penitent role to appease Detective Foxx. She regretted her decision to throw sex into the mix and hoped for the sake of the case, she didn't fuck up the Detective's offer to share information. "Perhaps we got off on the wrong foot, Detective."

"I don't play games, Agent. I know this whole adorable bad-guy routine is something you're used to getting your way with, but I can assure you, I am no more interested in you than you are in Agent Riley."

Game, set and match to Detective Foxx, Jordan thought. Very quickly, the rules of the game had been established. Jordan was benched before she even had the chance to swing. "Very well, Detective. No games."

Again, Rebecca's emerald eyes studied Jordan, this time looking beyond the façade and into her soul. This time she was almost convinced she had the upper hand...*almost.* "Agents, the information that I'm going to share with you is highly confidential. It stays here. Don't make me regret this."

They both nodded. They did not need to be told that protocol dictated that the information they received here would definitely be shared in their own circles, but it would stop there.

Rebecca pulled a file out of her drawer and opened it up. She handed Jordan a thin file. "We don't have much. So far, he's been clean. No DNA left at the scene."

"No sperm?" Matt asked incredulously. "Not even trace amounts? Nothing?"

"That's what I said, Agent Riley. This guy's good...or was." Rebecca smiled mysteriously. "Until last night's case."

"How so?" Jordan asked quickly.

"Last night he got spooked and pulled out...so to speak. The condom came off inside the victim..." Rebecca saw Jordan wince. "I'm sorry, I mean Ms. Keppler. It's the first break in the case we've gotten."

"It usually happens that way, Detective." Jordan opined. "The UNSUB thinks he's the first smart criminal and bam, he does something stupid."

"Did you get a hit in the Combined DNA Index System?" Matt interrupted. Jordan was emotionally involved already. He didn't think that her relationship with their boss was any closer than his. Sure, they were both lesbians, but that hardly qualified them as best friends. However, he knew his partner, and she was already invested in this case more than she should have been. That's when agents got sloppy, overlooked things, made mistakes when their brain stopped controlling the shots, and their heart took over.

"No, if our suspect has committed crimes before this, he's never been arrested." Rebecca thumbed through several more pages. "The only thing that kept Ms. Keppler alive was a homeless guy. It turns out they were in his alley. Spooked the perp before he could kill her."

Jordan swallowed the lump in her throat. Here they were talking about Julie as if she were just another victim, a number in the CDD's or FBI's database, like she was just one more faceless person in a long line of faceless people. She was frustrated beyond belief. She had never had to put a face to the victim, never had to personalize the case. She felt a mixture of helplessness and fury swirling around inside her gut. Her next words were spoken through gritted teeth. "How many?"

Rebecca looked confused. "How many what?"

"Victims. How many victims were there before Julie?"

"Six." Rebecca let the number sink in. She could tell it shocked them. "At least that we could tie to this case. That's over a span of two years. If he changed his MO at any time, we wouldn't have tied it back to this one."

Matt leaned forward. He could see Jordan's hands clenched on the arms of her chair, and he needed to give her a chance to cool down. "What's his MO?"

"This is where it gets bad." She looked at Jordan, concern on her features. "Are you sure you want to hear this?"

Jordan nodded her head. She forced herself to exhale, realizing that she had been holding her breath, only seconds from passing out. "I need to. If I'm going to be any help, I need to know what this monster is doing. I need to be able to get inside his head."

Rebecca nodded. She didn't know the exact nature of Special Agent Gray and Assistant Director Mitchell's relationship, but she imagined it went beyond the normal working acquaintance. "From what we can piece together from time of death, he strikes at night. He carries a knife, most likely forces them into an alley with that. Forces them down on their stomach, slits their throat, and as a final, demeaning blow, rapes them and takes the baby."

Jordan bit her lip. The more she found out, the angrier she got. She took several deep breaths and willed herself to calm down, stay impersonal and focused. "Any similarities?"

"They were all pregnant, other than that, nothing. Didn't work together, didn't travel in the same circles. Not much to go on." Rebecca smiled ruefully. "You can see why I want to catch this guy. He's a fucking monster."

"Can we get a sample of the DNA?" Jordan asked quickly. "We can run it in the National DNA Index System and see if we get a hit."

"Sure, as long as..."

Jordan put her hand up. "I know, as long as it stays in this office."

"Most likely he will strike again soon." Matt interrupted the latest push for power. "We have to figure he's pissed off about Julie. He's going to be out for blood, get his retribution for not getting the kill."

Jordan had to give consideration to Matt's idea. His major in college had been psych and had he not wanted to be in the field, could have had a perfectly decent career as an FBI profiler. Hopefully, they could put that to good use. She gave him a cautionary glance to keep him from divulging anymore. The FBI could have secrets just as easily as the CDD. "What's the time frame between each victim?"

Rebecca checked her notes. "At first, he was sporadic. The first three averaged every six months. The latest three happened within the last six months."

"So one every two months. He's moving further away from reality, and it's upping his need to kill." Jordan rubbed her chin thoughtfully. "Think you can provide us with a copy of the file? It's for research."

Rebecca covered her files protectively. "I'm sure you know I can't do that, Agent Gray."

Jordan leaned forward and put her elbows on the desk, bringing her closer to Rebecca's face. Her green eyes were suspicious of Jordan's move, as she expected they would be. She was entering her personal space. "We all agreed our main goal was to catch this guy before anyone else gets killed. I'm not asking so I can take something away from the CDD, Detective, I'm asking so I can try to save the next woman, and her child before he picks them."

Rebecca sat quietly, turning Jordan's words over in her head. She seemed more earnest in those few seconds than she had since she walked in the door. "Fine. I'll see that you get copies. I swear to you, Agent Gray, if any of this gets out and jeopardizes my investigation, I will have your head, FBI or not." Content that she had gotten her point across, Rebecca stood up. "Come with me."

Chapter 3

Content that she had gotten her point across, Rebecca stood up. "Come with me."

She ushered them out into the Bull Pen, the large area where the majority of the detectives sat, questioned witnesses, discussed case details and worked leads. It was still early, and aside from a few stragglers here and there, the place was eerily empty. Wooden desks arranged in some forgotten fashion filled the room. The uncomfortable rolling chairs that squeaked when a person moved, sat haphazardly behind each grizzled old desk. In the air, the smell of sweat and determination mingled with something else, something sweeter hung in the air.

Jordan saw several orange and pink donut boxes stacked on a desk near the back. Her eyes flicked around the room, searching for the owner. Her stomach grumbled of its own accord, and she remembered there hadn't been time to eat.

Rebecca stood still for a moment, a frown marring her features. "Rick?"

A few seconds later, a short, stocky man Jordan put in his early forties, came from around the corner carrying two coffee mugs. He shot Rebecca a sheepish grin. "Hey, boss."

Rebecca looked as if she may address the offense, but thought better of it. "Jesus, Jonesy. You keep eating this shit and I'm going to have to roll your fucking fat ass everywhere we go."

"Sorry, boss." Rick Jones, or Jonesy, to everyone in Grand, smiled and made an attempt to wipe errant flecks of glaze of his

29

face. His eyes shifted to Jordan and Matt, and he threw Rebecca a questioning glance.

She shook her head imperceptibly then introduced them. A silent message had passed between them, and Jordan knew without a doubt, there would be more conversation about them when they left.

"Agents Gray and Riley, this fat ass stuffing his damn face, is my partner, Rick Jones." She nodded towards the agents. "It would seem the *overly* generous FBI has offered some assistance in tracking down our serial killer."

Rick nodded swiftly with none of the censures that Rebecca had given them. Jordan nodded, and as Matt stepped forward to offer a quick, conciliatory handshake, she took a moment to study him. His suit was dated, and she could see telltale signs of forgotten grease stains on his shirt. His tie hung haphazardly. His hair, a few weeks past a haircut, hung over his collar. His face was lined with the deep crevasses of someone who had seen a great deal, and been through a lot more, and she couldn't swear to it, but would almost bet there was a flash of welcome relief in his eyes at help from the outside. Obviously not married or dating, she thought he fit the stereotype for a hardened old cop.

He smiled warmly, and Jordan was forced to amend her take on him. He pumped Matt's hand up and down as though they were lifelong friends, and Jordan half expected to see him pull Matt into a bear hug. Where Detective Foxx was cold and unapproachable, Detective Jones was the polar opposite. She saw the lines around his eyes crinkle when he smiled, and she was forced to admit that this was a man who smiled a lot.

He held up a box. "You guys want breakfast?"

Rebecca's jaw tightened. It was one thing to be civil. It was an entirely different thing to offer her squad's breakfast to the enemy. He reddened at the apparent faux pas, but couldn't take back the offer. Jordan and Matt saved him from further embarrassment when they politely declined. Jordan figured the poor guy probably already had it bad enough without them making it worse.

Jordan's gaze met Rebecca's inquisitive one, and she faltered, wondering what Rebecca saw in her eyes. The corner of her mouth turned up as if to say I can see inside you.

Rebecca answered with another roll of her eyes. "Let's get to it. Jonesy?"

They had obviously been together long enough that he needed no explanation. He pulled a large whiteboard towards them and flipped it around.

She flipped a whiteboard around and stood back. It was covered with the autopsy pictures of the six previous victims, all marked with a date. The only difference was that Julie's picture was one of her still alive, and yet, despite the fact that she had survived, Jordan still flinched at the sight. Detachment was one of the ways she dealt with crime, and this case didn't allow for that. It reached inside her soul with a cold hand.

Rebecca waited until they pulled chairs up and sat down. "This is what we have so far. First murder happened in June, 2009. Kate Stevenson. Twenty—seven year old white female. Second, in December of 2009. Amy Perez. Thirty—three year old Hispanic female." She pointed at each victim and provided their vital stats. "All pregnant, and in each case, the MO was identical, down to taking the baby. Jonesy?"

Rick jumped at her voice. It was obvious they had been together a long time, and in those years, he had come to know her very well and could probably read her mind, a valuable asset in a partner. He pulled a folder out. "Autopsies haven't helped much. Best guess, we are looking for someone tall, five—ten to six—two, buck fifty to buck seventy tops. Whoever this guy is, he's not heavy, but he is really strong. All of the women had injuries consistent with being restrained and forcibly raped. Not easy when you've got a knife in one hand and the other pinned over her mouth. The guy is methodical though, and the MO is the same in every case. He grabs them, throws them down and slits their throat before he rapes them, ensuring they bleed out quickly. Those are all done rather carelessly. However, the incision in their stomachs is different. It's almost as if he takes his time to make sure he doesn't hurt the baby in the process. The cuts are very clean, and there's no sign that he makes them quickly or in anger. Guy's a monster who hates women, but loves kids. Weird."

Jordan stepped closer. She studied each woman's face and the photos from each crime scene. "Any similarities, I mean besides the obvious?"

Rebecca shook her head. "Pregnant. The only other link is they are all lesbians."

"Hate crime?"

"We thought so at first, but we believe the nature of the crime is directed more at the pregnancy then at the sexual orientation."

"Did you look into the area anti—gay groups?"

"Very thoroughly. We interviewed dozens of people and got nothing. The only lead we had was a link to the sperm bank they had all used. Unfortunately, everyone that was associated with the clinic had solid alibis and no motive for murder, almost all the employees were female, we had to rule that out."

"What about someone else, even someone remotely connected with the clinic?" Jordan rubbed her chin. "Janitor? Tech? Delivery guy? Anyone?"

Rebecca exhaled loudly. "The CDD was very thorough in its investigation, Agent Gray. Believe me, we exhausted every possible angle, and we had nothing but dead ends. The attack on Julie Keppler was the first real break we got."

Jordan smiled apologetically. "I'm sorry. I didn't mean to imply that you hadn't done your job."

"Yes, you did, whether that was your intention or not." Rebecca bit back. "We've logged hundreds of hours on this case. I don't need some cocky FBI agent coming in and questioning the work we've done."

She pointed at the board angrily. "These women haunt me every day. I don't need to be reminded, that up until now, we've made no real headway in catching the killer."

"Again, I'm sorry, Detective. I know the CDD has done what they can. We're just here to offer whatever help we can." Jordan offered a conciliatory smile. "And you're right, I'm way too cocky for my own good."

She met Rebecca's blazing green eyes. She knew in that second that she did not want this woman mad at her. She couldn't risk getting herself and Matt thrown out on their asses. Susan wouldn't take failure in this case, not when it involved her wife. Jordan scrambled to find something to smooth things over and almost hugged Rick when he jumped in to save her.

"Agent Gray, you have to understand that this case has been one of the most difficult ones we've ever been up against." He met Rebecca's eyes, and in a move that surprised them all, nodded towards a chair. She gave in reluctantly. Obviously, this barely put together detective had the ability to calm her when no one else did and Jordan thanked him silently. "What Detective Foxx means is that we've lost a lot of sleep over this case and not being any closer to catching the guy hits you in the gut. Forgive us, if we take things a little personally around here."

Jordan shook her head from side to side. "It's my fault." She lowered her eyes from Rebecca's glaring gaze ruefully. "I know what it's like to have someone question how you do your job. Thank you for sharing your case files with us. We'll get out of your hair now."

Jordan grabbed Matt and started to leave. She turned back and met Rebecca's gaze, once again looking inside her. "Whatever we can do to help, please let me know. You have my promise that even though our intrusion is off the record, you will have the full resources of the FBI."

Rebecca nodded her headed slightly, a small sign that for the first time she might appreciate the help. "Thank you, Agent Gray."

Chapter 4

Jordan knocked on the door leading into Julie's room. She met Susan's eyes, giving her a slight nod to let her know that she and Matt had already met with the CDD already. She didn't take the folder with case notes out of her jacket for fear that it would upset Julie. "Assistant Director Mitchell."

Susan's wary eyes met hers, and she could see they were red—rimmed. "Susan, please. We're outside the office."

"Susan." Jordan's voice was decidedly low, given the sterile and ominous surroundings. She gestured towards Julie, who was still under heavy sedatives. "How is she?"

Susan stood up and rolled her shoulders. The ache that had started when her partner had been attacked hadn't stopped. She wasn't sleeping, and it showed. "Resting, finally. She's been having nightmares."

"As expected." Jordan rested her hand on Susan's arm. She met her eyes, not masking the concern in her own. "How are you holding up?"

"I've been better." Susan shrugged. "I'm sure when the shock wears off, and I finally sit down, it will all hit me. I'm certain I'll fall apart then."

"Call me if you do. We'll talk." Jordan's voice carried her concern. She suddenly felt closer to Susan, as if they were friends, and she wasn't her subordinate. They would return to that when protocol dictated, but for now, Jordan knew Susan needed a friend more than a coworker.

Susan let herself feel anger for a few brief moments then her body grew tight and Jordan felt her pull away, physically and mentally. Her eyes flicked to Julie then back again, satisfied she was still asleep. "Did you get any leads from the CDD?"

Jordan shook her head. "Not here. Let me get you a cup of coffee. There's a Starbucks right around the corner. You look like you could use a break."

Susan looked as though she might resist, but her weariness got the better of her. "A quick one, okay?"

Jordan nodded her acquiescence. "Fifteen minutes."

They rode the elevator in silence and didn't talk again until they were seated at a corner table, nursing Venti coffees. Jordan pulled the folder out of her jacket and slid it on to the table in front of Susan.

Susan eyed it suspiciously and raised an eyebrow in Jordan's direction. "This is it?"

"It's not much to go on, I know. I'm hoping that Julie can give us at least a somewhat decent description of the UNSUB."

Susan scanned the file quickly. The tips of her ears reddened as she read, the only sign that her ire was raising with every sentence. She finally shut the file and leaned back in her chair. "He's a fucking monster." She ran a hand through her unruly hair. She looked like she hadn't slept or showered in days. She leveled Jordan with her gaze, hints of helplessness juxtaposed by seething anger. "I want him dead."

"Is that my boss or my friend talking?" Jordan saw the mixed emotions in her eyes. "I know this is personal, but I need to know."

Susan shook her head. "I can't answer that. My heart wants this bastard dead for what he took from me, from Julie. I know he should rot in prison for his crimes, but why should he get to live when my baby is dead?"

Jordan watched the tears well in her eyes. Susan was making it even more difficult to keep her distance from the case. She was already too close to it. She needed to get that emotion under control, so she didn't make a mistake. "I'm sorry, Susan.

I'm so sorry for your loss. I won't sit here and say that I know what you are going through. However, I will promise you today, we will get him, dead or alive."

Susan saw the understanding in Jordan's eyes. "I know you will. That's why I asked you to do this for me." Her eyes dropped, and she rolled her cup around in her hands. "I know that I don't have to tell you what I want."

Jordan shook her head from side to side. Susan didn't need to tell her that officially or unofficially, it didn't matter. She wanted him to suffer and eventually die. If asked on an official basis, both knew they would never say those words out loud. They would swear only to catch him and having faith in the justice system. Neither one would ever voice anything other than blind faith in the law. "No, you don't."

"How did the Detective treat you?"

"Alright." Jordan smiled ruefully, her mind going back to yesterday's encounter. "She did make it quite clear that she didn't give a rat's ass that we were FBI, and her only reason for cooperating in the least, was her desire to catch this bastard. She's ballsy. She might be the best person to have taken the case. I don't see her giving up."

"I guess if she doesn't put up with your shit, she won't let anyone run over her." A hint of a smile played on Susan's face. Whatever their relationship, the two women had a lot of respect for each other. Jordan knew any teasing from her boss was because she genuinely liked her.

"Hey, she didn't fall for Matty, either." Jordan said defensively. She wasn't sure why it mattered that Detective Foxx had shot her down. She tried to tell herself to take the rejection and move on, but her thoughts had returned to the hot redhead more times than she was comfortable admitting.

"Don't get sidetracked, Gray." Susan said sternly. The corners of her mouth turned up slightly, but Jordan knew from the throwback to her last name that Susan wasn't joking, and she wouldn't be stupid enough to blow this case because she couldn't keep her libido in check.

Jordan fidgeted in her chair. "I won't, Assistant Dir…"

Susan waived a hand dismissively. "Jordan, please. I know I'm asking a lot for you and Matty to do this on your own time. I hope I'm not asking too much."

"You aren't." Jordan shook her head. Her eyes turned cold. "I want him just as badly as you do."

Susan gulped the remaining coffee and set the cup on the table. "I need to get back." She stood up, her eyes telling Jordan to stay seated. She tapped a finger on the file and met Jordan's eyes. "I'll call you when Julie feels like talking. I'm not sure if she got a look at him. It was pretty dark. However, maybe she can remember something."

Jordan watched her walk away; her shoulders huddled against the wind. Her heart went out to her boss. Her partner was safe, albeit hurt, but they had lost their baby. She hoped that the wounds she couldn't see would heal with time.

She pulled her phone out of her pocket and dialed a number and waited. When he finally picked up, she smiled. "Hey."

"Hey, boss."

Jordan smiled again. His moniker for her made her smiled every time. She wasn't his boss. In fact, he had shown her more than once that if anyone were boss, it was him. She stood up and stuck the file under her arm. "You busy?"

"Nah. What's up?"

She could hear his gravelly voice and wondered how he was as healthy as he was when he smoked like a chimney. It seemed almost illegal that her trainer was in better shape than she was, given her strict diet and exercise regimen. The only vice she allowed herself, besides cars and women, was alcohol. She figured she was going to die one day, might as well let liver failure take a shot at her. "You up for some sparring?"

"Yeah, sure." She could hear him talking to a voice in the background, decidedly female, and she chuckled. It was obvious she was interrupting some sparring already. "Give me thirty minutes and I'll meet you there."

"Sure thing." She ended the call and shoved her phone back in her pocket. She cinched her collar up around her neck in a vain attempt to block the wind. "Fucking cold weather."

She didn't realize she'd sworn out loud until a fellow pedestrian glared at her and tried to cover her son's ears. "Sorry." Only she wasn't remorseful. The kid probably heard worse in school anyway.

She crossed Michigan and headed back towards Mercy Medical. She was illegally parked in an unloading zone in front of the hospital and figured her fifteen minutes was passed being over. She increased the speed of her stride. The wind blowing off the lake was the coldest of the season, and she shivered uncontrollably.

She spotted her car and rolled her eyes at the pink ticket flapping under the wipers. She ripped it off her car and wadded it up, her irritation making her want to toss it on the ground to prove a point, but instead she shoved it in her pocket and got in her cold car. It turned over reluctantly, wanting to make a point that it didn't want to work in this weather any more than she did. She proved her own point and sped away from the parking lot before the engine had a chance to warm up and let it whine in protest.

A half an hour later, she was strapping on gloves, waiting for her trainer to show up. She threw several blind punches in the air, feeling the muscles in her shoulders start to warm up. She moved slower in the winter, or maybe she was just getting old. Thirty—six wasn't exactly old, but lately she felt it. The last few years had snuck up on her and a quick look in the room—length mirrors confirmed her suspicions. The wrinkles were starting to show.

She ran a finger over the laugh lines around her eyes and lifted her eyebrows, groaning at the creases on her forehead. "Ahh fuck, Gray. Don't let one crazy redhead make you feel old."

A loud chuckle from across the room got her attention,

and she spun around to see Tony laughing at her. Tony Wozniak, or Woz to his close friends. Retired FBI, at fifty— eight, the man looked better than most guys half his age. "See what women will do to you."

"Hey, Woz. How come it hasn't happened to you?" Jordan smiled and punched him in the shoulder.

"Whiskey, and maybe cigarettes. All the preservatives." Tony was the father she never had. Her own father had abandoned her mother years before, and most times, unless she thought long and hard, she couldn't even remember what he looked like. Tony had taken her under his wing long before she joined the FBI. In fact, there had been a time when she thought that maybe he and her mother might like each other.

His proclivity for women and smoking changed her mind rather quickly. Her mother, God bless her soul, didn't need another man coming into her life and leaving just as fast.

She watched him pull on his own gloves. He punched one hand into the other to make sure they were tight then repeated the process on the other hand. "You ready, kiddo?"

Jordan nodded, her feet already dancing on the pad below her. She put her mouth guard in and waited while he did the same.

She watched his eyes, admiration in them. She was cagey and a good boxer to boot. She could feel his respect for her. Their sparring matches usually ended in some well—placed punches on both sides, but more often than not, he could still take her. She thought back to her childhood and wondered if she hadn't wandered into this very gym twenty years ago, if her life would have taken the same course.

They danced around each other, throwing a few light punches, each feeling out their opponent. In silent agreement, they both raised their gloves and readied for the real match. She moved around him, her left hand resting just in front of her chin protectively. She jabbed with her right, and soon, she had landed several good blows to his ribcage.

He took advantage of her weak left shoulder, a result of a gunshot wound years earlier and took a poke at her unprotected jaw. She wheeled around, stunned momentarily. She shook her head, shaking off the stars.

"Come on, kiddo. Keep your left up. You gotta guard your moneymaker." He smirked behind his glove, and she felt her blood start to boil. Jordan was competitive by nature, and she hated to lose, especially to someone twenty years her senior, whether she liked him or not.

She brought her shoulders forward. Her eyes narrowed, and she focused on the small opening above his glove. She threw a roundhouse punch to his left ear and smiled when it hit home. His head whipped sideways, and his left hand flew to his ear protectively. She jabbed at his abdomen, and when he bent forward, she threw an uppercut at his chin. He reeled backwards, his hands in front of his face, and she went at him, her fists pummeling him everywhere.

She didn't mean to be so brutal, but the emotions from the case were flooding to the surface. She wasn't sure how long her arms jabbed, recoiled and jabbed again, but Tony's voice finally broke through her haze. "Whoa, whoa, whoa there, kiddo. Take it easy on your old man."

Jordan stood back and shook her head, dazed. "Sorry, old man."

He shook it off, waiving a gloved hand dismissively. He stuck his hand under his arm and pulled his glove off then pulled his mouth guard out. "Rough day?"

She smiled sheepishly and held up her gloved hands. "Sorry, they kind of got away from me."

Tony chuckled. "Wanna talk about it?"

Most times, when he offered, she would share whatever case she was working, and he would offer his opinion. This one she couldn't talk about. She shook her head. "Nah, just a lot of pent-up energy."

He quirked an eyebrow and smirked at her. "Energy, huh?

That's what you're calling it these days?" He knew her well enough to know that her taste in women was very similar to his and staying tied down to one wasn't in their blood.

Jordan laughed and wiped a bead of sweat off her forehead. "Guess I just need to get a few more rounds in. You up to it?"

Tony shook his head. "Can't, kiddo. I got a date tonight."

"Same girl I heard on the phone? Sorry about dragging you away."

"Nah." Now it was his turn to smile sheepishly. "New gal. Met her at my dry cleaners. She puts a hell of a crease in my pants."

"And now, you would like to see her crease up close?" Jordan teased and was rewarded with a laugh.

"Something like that." Tony pulled his second glove off and slapped them together on his leg. "Listen, kiddo, I've known you a few years now, and I can tell when something's up your craw. If you decide you want to talk about it, I'll be around."

Jordan watched him walk away and waived one last time as he threw a glance over his shoulder. She listened to his steps, wishing she could talk to him about her *unofficial* case. She knew he could offer invaluable insight, and so far, with the limited details in this case, any help would be greatly appreciated.

Instead of feeling settled and worn out from their sparring match, she felt uptight. She walked towards one of the gym's punching bags and was just about to take out her emotions on the heavy bag when a husky voice interrupted.

"I could use a partner, if you're up for it."

Jordan turned and was immediately struck by the owner of the voice. She had dark eyes and even darker hair, and it struck Jordan that she was very tall. She had at least a couple of inches on Jordan, which meant she was six feet tall at least. "Sure."

Jordan watched her approach, and her heart skipped a beat. The stranger was attractive, and if Jordan was correct, was regarding her with what she could only describe as mutual interest. Her eyes were chocolate brown, set in an angular face, framed by masses of flowing black hair.

"Thanks."

The stranger's voice was deep and husky, somewhat at odds with her feminine features. She looked down, concentrating on her gloves, which gave Jordan even more opportunity to study her. Her bare arms were lean and rippled with muscles. She was on the slender side, in need of a few extra pounds. Jordan could tell she was in incredible shape, though. Her eyes swept over her body, and as her eyes flicked back up to her face, she met her amused gaze.

"I usually hit the bags too, but I wanted to spar and there's never anyone here when I come."

Jordan shook her head, the heat finally leaving her cheeks. "Yeah, mornings are the best time here. You can usually find someone to go a few rounds."

"I'm Meghan, by the way." Her eyes studied Jordan, the interest in them still evident. Her gaze roamed over Jordan's body, and she unconsciously licked her lips.

Jordan felt the heat rise in her face again. She was used to women blatantly checking her out, but it had been a while since a woman had grabbed her attention so quickly. "Jordan." She spun around, needing to break the connection between them. "You ready?"

Meghan put her mouth guard in and punched her gloves on tighter. "Ready."

She stepped back on her right foot, planting her weight on her heel and dropped her right shoulder. She grazed at her chin with her gloved hand, a sign she was ready to spar.

Thirty minutes later, the women sank to the mats, completely out of breath and totally drenched in sweat. It was several minutes before either of them spoke.

"Wow, you are really good." Jordan said with admiration. "I don't even work that hard with my trainer."

Meghan chuckled softly. "Well I should have told you before. I boxed in college, and I kept it up for fun ever since then. I had an unfair advantage. You held your own alright, though."

Jordan blushed. The compliment, spoken so honestly, warmed her through and through. "I'm sure you were taking it easy on me."

Meghan sat up quickly, feigning innocence. "I did no such thing."

"Sure." Jordan sighed and pushed herself off the mat, her knees cracking in protest. "I'm gonna hit the showers. See you around?"

Meghan nodded yes. "Hey, if you're not in a hurry, you want to grab a drink? I mean, if you're available."

Jordan smothered a smirk. It had taken her all of thirty minutes to ask her out. *Guess I haven't lost my touch after all. Take that, Detective Foxx.* "I'm completely available."

Chapter 5

Meghan waited while the bartender set drinks down then held hers up to Jordan. "To whatever comes next."

Jordan clinked her glass and smiled as sincerely as she could muster. She knew exactly what came next. Sex. She could read between the smiles and the innocent touches. She could tell the interest was mutual, as was their desire for a quick and unencumbered night of passion. They hadn't exchanged last names. There was no need to pretend that this night would continue tomorrow morning.

"So what do you do, Jordan?"

The question had been asked nonchalantly, as if they were acquaintances meeting for coffee. But she saw something underneath the inquisitive look. Meghan was searching for something. What it was she wasn't sure, but Jordan felt the need for nondisclosure. "I'm an...investor."

That was generic enough and held some truth. She did invest her life, so to speak, to bringing justice where there was injustice. "How about you?"

Meghan regarded her closely. She knew she had been lied to, or at least the real truth had been withheld. She knew the game. She'd had these encounters before, more often than she would like. Sometimes, she even imagined that she could commit to someone, but then her true nature came through, and she would go in search of another one nightstand. "Banking."

It wasn't entirely untrue. She was a banker of sorts. She was actually the managing director of the Helping Hands

Fertilization Clinic. That wasn't something she told her dates though. It wasn't sexy, and more times than not, the conversation sparked an evening of delving questions, and she wasn't up for that tonight. No, tonight she wanted to separate her mind from her body and just fuck. One look at Jordan and she was sure she would accomplish that tonight.

"Sounds interesting." Jordan feigned interest in what she was sure wasn't really Meghan's profession. She downed her drink and waived two fingers at the bartender. When he had refilled them, she met Meghan's interested gaze. She ran her knuckles over Meghan's jaw. "Listen, let's not pretend this is anything more than sex."

"Fair enough." Meghan sighed with relief. "I wasn't sure if I would be able to keep up the conversation much longer."

Jordan laughed wickedly. "Your place or mine then?"

Meghan dropped a twenty on the bar and slid off her stool. "Mine, it's right around the corner."

Jordan followed her out of the bar and in the darkness of the night, slipped her arm through Meghan's. "Lead the way."

Two minutes later, they were ensconced in the warmth of an elevator, the nine—floor trip flying by quickly. Meghan opened the door to her apartment and turned on a hall light. She shut the door behind them and held out her hand. "I'll take your coat."

Jordan shrugged out of her knee—length leather coat and draped it over Meghan's arm. She let out a low whistle. "Nice place. The banking business must be pretty good."

Meghan smiled. *You have no idea.* "Can I get you a drink?"

"I'll take a beer if you have it."

Meghan led them into the kitchen and pulled two bottles out of the fridge. She twisted the tops off and handed one to Jordan, who took an appreciative swig.

"It's a local brewery. Goose Island."

"I know it well. My mom is a waitress there. Has been since I was a kid."

"Small world." Meghan set her beer on the bar and stepped closer to Jordan, pressing her against the countertop. She looked down at her, her eyes twinkling. She ran a fingertip over the collar of Jordan's shirt, dipping into the vee between her small breasts. She licked her jaw seductively, and Jordan felt her knees tremble. When Meghan's tongue dipped into her ear and swirled around it, Jordan shivered. "I'm going to fuck you now."

True to her word, Meghan slid a hand over her crotch. She let out a disappointed sigh. "You're not packing. I figured a butch like you would come equipped."

Jordan smiled ruefully. "Not tonight, darling. You didn't give me much notice."

Meghan shrugged. "No matter. Besides, I prefer to be the one with the cock." She opened Jordan's jeans and slipped her hand inside her briefs. Her finger dipped inside Jordan at the same time as her tongue teased its way inside her mouth. She was a skilled lover, and before long, Meghan had Jordan bracing the countertop, her fingers drawing out a fierce orgasm. When her breathing returned to normal, Jordan leaned against Meghan. "Fuck, your hands are dangerous."

"You know what they say, practice makes perfect." Meghan's voice was oddly devoid of feeling, and Jordan wondered if she were present. She met her eyes, and they had turned decidedly remote.

Jordan wasn't sure what prompted her next move other than the emotional distance making her even more turned on. "Then I guess I should get some more practice in."

She spun Meghan around and hoisted her body up on the bar. They were at eye level now, and she ran her tongue over Meghan's lips, darting inside her mouth. She undid her shirt and pulled her bra away. Leaning over, she captured Meghan's nipple in her mouth and swirled her tongue over it roughly. She heard Meghan moan, and when she spread her legs, Jordan stepped between them.

Jordan had questioned Meghan's skirt, given the temperatures, but it did allow her easier access, and she quickly slid the material up, exposing Meghan's naked sex. She licked her thighs, her nose taking in her heady arousal. She pushed

Meghan back roughly and slid her tongue inside her wet creaminess. She pulled her hips towards her face, burying her tongue even deeper.

Meghan could feel her muscles contracting and her arousal building deep inside until her clit was a painful peak. She pulled Jordan's face into her body roughly and started to ride her tongue. "Fuck, Jordan. Eat my pussy. That's right, eat my fucking pussy."

Jordan's own arousal though already sated came back with a painful ferocity. She felt her jeans rubbing against her clit painfully. She lifted her leg over Meghan's foot and started to rub against it, trying to assuage her own need. She slid two fingers into Meghan's aroused center and captured her clit in her mouth.

She stilled until Meghan moved against her, begging to come. She pulled her fingers out then slammed them into her body making her cry out. "Yeah, like that. Fuck me!"

Meghan was not shy when it came to sex, and that turned Jordan on even more. She increased the pressure on her clit and soon, Meghan's body began to tremble around her. She could feel her own orgasm coming close behind. She pushed Meghan to the edge then over as her own orgasm crashed through her body.

When she stopped coming, she fell against Meghan's body and smiled into her naked breasts. "Now that's my kind of sparring."

Meghan chuckled softly. "And that round goes to you. I'd say you don't need any more practice."

Jordan could sense the dismissal, and it didn't bother her at all. Yes, sex with Meghan had been great, but by prearrangement, they had both already decided this was all they wanted. She pushed herself away from Meghan and smirked. "Thanks, darling. I'll show myself out."

Jordan pulled the door closed behind her and smiled again. She ran a finger under her nose and inhaled deeply. Very immature and too much like a man, but she did it anyway. She wouldn't apologize for it either. She liked the way a woman smelled and tasted, and she lingered on the scent a moment longer before punching the button to call the elevator.

When she stepped outside, the cold hit her immediately, and she pulled her coat around her tightly. She shoved her hands in her pockets, wishing she had thought to bring her gloves. Despite the cold and the late hour, the city was still alive, and she decided she wanted another drink. She was about to pull her phone out to call Matty when it rang. She hit the accept button and held it against her ear with a shaky hand, unable to control her shivering. "Hello?"

"Special Agent Gray?" The voice on the other end was slightly familiar, and it only took Jordan a second to remember it.

"Detective Foxx. What brings you to my phone at this hour?" Jordan tried to ignore the slight flutter in her stomach when she said her name. She thought that Foxx was certainly a fitting moniker, but she suddenly wished that she was at liberty to call her Rebecca.

"We've got another victim." Rebecca's voice didn't waver, but Jordan imagined she detected a hint of anger. And why not? Anyone surrounding this case couldn't help but be angry.

"Where? I'll be there in fifteen minutes."

Jordan was surprised to hear that the body had been found in the same alley that Julie had been attacked in. She punched in Matty's number and told him to be ready in five minutes. They had another hit in the case.

Fourteen minutes later, she screeched to a halt behind an already active crime scene. She flashed her badge to the patrolman who was holding the press back from the crime scene. She and Matt stooped under the crime tape, and she spotted Detective Foxx's red hair. They stepped around officers and the medical examiner's van.

Rebecca looked up as they approached and smiled warily. "Come on. I'll show you the body."

She led them into the alley, and Jordan was surprised to see what she surmised was a homeless man lying face down. A chilling thought hit her square in the stomach. "Tell me this isn't the guy?"

Rebecca nodded. "We think so."

Jordan stepped closer and studied the pool of blood around his body. She crinkled her forehead. "Looks dry. This guy has been dead awhile."

"Witness says maybe since last night." Rebecca said somberly. She met Jordan's eyes, and a mutual understanding flashed between them. "Guy's homeless, most people don't notice them. Buddy of his says he didn't show up at the shelter last night and then tonight either. Figured something was wrong, maybe died of hypothermia, so he called 911. Apparently, he likes this alley. Bread store around the corner throws out the day-old bread. So we looked here first."

Jordan shook her head. "Fuck!" She rubbed the back of her neck in frustration. "You check out the body yet?'

Rebecca shook her head. "We are getting ready to. I wanted to wait until you guys showed up."

"Thanks." Jordan nodded her head in appreciation. "You got extra gloves?"

Rebecca handed her a pair of blue latex gloves, and she pulled them over her hands. Strangely, she wasn't cold anymore. Her heart was racing now, and it chased the cold away. She knelt over the body and began a slow study of the body and the area surrounding it. She knelt over to look at his neck. "Shit."

Rebecca jumped forward. "What?"

"Can we roll him over?"

Rebecca signaled for the rest of her CDD team and the M.E. "You guys okay if we roll him?"

The general consensus was yes, and Jordan and Rebecca eased him over onto his back. Rebecca jumped backward, her hand over her mouth. Matt, who came closer to help, stepped back quickly and swallowed, forcing the bile back down.

The man's face was a mess. His eyes had been carved out, and his lips had been sliced off. Jordan had seen a lot of shit in her life, but nothing like this. She looked up and saw Rebecca's eyes. She was angry and obviously trying to calm down before she looked closer.

"Talk about being in the wrong place at the wrong time." Jordan stood up and pulled her gloves off. "I don't think it's a stretch to say this is the same guy. Matty said he would strike again, and he's definitely pissed."

"He's getting messy." Rebecca suggested. "He's an emotional killer. It's only a matter of time before he slips up and when he does, I'll be there."

"We'll be there." Jordan leveled her gaze on Rebecca. "This guy's out for revenge. He's not going to accept that Julie didn't die, and he won't give up until he gets her. From here on out, I'm going to be up your ass."

Rebecca glared at her, anger evident in her features. The M.E. stepped around them, and Jordan was thankful for the space. She wasn't sure, which was worse, her mother's angry glare when she was younger or Detective Foxx's angry gaze. "I don't mean to step on toes, Detective. I just meant we have resources that, quite frankly, the CDD doesn't have the budget for. We can help…if you let us."

Rebecca's anger dissipated somewhat, and Jordan swallowed nervously. Why on earth, it mattered that she got her approval was beyond Jordan's imagination. "I think you need to pick your words more carefully. I already told you I would assist in whatever way possible, but you threatening to be up my ass is a surefire way to push me away."

Jordan smiled ruefully. "Perhaps you're right, Detective Foxx. I have a way of putting my foot in my mouth."

"Detective?" The M.E. was leaning over the body, and she waived them over quickly. "You're gonna want to see this."

She gripped his chin and pulled his mouth open.

"Holy shit." Jordan winced, unable to remain calm given the latest cruelty.

His eyes had been cut out and shoved in his mouth, a clear message that his unfortunate sighting and subsequent telling of Julie's attack had gotten him brutally murdered. He would end up just another person with no name or story that would be forgotten by tomorrow.

Rebecca spun on her heel and marched away quickly. She waited for Jordan to catch up. "Whatever the FBI can do to help, do it."

Jordan nodded. She knew from the two brief encounters with Detective Foxx that she was a proud woman, fiercely protective of her territory. To ask for help, even that which had been previously offered, required a quiet strength that few possessed. Jordan imagined that doing so had knocked her down a few notches, and her admiration for this woman grew exponentially.

"Come see me tomorrow. Bring the autopsy results. We'll see what we can put together on this guy." Jordan offered quietly.

Rebecca smiled and thanked her reluctantly. She didn't want to need help, especially Jordan's help. She couldn't decide which was worse, Jordan's overt attempt at seduction in an attempt to get her way, or Matt's subtle way of playing good cop to Jordan's bad cop. What irritated her more was that she found herself actually tempted to take Jordan up on her offer.

She didn't have much time outside work for relationships. She wasn't sure she even wanted one. If she guessed correctly, sex was all Jordan was offering, and that was really all Rebecca had or wanted to give. Truth be told, she missed it. It had been months since she had touched another woman, and she was hungry to taste someone's arousal, to have a woman's touch bring her to orgasm.

Shaking her head, she dismissed the thought of her and Jordan as quickly as it had surfaced, trying to ignore the nagging tug in her chest or the pulsating ache in her clit. That was just what she needed, something else to cloud her judgment and keep her from devoting her time to the real problem. This case.

Chapter 6

"So, what do you think?" Jordan fiddled with her radio trying to find something that wasn't Justin Bieber pop.

"Guy's fucking crazy. He's definitely got an ax to grind. I'm not sure where the hate is coming from though. It's probably a good idea to bring Detective Foxx in to speak with our profiler."

"Already suggested it." Jordan laughed softly. "She wasn't happy about it."

"She can't argue with that. The FBI has resources they will never have." Matt's tone was adamant, but there was a hint of something softer buried between the words.

Jordan studied Matt's profile in the dim lights of her console. Her 370Z hummed along the quiet night streets, and she preferred to keep the peace between them, but a thought nagged at her until she opened her mouth and it spilled out. "You like the Detective, huh?"

For a moment, she thought he would not answer, and she had almost given up when he looked at her out of the corner of his eyes. "Yeah, I do."

Jordan glanced over and saw the telltale puppy-dog look in his eyes, a look she knew well. "Shit, Matty. You really like her. Is that going to be a problem?"

He shook his head. "I have it under control, okay?"

"Good." Jordan slowed down and stopped in front of his building. "I don't think she's the type to mix business and pleasure. Don't get yourself hurt."

She could see his jaw tighten, his only sign her words affected him. He ran a hand through his hair. "I said I got this."

He opened the door and stepped out without another word. She watched him let himself into his building, a slight slump in his shoulders belying the fact that the bravado he showed her was just a façade.

"Whatever." Jordan gunned the engine and pulled away on screeching tires. She felt reckless tonight. A few hours ago, she had been knee-deep in a frenzied bout of sex with a woman she found attractive and uncomplicated. That should be enough. Instead, she was worried about Matty and Detective Foxx. What she should have worried about was following Matt's lead and starting to care too much for the Detective herself.

Jordan pulled into the parking garage that connected with the tower she lived in. She parked and was just about to go in, when she realized she was so wound up, there was no way she could settle down tonight. She punched the elevator and when the doors opened, she hit the ground floor instead of going up.

She wasn't sure where she wanted to go, she only knew it was anywhere except her home. She wandered up the dark street, her senses on high alert. Downtown Chicago was safe most times, but the events of the past few days made her leery. Subconsciously, she patted her side. She felt the hard casing of her holster. She fingered the grip of her Glock and let out a breath.

She wasn't sure why she needed to feel it attached to her side to feel safe. Maybe it was more to reassure herself that it was actually there. Her hand strayed to her left shoulder. The scar was still there. The one time she had been unarmed was the one time she had been shot. It was stupid really. She was getting her weapon serviced, and she had stumbled into a robbery unarmed. She was actually lucky the bullet had only hit her shoulder and not six inches lower.

She shook her head, realizing she was doing it again, reliving the past. She tried not to do that. *Don't stop thinking about tomorrow.* Her mantra, one she stole from a Fleetwood

Mac song. Besides, looking into her past just made her angry, and she didn't want to feel anger. She functioned better when she stayed level—headed.

It wasn't until she heard the bartender ask what she wanted that she realized she had ended up in her favorite dive, Franks. She ordered a whiskey on the rocks and made it a double. She eyed the pool table and figured she could challenge herself to a round or two. Between that and Jack Daniels, she may be able to stop her mind from replaying everything she had seen in the past week.

The cool wood sliding between her fingers and the resounding crack and subsequent drop and roll of the seven ball calmed her frazzled nerves, or maybe her second double in as many minutes. She lined up the two ball and sent it into the corner pocket with a satisfying thud.

"So, you're a night owl too?"

Jordan looked up and saw Rebecca leaning against the doorframe. If she was surprised to see her there, her face didn't show it. Instead, an almost friendly smile had replaced the ever—present glare that Jordan was getting used to. She had changed into faded blue jeans and a worn out button-down shirt. Jordan had to admit she looked incredibly sexy away from work.

"Yeah, I don't sleep much anyway, and this case has me all riled up."

Jordan watched her push off the doorframe and walk towards her. She set her beer bottle down and grabbed a stick. "Up for a game?"

Jordan quirked an eyebrow in disbelief. "Sure. Although, I didn't think you liked me enough to suffer my company."

Rebecca laughed, and Jordan felt herself shiver. Her laugh was definitely sexy, just like the rest of her. "Forgive me, Agent, but you will learn pretty quickly that I take my job very seriously, and I don't like it when I'm stuck in a pissing contest over whose jurisdiction it is, when all I want to do is make the streets a little safer. Besides, beating you will be much more enjoyable than beating myself."

"Please call me Jordan." Jordan studied Rebecca's face as she re—racked the balls. She stood with her hands rested on the top of her stick. "If that's not overstepping my bounds."

Jordan winked as she said the words and Rebecca couldn't help but smile. Outside of work, Jordan was even more of a distraction, and she welcomed the warm feeling that was starting to spread through her body. She wasn't sure if it was the beer or Jordan, but she didn't care. "Alright, Jordan it is…outside work."

Jordan covered a smile. Even off—duty Rebecca couldn't let go of her control. "Are you always this competitive?"

Rebecca met her gaze and had to force herself to pull away. She realized that looking into Jordan's eyes was a bad idea. She could see getting lost in them, and that wasn't something she would allow herself to do. "With four brothers, I had to be."

Jordan nodded toward the table. She studied Rebecca's movements, imprinting them in her brain. Her movements were fluid, almost feline, with a calculated fluidity that made Jordan wonder if she hadn't been a ballerina at some time. She watched her lean over the table, the stick held gently between her thumb and forefinger. She pulled back and sent the cue ball flying with deadly accuracy. By the time the break had come to a stop, she had dropped the six and thirteen balls respectively. Rebecca stood up and sent a devilish grin towards Jordan. "You're in trouble." She circled the table. "I'll take solids. Two ball, corner pocket."

"You didn't tell me you were a hustler." Jordan teased and watched her deftly sink the two ball. "So, you have four brothers, huh? Where did you fall?"

"Middle." Rebecca lined up another shot and sunk her third solid. "We were all born pretty close together, and growing up, I just kind of thought of myself as one of the guys. If they played football, I thought I had to play as well."

"And win of course." Jordan's eyes twinkled playfully. She liked this version of Detective Foxx. The sexy redhead was quickly making her blood boil. She stole a glance to see if maybe the feeling was mutual, but Rebecca was already lining up her next shot. After a particularly difficult bank attempt into the side pocket, she gave up the table.

"Guess I can't win 'em all." Rebecca's face broke into a smile. She felt free for the first time in days. Jordan had a way of putting her at ease and making her forget, for a second, she was a cop. "So what about you? Any brothers or sisters?"

A cloud passed over Jordan's face then disappeared just as quickly. "Nope. Just me and my mom, when she was around, which wasn't much." She lined up over the cue ball and sent it flying, smashing into the eleven and slamming it into the hole so hard it bounced up in protest before dropping with an obliging thud.

Rebecca wanted to push, but she sensed that subject was off limits. There was no mention of her father, which made her heart catch. Rebecca's own father had been a huge part of her and her brother's lives until he passed away two years ago from lung cancer. She felt Jordan withdraw and needed to bring her back. She liked the warmth and comfort she felt with her, and she didn't want to let it go as quickly as she had felt it. "So, what brings you to a place like this? And no, that isn't a bad pickup line."

Jordan's face broke out in a grin, and Rebecca could see where women would find her quite handsome. "Damn, I was hoping you were hitting on me."

Her gaze seared through Rebecca, and she had to swallow the lump in her throat before she could speak without her voice shaking. "Not gonna happen, Agent Gray. I'm not interested in dating you."

Jordan furrowed her brow then quickly pulled her eyes from Rebecca's face. She wondered if she was not interested in her or not interested in women. It didn't matter though, Jordan wasn't interested either. At least, that was what she kept telling herself, although her heart pounded a little faster when the Detective was around. "Good. We won't have to worry about our relationship getting in the way of working together."

Rebecca hid her disappointment. She wasn't sure what she had expected Jordan to say in response to that, but agreeing with her wasn't Rebecca's first choice. "Glad that's settled."

Jordan felt a tug in her chest again. She pushed it down. "I live right around the corner. It's kind of been my haunt for the last few years. How about you? Is this your first time in here?"

"Nah, just haven't been here in ages." Rebecca took a swig from her beer and watched Jordan miss just to the left of the side pocket with her fourteen ball. "Normally, I hang out with the Jonesy and the guys at Stan's, but tonight I needed to get away from work. You can't there. I live right around the corner on Arlington."

"No shit." Jordan laughed. "I live on Halstead."

"So let me guess, you're here a lot?" Rebecca leaned over and lined up her shot and sent the four ball cleanly into the corner pocket. "This place suits you."

Jordan quirked an eyebrow. "I'm not sure if I should take that as a compliment."

Rebecca chuckled innocently. "It is. It's uncomplicated…like you."

"Guess that pretty much sums up my life." Jordan smiled sheepishly. "Things were too complicated growing up and I like it much better this way. Keeps me from going crazy."

"It's hard in this line of work." Rebecca tapped the seven into the side pocket and studied the table. She walked around and stepped in front of Jordan to line up her next shot. She made the mistake of getting too close to Jordan, her breasts brushing across her arm. She tried to ignore the jolt of electricity that shot through her body. Suddenly, she was aware of their closeness, and she tried to back away, but she felt her bottom hit the edge of the table.

Her next mistake was looking up into Jordan's eyes. Instead of her practiced air of nonchalance, there was a hint of desire, and it made Rebecca shiver. Jordan licked her lips and didn't break the connection that crackled between. She leaned in closer, and Rebecca could feel her warm breath against her cheek. She smelled like whiskey and peppermint gum and something else she couldn't quite place, but it reminded her of danger.

Jordan was enjoying this closeness too much, enjoyed making the Detective uncomfortable. She could have easily captured Rebecca's mouth against hers, but she was enjoying the hunger that was building inside her even more than what she surmised would be a rebuffed advance anyway. She leaned in closer and when she thought Rebecca could take no more, she reached around behind her and grabbed the chalk.

She stepped back and heard Rebecca exhale the breath she had been holding since Jordan had paralyzed her with one glance. When she spoke, her voice was an octave lower and there was no mistaking the naked hunger in her husky voice or the silent challenge in her eyes. "I believe it's your move."

Five little words and Rebecca's carefully constructed life started to tremble. It wasn't the game Jordan referred to, although this felt like a game. Jordan was the hunter, and she was her prey. No, Jordan's eyes spoke volumes and her carefully spoken words let Rebecca know that whatever happened next was indeed her move.

Jordan moved to the opposite side of the table, allowing her plenty of space. However, it took several moments of deep breathing before her heart slowed enough to allow her to even turn around and face her again.

Rebecca was certain she had gotten herself together, but when she leaned over to shoot, she sensed the slightest tremor in her left hand and when she shot, her line of fire was a hair off course. Her concentration was broken, from the game anyway. She was forced to admit it had found a new point to center its focus around. It was too much for her, and with a laugh that sounded entirely too forced, she set her stick on the table and smiled. "I think I'm going to call it a night."

"Scared huh?" Jordan teased. "You should be. I'm better than you think."

Rebecca walked away quickly, leaving Jordan shaking her head in disbelief. A thought had sprung from somewhere in her subconscious and had started to grow, until for want of saving her sanity, she was forced to run before she did something she knew she would regret. She was forced to admit that Special Agent Gray had overstepped her boundaries in work and in pleasure, and it made her uncomfortable.

Chapter 7

It's bone—chillingly cold tonight. I lean further into the entryway hoping it will block the icy wind that is rushing around me. Funny that the cold manages to break through my senses and register at all. Normally, my mind is so focused on the hunt that little else matters, although tonight the cold hits me, and I shove my hands into my pockets to warm them. They brush against steel and my focus returns. Tonight is the night, the night she will die.

I mentally stop my body from shivering. My teeth no longer chatter loudly and once again, I can hear the voice talking to me. *Yes, tonight is the night. Tonight, she will pay for her sins.* I repeat the words again. Tonight is the night, the night she will die.

She doesn't know that I've been watching her, many months now. I see her face clearly at the moment, the lights of the deserted street casting an eerie glow over her features. It isn't long before my nostrils get the first hint of her scent. She smells fruity, cloyingly sweet, and oh so overbearing. A mere intake of breath and my stomach is sick with her smell. I blink and try to clear my head, as I hear the telltale staccato of her heels pounding against the cold pavement.

If she sees me, she dismisses me just as quickly, another soul looking for shelter from the frigid cold. Had it been a warmer night, she might have felt the evil around her, shuddered involuntarily at the darkness that enveloped her, but not tonight. Tonight, she is focused only on the streets she hasn't traversed yet, and she takes no notice as I slip from beneath the shelter of the narrow portico and begin the hunt.

I am a lone wolf, a hunter in search of the kill. Only the taste of death can quiet the voice inside my head. He speaks softly now, not wanting to drown out my own thoughts. When he speaks, I have to stop and focus and listen, and this does not allow me to move, and I must move. Tonight I must kill.

I sniff the air and the cold burns my nostrils. I am not close enough to cause alarm, but I can still smell her and her scent angers me again. She smells like her, and I hate her. My eyes have narrowed now. The only thing in my focus is my prey. A stranger bumps me as he emerges from a door, trying to catch a nearby cab. I can feel my blood begin to boil, but the voice speaks up, and I'm paralyzed.

He is not our prey. Do not lose focus of the prey. She must die and we both know why.

No, I know. I shake my head and reassure him that my focus has not been lost. I sniff the air once more, and I imagine I can smell her fear. She turned around at the sound of the scuffle and for a brief moment, I imagined a spark of recognition, but she turns around just as quickly, and I breathe a sigh of relief.

There will be no mistakes tonight, no interruptions. Tonight, my prey will die. I will make sure of that. She is close, and her life cannot continue. She cannot be allowed to give birth. She is not worthy. None of them are worthy. They are abominations, forsaking God's natural plan for them.

Can't they see it? Can't they understand why they must die? Why God has chosen me to end their sinful lives? I am a hunter for God. He has chosen me and tonight he has chosen her for the sacrifice.

I can see her step falter. Perhaps she has finally realized that she is being stalked. I can see her speed up. My dear, you must know running is futile. I will catch you. You will be mine. My stride lengthens, and the gap between us narrows. The wolf is hungry tonight, silently stalking its prey. A low, guttural growl escapes from my lips and is carried off on the wind.

It is time. I can see ahead that she realizes what I am. I am death, and it is her time. She opens her mouth to scream and only air escapes. She is paralyzed with fear, and I feel my heart smile. She has seen my knife and knows that she cannot run, she cannot hide. I grab her around her bulging waist, and my hand feels the life within in her. A life brought about by her sin. She opens her mouth to scream, and I wrap my hand around her mouth to silence her.

She is fighting me. Her will to live has kicked in, and her will to protect her unborn child is strong. She wrenches away from me and starts to run, and I realize that tonight will not be easy. I spring at her with unearthly speed and let out a low howl. She tries to knee me in the groin, and I punish her with a backhand that sends her staggering to the cold ground below.

It is late, and the streets are deserted or certainly some unlucky passerby would hear us struggling. That last time this happened, he was punished for it. I cannot be deterred in my quest for retribution. I am kneeling over her, and the smell of her fear has made me hard. I can see her eyes that she knows what is about to happen to her.

"Do not be afraid. You are very special. You will get to atone for your sins." My hand is clamped over her mouth, and she shakes her head from side—to—side with the fury of a trapped animal who knows it is about to die.

I brandish my knife over her and the low lights from the alley glint off of it. She sees the sharp edge, and her eyes widen, knowledge that these are her final moments dawning on her. She wraps her hands around her stomach, and I can feel her lips moving against my hand, begging for mercy. I am not the one whom she should ask for mercy.

I move my hand, and the edge of the knife slices along her neck, the first drops of blood steaming against her cold skin. I sniff the metallic scent and it lights through me like wildfire. I lean in closer and meet her scared eyes with my own dark gaze. A hint of recognition passes over her face. "Yes, you do know me. You must know now why you have to die."

My weight on top of her and the life seeping out of her has made her tired, and she has stopped moving beneath me. Her eyes blink heavily, so I slap her with a gloved hand. "Oh, no, no. Don't go to sleep. You won't want to miss this. This is the best part. This is the reason you must die."

I reach for the button on my jeans and pull it open hastily. The sound of the snap releasing echoes through the alley and hardens my erection. She has not made this easy. The bitch is wearing pants, so I am forced to my knees to slice them away from her body. She summons all her strength, and her fist flies and connects with the corner of my face. I punch her in response. My eye is pounding from the blow. "Do you know at all why I chose you?"

She shakes her head again. The fear is gone from her eyes. She has resigned herself to her fate. I rub her stomach, and I can see the hatred well in her eyes now. The life that she was given, her miracle and I have the gall to touch her. I reach in and pull my erection out and poise it outside her body. "You fucked up. Your baby, she is not a gift from God. You think that you can turn your back on God and get pregnant without a man? You are wrong, and you must give your life as retribution."

I can see realization dawn on her. I drive my cock deep inside her with a low growl and pound inside her angrily. This is her sacrifice, her means to forgiveness. God is using me to exact punishment for her sins and with every furious stroke, her last precious breaths ebb away, and as I pull out, her eyes roll back in her head, and she pays her debt.

I stare down at her lifeless body, and for the first time today, the voice is quiet. I cannot afford to linger any longer. I know the danger of getting caught. I slice across her belly and reach into her still warm body. I can barely watch this part. It doesn't get better. Blindly, I fill a plastic bag and bury it in my coat. I wipe the knife against her leg, her blood smearing on what is left of her cashmere pants. I cast one more glance over my shoulder and leave the alley, an angry sneer curling my lip.

Her scent still lingers, and I wave my hand in front of my face before realizing it's on me. I try to breathe through my mouth, but the cold hurts my teeth, and I shut it just as quickly. The street isn't clear anymore. The cold is making my eyes water, and everything is blurry. I brush my hand over my eyes and wince at the tenderness around my eye. I touch it gingerly, feeling the first sign of swelling beneath my finger.

"Shit." A black eye will be hard to explain, and suddenly, I'm angry again. But my fury is not directed at her. It is directed at my wife. My ex—wife.

"No, you don't understand. I want to have children."

I regard her helplessly. We have this same argument daily. *"I can give you a baby."*

She laughs mockingly. "Can you? We've tried, and I'm still not pregnant. I can't wait any longer."

I follow her out the door. "So, now what happens? You're just going to leave? And go where?"

She flees to the waiting car and throws the door open. She gets in without so much as a second glance in my direction. I see the driver lean forward. It's not her mother, whom I assume she would be running away to. It's a man, and immediately I know what she is up to. I couldn't get her pregnant no matter how many times we tried, so she has picked a man she feels is more virile.

"Hey, buddy, watch out!"

I wake up and realize I have walked to the Loop. I see a man shove his way around me, as I have stopped in the middle of the stairs and am standing like a statue, watching his car drive away again.

Chapter 8

Jordan checked the display on her phone and grimaced. Detective Foxx was obviously still pissed about her little display at the bar, and she was about to get an earful. She sighed and pushed the Receive button. "Special Agent Gray."

"We have another murder." Rebecca's voice trembled, and Jordan could tell how angry she was. Not at her as she had suspected, but at the killer she hadn't managed to make any headway on.

"Where are you?" Jordan heard the concern in her voice, and she realized that somewhere between trying to flirt with Detective Foxx for information and almost kissing her, she had started caring about her feelings. "Shit."

Rebecca answered without hesitation, and Jordan breathed a sigh of relief. Obviously, her cursing was for her feelings surrounding the case and not Jordan's behavior. Jordan scribbled the address down. "I'll be there in ten."

She hung up and called Matty. He answered drowsily, and Jordan gave him a quick recap. She could hear him moving around and knew he was trying to find something to wear. "See you in ten."

It was a given now, Jordan and Matt would be called to the crime scene. Rebecca no longer worried about their presence there. To the casual observer, they looked like a couple of detectives. It would only be if someone started digging and put two and two together that anyone would catch on to the fact that the FBI was showing up at cases that weren't their jurisdiction.

When Jordan skidded to a stop in front of the crime scene, the place was already crawling with Chicago's finest. This part of the city was eerily familiar to her. Her gym was right around the corner, and she shuddered involuntarily. She didn't wait for Matty, instead locating Detectives Foxx and Jones just inside the yellow crime tape.

She had walked past this alley many times and wasn't prepared for the site that awaited her. The victim, a woman in her early thirties, was lying on her back, her lifeless eyes staring out vacantly. Her body was covered with a thin sheet, but Jordan could see the blood on the ground near her face and around her midriff. She covered her mouth and swallowed bile.

Detective Foxx materialized beside her. "We covered her in case reporters showed up. I can have them remove the sheet."

Jordan nodded weakly. She watched them pull the sheet back, and the first glance made her look away. She took several shallow breaths and turned around. The woman's stomach had been sliced open, and the blood covered her body. "Fuck."

"I'm sorry. I forgot you had only seen crime scene photos of the other victims, and Ms. Keppler got lucky. I should have prepared you."

"Shit." Matt slid to a stop behind them and pulled back quickly.

"Special Agent Riley." Rebecca watched him over her shoulder. She felt sorry for him. She wasn't sure how long he had been with the FBI, but something told her, he wasn't used to the kind of cases she saw. She gestured to the M.E. "Cover her back up."

"Pregnant?" The question was almost a whisper and Jordan cleared her throat. "Was she pregnant?"

Rebecca nodded. "We can't be sure until the autopsy, but it's a pretty good guess she was."

"And he…he took the baby?" God bless him, Matt was trying. Seeing crime scene photos was one thing. Seeing it firsthand was a perspective he wasn't exactly comfortable with. He saw the response in Rebecca's face and stumbled backwards.

Rick put a protective hand on Matt's shoulder. "Listen, Riley. Why don't we check the area outside the alley? See if he got careless and dropped something. Maybe you can find someone that saw something." Rick knew they would find nothing, but he could tell Matt needed a distraction.

Jordan watched him walk away, thankful for a reason to get out of the alley. "Take the sheet off."

She knelt over the body. The smell of blood repelled her. She saw the remains of her torn pants and knew without being told that this woman had been violated sexually as well. She shook her head. "Do we have an ID?"

"Yeah." Rebecca pulled a pad out of her pocket. "Purse was on the sidewalk outside the alley. That's how they found her. Name's Elizabeth Hudson."

"Does Ms. Hudson have a husband?"

Rebecca shook her head. "We're tracking him down. The only contact number in her purse is a cell, and he's not answering."

"Hell of a way to find out about your wife and kid." Jordan ran her hand over her jaw. "I don't mean to be an ass, but I'm thinking it's time to lay everything out on the table. Whatever issues we have, catching this guy needs to come first."

Rebecca narrowed her eyes. "I don't need you to tell me how to do my job. I'm well aware of how important catching this guy is."

"Whoa!" Jordan held up her hands defensively. She stepped closer and lowered her voice. "I realize I may have rattled you at the bar, but that's no reason to make this investigation more difficult."

"First off." Rebecca held up her finger. "You did not, nor can you, ever rattle me, and second, don't for a minute think that I would let whatever personal issues you have get in the way of an investigation. It may behoove you to remember that you came to me, *Special* Agent Gray, not the other way around. My continued allowance of your involvement is a personal favor to your boss, nothing more."

Jordan's mouth dropped in shock. Rebecca lived up to every stereotype about redheads and tempers. She toyed with putting the Detective in her place and decided against it. What she really wanted to do was laugh. It had been a long time since anyone had spoken to her like that, and truth be told, when Detective Foxx got all worked up, she was downright beautiful. "I'm going to check on Riley. Please let me know if there are any developments in the case."

Jordan spun around and walked off in search of her partner. She had a name at least and figured that a little homework of her own might produce a lead. First thing she was going to do was a little research on the victim's husband. It wasn't so far—fetched to imagine that the husband had something to do with it. Some lunatic commits a string of murders to cover the one that mattered. It was a sick thought, but Jordan had met enough wackos that she would buy anything these days.

She caught up to Matt and grabbed his elbow. "Come on."

He looked relieved. This case wasn't sitting too well with him. He preferred the high tech cases, the ones that required chasing white—collar criminals. The ones like this almost sent him over the edge. He didn't do blood and guts.

"So, what's your take on this?" Jordan asked after a few moments of silence, broken only by the well—tuned hum of her 370Z.

Matt shook his head. "This guy's a fucking nut job. I've never seen someone mess women up like this. You gonna ask Redmond?"

Julien Redmond was a criminal profiler and a genius at giving them something out of nothing. Asking him meant alerting someone else that she and Matt were working a case that wasn't technically the FBIs to work. Normally, she would worry about that, especially since Assistant Director Mitchell had specifically said *under the radar.* The less she pinged on the radar, the better. "I thought about it. Detective Foxx hasn't given me the go ahead, but something tells me we are going to have to do some investigating outside of what we share with the CDD."

"Think that's a good idea?" Matt asked quietly.

Jordan shrugged. "Maybe, maybe not."

"Don't tick her off, Jordie. In case you hadn't noticed, she's not exactly thrilled the FBI is sticking its nose in where it doesn't belong." Matt's tone held a friendly warning, but buried beneath that was something else. Something Jordan couldn't quite put her finger on, but it was something akin to admiration, maybe even like. "She's given us more than I thought she would; now she's even letting us into the crime scenes. That's more than the CDD has let us do before, and I'm guessing if we fuck it up, the shit will hit the fan."

He didn't have to say Assistant Director Mitchell would have their heads on a silver platter. It wouldn't matter anyway, if Jordan messed everything up, she would feel worse about it than her boss could ever make her feel. Besides, staring into those lifeless eyes tonight had triggered a primal need inside her, and she knew that whatever it took, she would catch him. She would make him pay. "You don't have to tell me, alright? I was there. I saw her face. I know what this means to her, to Julie and now to Detective Foxx. It's personal. Believe me, I don't intend to mess this up."

"Good." She could see Matt's appeased smile in the dashboard's glow. "Listen, I gotta ask you about Detective Foxx. Do you think she would…well, you suppose…"

Jordan had a sneaking suspicion of what he was trying to say and rather than help him, she opted to remain silent and prolong his misery.

"Hell, after this is over, I want to ask her out. You think she would be interested in me?"

The look he gave her was so innocent and hopeful that she didn't think she could crush his feelings now. She had only seen him interested in one other woman in the time they had been partners. That had ended badly, and if Jordan was even half way right, this one wasn't starting out so good either.

"I don't know, Matty. I think you would have your hands full with that one." It was the safe answer she knew, but something told her to go with safe for now. "She's certainly attractive, though."

"Yeah, yeah, she is." Matt agreed appreciatively. "Can you imagine the make-up sex a fight with her would lead to?"

Truth be told, Jordan might have already thought of that. Detective Foxx didn't do anything half—heartedly. She could only assume that her bedroom manner mirrored her fiery personality. "Just keep this idea of yours on the DL for now. I've already overstepped our bounds with her, and I don't want to give her anymore reason to shut the door on the little bit she is feeding us."

"No, I know." Matt shook his head up and down. "So, tomorrow we find the husband?"

Jordan smiled. She and Matt often thought alike, and tonight was no different. He had already figured out what she decided they would do anyway. "Yep, and we'll see what Redmond thinks about this guy."

Somehow, they drove to his place without realizing it. "Get some sleep, Matty. It's gonna be busy tomorrow."

"Ha, ha, I will." He slid out of her car and poked his head back in. "I'll bring coffee."

"Thanks." She threw him a mock salute and put the car in first, easing her foot off the clutch and lowering the gas pedal with skilled precision.

Here in her car, gliding through the deserted streets, was her sanctuary. At least, it should have been. Tonight, she couldn't turn her mind off. She couldn't make the events of the last few days stop colliding like pieces of flotsam floating around in troubled waters. She needed something to take the edge off, and when her car pulled up in front of her local bar, she knew she had no choice but to try and silence the voices with a little help.

Jordan slid on to a barstool and ordered a whiskey. She held up two fingers signaling she wanted a double. She didn't nurse the first drink, merely leaned back and threw the contents of her glass down her throat. It stung momentarily, and when she winced, there was a second that her mind was empty. That was the peace she was looking for and had been evading her lately.

She was about to order another when a flash of red on the TV at the end of the bar caught her attention. "Hey, turn that up."

The bartender slid a remote down the bar and nodded when Jordan held up two more fingers. When he set the drink in front of her, Jordan's attention was already on the TV. A local reporter was interviewing Detective Foxx, who looked none too happy to be in front of the cameras.

"Do you have any suspects in this case?"

Rebecca gave the standard answer. *"We're investigating all possible leads."*

"Detective Foxx, this is the seventh victim. The citizens of Chicago would like to know if the Chicago Detective Division is getting any closer to making an arrest in the attempted murder of Julie Keppler and the other homicides?"

Rebecca looked as annoyed as Jordan felt. She hated when a reporter spoke in an overly concerned voice when beneath that plastered on fake smile, their fangs were ready to come out. *"I'm afraid I'm not at liberty to reveal that information."*

"Detective Foxx, can you tell me if the CDD believes this is a serial killer? Are there similarities in the case to the other murders?"

"No comment." Jordan noticed that Rebecca's lip was pursed angrily, and she figured the reporters might want to back off.

"Detective, the Mayor is calling this the most violent crime spree in Chicago history. Do you believe there is more than one person involved?"

"I'm not at liberty to say." Rebecca's eyes narrowed.

"When did the FBI become involved in the investigation? Is this a joint task investigation? Has the CDD requested the FBI's help since they have made no progress in catching the killer…or killers?"

Jordan thought Rebecca might have rolled her eyes, but she couldn't be sure. She looked pointblank at the reporter. *"I'm not going to speculate about the details of the case. I'm sure you understand that any information that is leaked could jeopardize this case and put more victims at risk."*

Not satisfied, the reporter pushed forward and hit Rebecca with a string of questions. She flicked her hand at one of the cops, and he quickly stepped in between Rebecca and the over—zealous reporter.

Jordan felt the corners of her mouth creep up. The cameras were still trained on Rebecca's back, and she could swear she could see the hackles standing up on her neck. "I'll give you credit, Detective Foxx. You don't take shit from anybody."

Thirty minutes and three double whiskeys later, Jordan was starting to relax. She looked at her watch and sighed. She took two twenties out of her wallet and threw them on the bar. It took her a record nineteen minutes to get home, shower, and when her head hit the pillow, Jack Daniels had somehow managed to make her forget everything she had seen today.

Chapter 9

Jordan yawned and smacked her lips together. Her tongue felt like a piece of dried-out leather. She twisted her body and dropped her feet over the side of the mattress, the rush of blood sending her headache into overdrive. She dropped her head in her palms and groaned loudly before she pushed herself up and started the shower. She loved whiskey, but last night, it had knocked her on her ass.

She showered, checked her messages and pulled into work a surprising three minutes after nine, which was earlier than most days. She walked into Matt's office and took her coffee with a nod. It took her half the cup, and a good ten minutes before she acknowledged him. "Thanks."

Matt chuckled softly in deference to the look in her eyes. "Looks like you need it."

Jordan shook her head. "Busy night."

"Besides the murder?" Matt asked incredulously.

Jordan looked askance at Matt as if to say you know me better than that. "Yeah. Workout before and drinks after."

Matt had the good taste not to ask about the workout. He knew the kind of exercise his partner liked to get and more times than not, he interrupted her workouts. "So, Mitchell wants us to interview Julie today. She says she's finally up to it."

"We might as well do that before we see Redmond. Besides I'm still waiting for the autopsy report for the Hudson case." It had only happened last night, and that quickly, she was just another victim.

Jordan downed the last of her coffee and chucked the cup into the trash can. She pushed herself up with a sigh. "Guess we might as well get this over with."

Matt could sense her hesitation. "Yeah, I'm not looking forward to this either."

Jordan pulled into the freight zone at Mercy and stepped out into the cold. The wind had picked up again off the lake, and it froze her bare fingers. She cinched her leather coat around her and wished that she had worn something heavier. "This fucking cold is killing me."

Matt punched her in the arm with his gloved hand and pulled the collar of his thick North Face coat up. "Dude, I've been telling you for how many years. That coat ain't good for shit except looking good."

Jordan glared at Matt. "Looking good has kept me warm many nights, brother."

"Whatever." Matt rolled his eyes and pushed through the revolving door. He hadn't gone to see Julie again, and his stomach roiled nervously. Hopefully, he would handle it better than his reaction to the crime scene last night.

They rode the elevator up in silence, all previous joking put aside. Jordan wrapped on the door softly, in case Julie was sleeping. Neither was surprised when a haggard looking Assistant Director Mitchell pulled the door open a few seconds later. She offered them a wary smile.

They stepped in almost silently in deference for Julie, not wanting to wake her if she was still asleep.

"Hey, guys." Julie's voice was low and still raspy, but she looked one hundred times better than when Jordan had seen her a couple of days ago. The bandage still covered the length of her neck, but her color was returning. Behind the weak smile, they could see the immense sadness in her eyes that no amount of pretending could cover.

"Julie, hi." Jordan gave her a small hug, careful not to hurt her. Matt, much more uncomfortable about the situation, stood back and nodded aloofly.

"Hey, Julie." He tried not to appear too out of place, but the constant shuffle with his feet gave him away.

"Jeez, Matty." Jordan shot him a look. "Chill, will ya?"

He smiled sheepishly and sloughed off to the corner to occupy one of the empty chairs.

Jordan turned back to Julie and smiled. "How ya feeling?"

Julie swallowed and winced at the movement against her stitches. "Been better. However, I'm alive, and I guess that's more than I can say for the other women."

Jordan gave a slight nod in agreement. "So, do you feel like talking?"

Julie's eyes left hers and landed on Susan's face. There was a slight tinge of red in her cheeks, and Jordan was alert enough to know that Julie didn't want to talk in front of her partner. Jordan couldn't blame her. Right now, the anger and hatred in Susan's eyes were enough that she thought Susan possible of murder herself. Hearing the details would only aggravate the situation.

Jordan stepped over to Susan and held her gaze. "Listen, why don't you and Matt grab some coffee? I got this."

Susan looked as though she was going to refuse, but in the end, she let Matt drag her from the room. Jordan watched her leave then shut the door behind them quietly. She preferred the details of her conversation stay in this room. It wasn't unlike reporters to lurk in hospital hallways trying to get the scoop.

Jordan pulled a small tape recorder from her pocket. She held it up to Julie and raised her eyebrows questioningly. "You mind if I tape this?"

Julie shook her head from side to side. Her lip quivered and she sucked her bottom lip into her mouth in an effort to hide her fear. She may have looked okay, but she wasn't. She was sure she may never be okay again. She couldn't close her eyes without reliving her attack, smelling her attacker, feeling him inside her.

Jordan pushed the record button. "Listen, we can stop whenever you want. We don't have to get this all done today. If it gets to be too much, just stop me."

Julie nodded.

"November 19th, 2011. Special Agent Jordan Gray interviewing Julie Keppler, regarding her attack on November 15th, 2011."

She rewound the tape and played back what she just said to verify that the tape recorder was working. Jordan didn't do notes. That seemed to make people uncomfortable and besides, most of the time, she couldn't read her own chicken scratch. "Let's go back to that night. Just try to remember as much as you can."

"Okay." Julie flinched subconsciously, the feeling of a cold wind ran through her. As much as she could remember? Better to ask her what she didn't remember. The details were crystal clear. Remembering wasn't the problem.

"Take me through everything that happened, and remember, if at any point you need to stop, just tell me." Jordan's voice dropped an octave and had taken on a soothing quality. That was one thing that she used to her advantage. She could put people at ease, get them to open up. It made her invaluable as an interrogator.

"I was coming home from work late, so it was already dark. I remember how cold it was, so chilly for November. All I wanted was to be home in a hot bath. Normally, I walk home, but that night it was sleeting, so I decided to call a cab. The wait was ninety minutes."

"So, you walked anyway?" Jordan broke in, feeling the need to calm Julie down. She watched her hands grow increasingly fidgety, and she could tell that already she was anxious.

Julie shook her head. "Yes. I remember thinking that I felt like someone was watching me, following me, but I was certain it was just my mind playing tricks on me. I should have listened to my gut."

Jordan squeezed her hand. "It is hard not to look back and think that. Most people are born with a sixth sense that alerts us to that, but we aren't trained to listen to that inner voice, to use it to protect us. Don't chastise yourself for that."

Julie smiled warily. "By the time, I finally figured out I wasn't crazy, it was too late. He was already there. I remember trying to scream and no sound coming out. There was no one around to hear it anyway. I tried to run, but I stumbled and fell. Damn high heels."

Jordan could hear her voice quiver, and it broke her heart. She couldn't imagine what Julie was going through, had no way to comfort her. Instead, here she was making her relive the whole thing. "What happened next?"

"The pain, I remember the pain in my stomach and praying to God that my baby…that my baby was alright." Julie tried to swallow the sobs threatening to escape, and every word shook as she spoke. "I'm sorry, it's just…"

Jordan grabbed her hand again. "It's okay. We can stop."

"No." Julie swiped at her eyes and took a drink of water. "I need to get this out, so I can start to heal."

Jordan didn't let go of her hand, and subconsciously she rubbed her thumb over Julie's hand protectively. "He…he held me down on the ground with his knee. He cut my throat and then he…he…ripped my hose off and he…his…he…" Julie's voice disappeared, the memory paralyzing her ability to speak.

Jordan stopped her. She didn't need to make her say it. Most likely, the tape would never be used as evidence, only for Jordan in her investigation. "Do you remember anything about him? Did you get a look at him?"

Julie shook her head. "It was too dark. I didn't get a look at his face. I know he was tall and skinny, probably six or seven inches taller than me and not much heavier. But he was strong, freakishly strong. His voice was odd in a way. I can't quite put my finger on it."

"You heard him talk?" Jordan asked, surprise evident in her voice.

"Yes. He asked me if I really thought I was special, and told me that I was a fucking bitch, and that I needed a penis to get pregnant."

"Anything else?" Jordan leaned forward and pushed softly.

"No, that was it." Julie's hand was clenched around Jordan's so tightly, she was starting to cut off the circulation to her fingers but Jordan didn't pull away.

"So, what happened to scare him off?" Jordan knew, but any little bit of information could be helpful.

"I don't know. I'm sorry. I passed out and when I woke up, I was here. I didn't know what happened, that is until Susan told me. That homeless guy died for protecting me. It's just not fair." Julie's lips were a narrow, thin line, and she bit back tears.

Jordan reached over and turned off the recorder. "I'm sorry to make you have to do that again. If there's anything else you remember, even if it's something you don't think is important, let me know."

A soft knock sounded at the door, and Jordan opened the door. She could see the silent question in Susan's eyes, and she nodded. It had been hard, but Julie had given her everything she could. Now it was up to Jordan to find the killer. Given the lack of details, no DNA evidence and the number of people in Chicago, it somehow felt like looking for a needle in several haystacks.

Jordan looked back over her shoulder. Susan had already assumed her protective position at the side of Julie's bed. Anyone could see they were united in their grief, agonizing over their loss and trying to build on the positive. Jordan knew, if at all possible, she would find justice for them and in doing so, hopefully give them much-needed closure to move on.

Chapter 10

Rebecca stood opposite the M.E., watching her make her first visual pass of Elizabeth Hudson's body. They still had not located her husband, which hadn't bothered Rebecca at first, but seemed eerily suspicious now.

There was a camera recording the entire process, and the M.E. noted every step of the autopsy. *"Date of the autopsy is November 19th, 2011, 10:53 AM. Performed by Sylvia Knowles, Medical Examiner. Manner of death is homicide. Cause of death is exsanguination due to an incise wound in the neck, severing the carotid arteries and an incision in the abdomen. Victim is a Caucasian female, approximately thirty—four years old. Generalized pallor and evidence of exsanguination, bi—lateral incision across the neck and abdomen. Left lower lateral chest-wall abrasions and contusions, consistent with injuries sustained."*

Rebecca watched Sylvia study the body, noting every bruise, cut or other mark that appeared out of place. When she mentioned the pregnancy and subsequent loss of the child, Rebecca bit back tears. She couldn't help but see the woman Elizabeth Hudson was just hours before, filled with energy and no doubt ecstatic about her upcoming birth. Now, she was a pale shadow of her former self, the blood that was once life—giving had been shed heartlessly. The life that, until recently, had flourished within her was gone.

"I'm going to do the rape kit next. Wanna stick around?" Sylvia watched for her reply behind her glasses. "I know we won't get anything, but I have to do it anyway."

Rebecca's belt vibrated loudly, and she pulled her pager out checking the display. "Nah, I got to make a call. Just call me when you finish."

Sylvia nodded, her attention already focused on the victim again.

Rebecca shook her head as she walked out. It took a special person to be a Medical Examiner. She knew without a doubt it was a calling that she would never have answered. Despite her hard—ass exterior, the hardest part of the job was separating herself from the victims, trying not to figure out their story. She knew she couldn't look at a person lying on the table and detach herself. It wasn't in her make up.

Rebecca pulled her phone out and dialed the number on her pager. "Foxx."

"Detective, it's Special Agent Gray. We tracked down Elizabeth Hudson's husband."

"Correct me if I'm wrong, Special Agent Gray." Her voice was razor sharp. "But I was unaware that the FBI was tracking anyone down."

"I just assumed that given the wide scope of the FBI's reach and your full plate, you would appreciate some assistance." Jordan hoped her tone didn't sound as sarcastic as she felt.

"You need to stop assuming that we need the FBI to swoop in and save the day. I can assure you that my team can handle this." Rebecca's tone had tempered some, but she was still on edge. No matter how long she had been at it, no matter how good a detective she was, there was always some invisible voice whispering in her ear that she just wasn't good enough. Usually it was some dick reminding her that she was a woman, and women are never as good as men. Today, it was Jordan's voice taunting her. The FBI had managed to do what the CDD hadn't. It tracked down Elizabeth Hudson's missing husband. It was just another reminder she had grown up amongst her father and brothers, who somehow always managed to be better than she was. It wasn't that they competed with her. It was her own insecurity and need to be something she wasn't. Rather than accept that she could succeed as a woman, she had lived in a self-imposed shadow of doubt and some unattainable goal that haunted her every day.

"So, does that mean you don't want to know where he is?" Jordan could tell she was baiting her, and she didn't really want to stoop that low, but damn it, that woman got under her skin. Did she want to catch the killer or not? And something as simple as tracking someone down shouldn't raise her ire as much as it did.

Rebecca let out a loud sigh. "Tell me what you got."

"Well, I'll assume you already know his name."

The smile in Jordan's voice was obvious, and it at least got Rebecca to loosen up some. "Yes, I do." Rebecca answered smugly. "Richard. Works for some law firm here in the city."

"Yep. Apparently, the law firm he works for handles a lot of overseas clients. He travels a lot, and my people picked him up at O'Hare. Guy was getting ready to fly to Singapore."

"Interesting considering his wife was killed last night." Rebecca's sixth sense was starting to act up, a sign that maybe she finally had a lead.

"Exactly what we thought." Jordan concurred quickly.

Rebecca pinched the bridge of her nose, her brain working on overtime. "Did he happen to mention where he was or why he didn't answer his phone?"

"Oh, he was very forthcoming with that. Had an early flight out of O'Hare, and apparently he hates traffic, so he spends the night at a hotel near the airport. Didn't answer his phone because it was off."

The hair on the back of Rebecca's neck was standing on end. "That's convenient. Did you tell him about Elizabeth?"

"Nope, I figured you would want to see his face when we told him." Jordan had thrown *we* in hoping that maybe, just maybe, with the help she and the FBI were able to give in tracking down Richard Hudson, Rebecca would return the favor and let her sit in when they told him about his wife.

"We?" Rebecca chuckled sarcastically. "You just think your part of my team now, huh?"

"Wishful thinking." It was true. She was wishing she could spend more time with the enigmatic Detective Foxx. She wanted it to be about the case only, but a more personal reason was starting to creep into her consciousness. "Besides, it might help to have backup."

"And why might I need backup? Detective Jones has covered my ass this long, and I'm still alive."

"Because of the second part of the news I wanted to tell you. Richard Hudson has a rap sheet."

"Whoa…what do you mean?" Rebecca's tone belied her disbelief. "We didn't find anything."

"And now do you see why I'm important to you?" Jordan asked smugly.

Rebecca begrudgingly admitted to herself that maybe having the FBI around wasn't too bad. "So what did you find on him?"

"You didn't find it because his record has been expunged. Dad evidently had money and knew someone in the DA's office. Apparently, this guy has a bit of a temper. Put his ex—wife in the hospital a couple of times. She tried to file for divorce, but he messed her up really badly. Bad enough that she filed for a restraining order."

The wheels in Rebecca's mind were spinning rapidly. "Think we can talk to her?"

"I wish." Jordan said ruefully. "She died six years ago."

Rebecca's heart stopped. "How did she die?"

"Funny you ask." Jordan's tone suggested it was anything but funny. "Attacked in an alley, had her throat sliced. Killer was never found."

Rebecca's interest peaked. The same MO as their current perp. Certainly it wasn't a coincidence. "And Mr. Hudson?"

"Alibi'd out. Can you believe that?" Jordan's incredulous tone suggested she believed that his alibi had been of a very convenient and much too suspicious nature to be a coincidence.

"Nothing surprises me nowadays." Rebecca grabbed her coat off a chair. She tucked her phone under her chin and shoved her arms into her coat.

"So, you wanna meet me at headquarters?" Jordan asked hopefully. "I think it's about time we tell Mr. Hudson what an unlucky fellow he is."

"Sure. Will Detective Riley be joining us?" For some reason, Rebecca had the oddest feeling of wanting to be alone with Jordan. The thought of Detective Riley joining them seemed like more of an inconvenience then a benefit.

"Not today." Jordan wasn't quite sure what to make of the question. She didn't think Rebecca was interested in him or any other man, for that matter, but maybe she read it wrong. "Let's just say he's covering both our asses while I am working on this case. I think he doesn't mind not being buried in this case anyway. He doesn't do blood and guts too well."

Rebecca's husky laugh came through the phone and sent shivers up and down Jordan's spine. "Yeah, I kind of gathered that from his reaction last night. Jonesy is following up on another lead as well."

A thought struck Jordan, and she took a leap of faith. "Since it's just the two of us, how about I pick you up?"

Rebecca almost declined, but on a whim and in the interest of time, she accepted. Twenty minutes later, Rebecca was ensconced in the soft leather of Jordan's Nissan 370Z. Richard Hudson was being detained at the airport, and Jordan was chomping at the bit to see his face when he learned his wife had been murdered. She stole a sideways glance at Rebecca and wasn't surprised to see her jaw muscles flexing uncontrollably. "Listen, I know I have a bad habit of butting in where I don't belong, but I figured in light of our shared desire to catch this guy, you might be willing to overlook that."

Rebecca's fist flexed into a tight ball. "It isn't that. I'm talking myself into behaving when we get there. I'm so ready to catch the fucker who is doing this, that I'm afraid anyone who even smells a little suspicious might catch the brunt of my anger."

"Temper, temper, Detective Foxx." Jordan directed her car onto the highway and instead of merging into the traffic, shot across several lanes and let the speedometer rest at eighty—five miles an hour. "I've been doing the same thing. Ever since I found out that Julie had been attacked, I've been fighting to keep this case from becoming too personal."

Rebecca finally turned to her and searched her face. "How's that working for you? 'Cause so far, I'm failing miserably. I want to slice this guy's dick off and shove it down his throat."

"Wow, tell me how you really feel." Jordan's tone was teasing, but she felt the same way. She followed her comment up by balling up her own fists.

Rebecca smiled evilly. "I can't help it. I'm tired of seeing the same thing day in and day out. Some guy goes on one bad date and decides to start taking it out on random strangers. Then more times than not, he pleads insanity and spends a few years in some cushy mental facility before he gets released back out on the streets and starts the whole thing all over again."

"Not this time." Jordan's tone held an unspoken warning. In all her years, particularly those spent surviving on the streets, she didn't fail. She wouldn't allow herself to fail her boss, and especially not Julie.

As much as Rebecca wanted to find him and gun him down herself, her sworn duty as an officer of the law required her to apprehend him, build the strongest case possible and then trust that justice would be served. "You can't go all rogue on me, Special Agent Gray. I've got my superiors to answer to and having to tell them that some hot—headed Fibbie shot my UNSUB in cold blood isn't going to go over well."

Jordan was silent for several minutes, not acknowledging the comment. She wasn't a hothead, didn't shoot from the hip.

That wasn't her style. She was methodical, cold, calculated. That's what kept her alive all these years. She also didn't defend herself to anyone, least of all a Detective with a chip on her shoulder.

Rebecca could sense she had hit a nerve, and she felt immediately guilty. Not enough to give her an apology, but enough to try to smooth things over. As much as she resented the FBI's involvement, she did appreciate what help they had given her and jeopardizing the relationship didn't seem as important as it once had. "Listen, since we are going to be working together pretty closely for a while, I'm going to do something I don't do...ever. Call me Rebecca."

It wasn't much of an apology, especially since Jordan had already done away with formalities...at least in her head. Jordan quirked an eyebrow, not sure that she had heard her correctly, but when she saw the smile on Rebecca's face, she knew she had heard right. It was the first genuine smile she had seen from the woman since they met. "I'd like that." When she said it, she meant it. It was one step closer to getting to know the mysterious redhead sitting next to her. "And you can still call me Jordan."

"So, Jordan, how do you want to handle this?" It was another attempt by Rebecca to smooth things over, one that surprised even herself. Normally, she could give a rat's ass what anyone else's opinion was. However, here she was, asking for Jordan's, and if she didn't know any better, she was willing to accept her input, not just trying to appease her.

Jordan swallowed a lump in her throat. She was shocked for the second time in as many minutes. First, they were on a first-name basis, and now Rebecca wanted to talk about what was happening between them. "Well, I don't know for sure, I've never dated anyone I worked with."

Rebecca's laughter filled the car.

"What?" The look of genuine surprise on Jordan's face was priceless.

"You thought I meant how we would handle something between us?" Rebecca wiped tears from her eyes. "There is no something between us, Agent. Get that through your thick skull. What I meant was how do you want to handle the Hudson thing?"

"Oh." Jordan couldn't think of any response that would make her faux pas any less embarrassing. "How about I just be your wingman? Let you take the lead."

The corner of Rebecca's mouth turned up slightly. Jordan was good. She could tell that Rebecca wanted to be in command, and she was content to stand by and let her take the lead. "I think that's a good idea. Just watch him. If he so much as flinches the wrong way, you cover me."

The drive to O'Hare was completely ignored during their conversation, and Jordan had pulled into the loading zone and flashed her badge before Rebecca knew they had even stopped driving.

When they walked into the room, Richard Hudson jumped up and started pointing angrily. "It's about fucking time. Maybe you can tell me why I'm being detained?"

Rebecca's eyes met Jordan's, and they exchanged a knowing glance. The rumors of his temper had not been exaggerated. "Mr. Hudson, please have a seat."

"I've been sitting for two hours." He started pacing the room. "Now somebody start talking. I know my rights, and you have no authority to keep me here."

Rebecca didn't budge, her eyes held his until he realized that he wasn't going to get any explanation until he cooperated.

Rebecca took the seat across from him, and Jordan opted to stand in the corner of the room, her behavior almost that of disinterest to the casual observer. However, her focus was on him, and she had already taken in details that many might miss. In his agitated state, he wrung his hands together with enough force to drain the blood from his fingers. He also had a nervous tick that made his right eye twitch. Despite being directly across from Rebecca, his eyes darted nervously between them. All of those could be signs of guilt, or merely the machinations of an innocent man who had been held up and provided no details about his sudden detaining. Time would tell.

"I'm Detective Foxx and this is Special Agent Gray." She pulled a folder out and left it on the table unopened. "I'm sorry to have kept you here."

He looked as though he wanted to say something about being detained, but thought better of it when he saw the look in Rebecca's eyes. "What's going on? Why am I being held here?"

"I'm sorry to have to tell you this, but your wife was murdered last night." Rebecca's gaze was trained on his face, looking for a sign of guilt, for anything that seemed out of the ordinary for a man who just learned his wife had been murdered. If there was a tell, he hid it well.

"What? Oh my God." Richard Hudson's mouth opened and closed. His eyes registered shocked disbelief. "No, no, not my Elizabeth." He buried his head in his hands. "What about...what about my baby?"

"I'm sorry, Mr. Hudson, the baby did not survive." Rebecca didn't think it was a good time to bring up the fact that the baby had been taken.

The sound of soft sobs filled the room, and Jordan used the opportunity to study him. The sobs sounded convincing, but then she remembered he had done this once before. Grief could be faked. She had seen it done in the past.

"How did it happen?" His sobs quieted to soft inhales of breath and an occasional hiccup.

"Are you certain you want to know?" Rebecca voiced her concerns, not sure that he would be up for hearing details of her murder. That was assuming he was innocent and not the UNSUB they were looking for.

"She's my wife, Detective Foxx, I need to know how she died." His eyes held hers, and Rebecca knew that she had to tell him. He needed to know as a means to move forward.

"Her throat was cut and she bled out."

"Is that it?" His hands wrung together slowly, as if steeling himself to hear the news.

"I know what's been all over the news. Was that all that happened?" His eyes pleaded with her for the truth. It was at this particular moment that Jordan started to doubt his act. Was he interested in how his wife had been attacked because he loved her and he needed to know, or was he a psychotic killer who knew the details and got off on them being repeated back to him?

"No." Rebecca looked over her shoulder, her eyes asking Jordan a silent question. She interpreted her nod as a sign to tell him everything. "She was raped and the killer took the baby."

Richard Hudson looked as though he might vomit. Anger flared in his nostrils, and Rebecca could see in his eyes someone capable of murder, maybe not his wife, but someone.

"I'm so sorry for your loss." At that moment, she did feel sorry for him.

"I want to see her." His tone was cold, and she sensed a small amount of the man that had a prior arrest record for physical violence.

"I'm not sure that's a good idea." It was true. Rebecca didn't think it was a good idea to show him Elizabeth's body. As angry as he was now, she knew seeing his wife lying on a cold autopsy table might bring out the devil in him.

Richard Hudson jumped up, and his chair slammed back into the wall. He leaned over the table and stuck his finger in Rebecca's face angrily. Before she could even react, Jordan had come around the table and grabbed him by the arm, hauling him back roughly.

"Mr. Hudson, while I can appreciate your grief, you will do well to remember that assaulting an officer isn't a good way to get what you want." Her voice was low and even, and she left no doubt that she was willing to do whatever it took to see that Rebecca was okay.

"Agent!" When Jordan didn't pull away, Rebecca shouted again. "Agent Gray!" Rebecca slammed a folder down on the table loudly. "I can take care of myself. If Mr. Hudson wants to see his wife, I'm sure we can arrange it."

She wasn't sure what made her agree to it, especially after he had thrown himself at her. Something in his eyes made her change her mind. She wanted to see how he reacted when he saw the body. Perhaps then she would be able to judge his guilt or innocence. She was buying into the whole grieving husband act, and she didn't want to be wrong.

"If you don't mind, I'll have one of my uniforms escort you to the morgue."

He merely nodded and sat down in the chair dejectedly.

Rebecca followed Jordan out of the room. "You want to tell me what the hell that was?"

"He came at you." Jordan knew she sounded defensive, but Rebecca had accused her like she was the bad guy.

"He didn't come at me. He was emphatic. The guy just lost his wife. Give him some slack."

"That slack could have gotten you hurt. You saw the look on his face, and you know his history." Jordan felt the need to defend her actions. "Besides, I'm not sure I buy the whole grieving husband bit."

"Really?" Rebecca studied her profile until Jordan met her gaze. "I didn't get that."

"I can't put my finger on it, but I don't like him." Jordan's time on the streets left her with the ability to read people. She was usually a pretty good judge of character, and she bristled at the fact that Rebecca doubted her judgment.

"If he is the guy, he's a pretty damn good actor." Rebecca opined. "I bought his act. Besides, we didn't get a hit in the Combined DNA Index System for the DNA, and Richard Hudson has a record."

"*Had* a record. As far as the CDD is concerned, his record is nonexistent, so you wouldn't have gotten a match. But that doesn't make him any less violent."

"Violent yes, but not necessarily a killer." Rebecca felt like playing the devil's advocate, getting under Jordan's skin. "Besides, it seems nuts to kill seven other people, just to cover the murder of his wife."

"Stranger things have happened. I'm still having Matt run the sample you gave us against his DNA in the National DNA Index System."

Rebecca rolled her eyes and walked away leaving Jordan running to catch up.

Jordan caught her arm. "Listen, come back with me. I had our profiler look at the case files, and I think he has some thoughts on our UNSUB."

"Fine, but after this, you are buying me lunch." Rebecca's lip curled up slightly, and Jordan felt warmth effuse her body. This new feeling of wanting more than just sex with Rebecca was quickly becoming part of who Jordan was, and she wasn't too thrilled with it.

"I guess I owe you at least that much…" Jordan smirked. "…for making this whole working together thing so incredibly enjoyable."

"Funny, smart ass. Let's get this whole profile thing out of the way. I'm getting ready to start, and I'm totally craving something chocolate."

Chapter 11

"Julien, this is Detective Rebecca Foxx with the Chicago Detective Division."

Rebecca stepped forward and shook hands with an attractive gentleman, whom she put at close to fifty. His hair was brown with slightly grayed temples and when he spoke, she had to keep from rolling her eyes. What was it with hiring people with foreign accents? It reminded her of commercials that used foreign actors because supposedly some survey indicated people actually bought more of a product if the actor had an accent. "Pleasure to meet you, Mr. Redmond."

Jordan directed Rebecca towards a chair and handed her a bottle of water. "So, Julien, what do you have?"

"Well, originally I thought he was targeting lesbians, but the most recent victim changed that idea. I believe we are looking for a male in his mid to late thirties. One who is very angry and is lashing out at whoever or whatever is around him. I believe he might be suffering from some form of impotency. The thought of being less of a man has made him resentful."

Julien expanded his thought. "I believe that he may have been married at one time, perhaps even still married. He feels emasculated because he cannot father a child. Something happened to push him out of reality. Given the fact that the space between murders has shortened, he is losing touch with reality. It's quite possible that his wife left him for another man, one who could get her pregnant, and he sees that as another sign of personal failure. He also believes he is above the law, or at least above getting caught. He leaves his victims in plain sight, which leads me to believe he feels superior to law enforcement. That he is too smart to get caught."

"What do you make of him taking the babies?"

"He feels a certain need for the familial bond with the child. Perhaps he believes that the child is his own, perhaps filling the parental void that was left by his inability to father a child. He does it with almost tender precision, and I would guess his treatment of the fetus will border on loving. That is his one act to erase the violent death that he just committed."

"Violent. That fits Richard Hudson." Jordan couldn't help the feeling that he was involved in these cases, much more than Rebecca was willing to admit.

"Like I told you before, that doesn't make him our killer." Rebecca held her gaze until a slight blush crept into her cheeks. No matter how hard she tried, she was not as immune to Jordan's handsome looks as she wanted to be.

"One other thing, ladies. He was interrupted when he attacked Julie Keppler. I have seen the crime scene photos from the homeless man. He is very angry that he was not able to kill his mark. He is not going to accept failure. He will try to kill her again, if at all possible. Combine that with the fact he knows that the condom with his DNA was left at the crime scene, and you have a killer who is mentally unstable at best. Julie could very well be in danger again."

"Have you spoken to Assistant Director Mitchell about that?"

Julien shook his head. "Not yet. I was hoping we would not need to address that with her."

"I don't want to have to, but I think you're right. We need to make sure she is guarded at all times." Jordan turned her gaze toward Rebecca. "I think we need to dig a little deeper and find out what Richard Hudson is hiding. I can't shake the feeling he isn't as heartbroken as he pretends to be."

Rebecca opened her mouth to respond, but stopped when her hip started to ring. Rebecca pulled her phone out of its holster and took the call. "Foxx."

When she finished talking, she hung up and pushed back in her chair. "Uniforms already brought Hudson to the morgue. They're sitting on it until I get there. Wanna take me for a ride before lunch? I want to see his reaction to the body."

Jordan opened her mouth to answer and caught the warning look in Rebecca's eyes. For now, she had to leave that comment alone. "Sure." She glanced to her left. "Julien, thank you."

"It was my pleasure, Jordie. Detective Foxx, it was a pleasure meeting you as well."

Rebecca followed Jordan outside. Her eyes fell to Jordan's shapely bottom. Standard issue, black khakis should not look that good on anyone, but Jordan made them look sexy. She unconsciously licked her lips, and somehow had the wherewithal to lift her eyes before she walked out the door. She ignored the knowing smirk on Jordan's face, hoping she hadn't caught her staring. Oddly enough, that was the last thing she needed, but the one thing she wanted. *God, I need to get laid.*

"So, are you starting to believe me?"

"Maybe I'm not buying the whole guilty thing yet, but I'm a slow learner." Rebecca waited while Jordan opened the door for her, still not accustomed to being treated like a lady. "You might have to teach me."

"I'm a great teacher." Jordan teased lightly. She walked around the back of the car, a smile on her face. If she didn't know any better, Rebecca was actually flirting with her, and it felt damn good. She started the car and revved the engine loudly. Nothing like a little female attention to get the blood running hot.

Rebecca studied Jordan closely, watching her movements. She did everything with as little wasted energy as possible. Her hand draped over the steering wheel casually, occasionally gripping it tighter to take a turn. Her eyes took in the tight muscles straining beneath her khakis. There was no hiding the fact that Jordan had a great body and when Rebecca pictured her tongue gliding over her taut skin, she shivered.

"Cold?" Jordan reached over and turned the heat up.

"No." Rebecca's face was tinged pink. "Just thinking about the case. You really think that Richard Hudson did it? It seems kind of extreme, don't you think?"

Jordan shrugged noncommittally. "Maybe not. However, I do think the guy is hiding something. We already know he has a temper. It may be a stretch to say he killed seven other women just to cover his wife's murder. But my gut is telling me he is dirty."

"Guess we will see." Rebecca watched Jordan ease into a spot outside the morgue. She stepped outside and sucked in a breath at the rush of cold air. "I suppose it would have been too much to ask him to wait until summer to go on a killing spree."

"Oh yeah." Jordan shoved her keys in her pocket and pulled her coat tighter. "When you meet a criminal who wants to do it our way, let me know."

Rebecca smiled. "And we'll call it the Burger King of crime. *Have it your way.*"

Jordan started laughing, and Rebecca had to admit even her laugh was sexy. She shook her head, trying to get Jordan out of her thoughts and maintain her distance. "You ever been to a morgue before?"

"Once. It's been a long time." Jordan's mind flashed back to her first year at the FBI. She and Tony Wozniak had been investigating a crime ring around the city, and one of their informants had gone missing. Turned out, he wasn't lost, just dead. They had the unfortunate job of identifying the body, her stomach turned at the memory. It was the first time she had seen a dead body, and this one was especially gruesome. He had learned the hard way that being caught as a snitch was a very bad thing.

"Well, you will find it hasn't changed much." Rebecca came to a stop in front of two Chicago Police Officers. Jordan could tell from the chilly reception, this was another place that

Rebecca's presence wasn't liked. She shook her head. It was tough to get anywhere in a man's world. Rebecca had done it, but she hadn't made many friends along the way. "You got him?"

One of the uniforms nodded his head behind him. "Had to take a leak."

"Okay. Listen, thanks for bringing him down. I'll handle it from here."

"Sure thing, Detective."

Jordan saw him smirk as they walked away. "Nice guys you work with."

Rebecca shrugged. "Some of them can be. It just depends on who you get."

Jordan opened her mouth to respond, but kept quiet when she saw Richard Hudson walking back down the hallways.

"Are you sure you want to do this?" Rebecca offered him one more chance to refuse, knowing the scene on the other side of the doors was not something any person, let alone someone whose wife had just been brutally murdered, should ever have to see.

"Yes. I need to see her." His tone was quiet, but adamant.

Rebecca led him into the examination room and nodded at Sylvia. She stopped at a table with a white cloth draped over the obvious outline of a body. Her eyes met Richard Hudson's one more time and when he met her inquiry with a silent nod, she pulled the sheet back.

The y—shaped incision across and down her chest was enough to catch most people off guard, and if that didn't, the closed incisions across her neck and abdomen would certainly tell the story of her brutal death. Her skin had an unnatural grayish tint that was reserved for the very ill, or in her case, the fallen. She lay so still, that if not for the mutilation of her body, one might suppose, she was just sleeping.

For the first few moments, Rebecca thought he might not react at all, and she had started to question his innocence, but then an ungodly moan had filled the room.

An unnatural pallor crept over his face as his eyes took in every inch of her. She could see his hands tighten reflexively, until they were balled into such tight fists that she felt like he might lash out again. His body, once still in calm repose, visibly shook, and she thought she could feel the tremor.

His last look at her reminded Rebecca of a wounded animal trying to understand why it had been hurt. She barely heard the uttered why before he sank onto his knees and dropped his head in his hands, sobbing uncontrollably.

Chapter 12

"Two, with mustard." Jordan pulled her wallet from her back pocket and handed the vendor a couple of bills. "Keep the change."

"You know when I said you were buying me lunch, this isn't exactly what I had in mind." The words came out almost as a stutter against the cold Chicago air. The wind blowing off the river sent chills up and down Rebecca's spine. Truth be told, she hated winters here in Chicago. Growing up in southeast Texas meant she had never experienced a real winter aside from a few freak storms. When she had opted to go to Northwestern for school, she got the shock of her life the first winter she had been here. It was almost enough to drive her back south to the warmer, balmier Texas temperatures. Almost.

Jordan handed her a hotdog and smiled. "Come on. You'll love it, I promise."

Rebecca took the food with a shaky hand. She didn't bother taking her gloves off, so when a glob of mustard stained her glove, she swore silently. She took a bite and moaned appreciatively. "So, it's good, okay. Can we at least sit in the car?"

"Nope." Jordan smiled cryptically and pulled her closer towards the bridge on Michigan Street overlooking the river. "Gotta get the whole experience."

They walked until they were midway across, and Jordan leaned her elbows on the cold concrete. They could see Lake Michigan in the distance, and Jordan shivered involuntarily.

Despite the cold temperatures, the Magnificent Mile was a hurried rush of people, and they ate in silence, watching the world pass them by.

"See, I told you. It's fucking freezing." Rebecca stuffed the last bite of her hotdog in her mouth and chewed quickly.

"Hungry?" Jordan said with a throaty laugh.

"Starving. But I was afraid if I didn't eat fast, I was going to be eating a meat flavored Popsicle, and I have to admit, I've never had a taste for those."

"Hmm."

"Hmm, what?" Rebecca queried.

"Hmm, that answers one question." Jordan finished her dog and said the next words around a mouthful. "Whether Detective Foxx is really one of the guys or not."

"Ahh." Understanding dawned on her face. "You thought maybe because I didn't fall for your tortured bad-guy act, that perhaps I liked dick."

Jordan laughed. "Something like that. Of course, Agent Riley will be sorry to hear that. He's nursing a little crush on a certain beautiful redhead."

Rebecca studied her face as if trying to figure out if Jordan was just teasing her. An uncomfortable look broke out across her features when she realized she was serious. "Well, that will make it a little more awkward when he's around."

"Don't worry about him too much…until after the case." Jordan caught Rebecca's furrowed brow. "That's when he is planning to ask you out."

"Argh." Rebecca dropped her head in her heads dramatically. "God this happens all the time. Why do all the guys have to fall for the bitchy, red—headed Detective?" Her voice held just enough sarcasm to be humorous.

"Don't give him too much grief. It's pretty easy to get a crush on you." Jordan admitted with a rueful smile. "I'm sure he isn't the only one that has fallen for the tough as nail's Detective."

Rebecca met her eyes and looked for a sign that this time, she was teasing her. She found none. Realization dawned on her, and she mentally chided herself for the feelings she was starting to reciprocate. This was suddenly becoming very complicated, and Rebecca didn't do complicated.

Jordan sensed her discomfort and changed the subject quickly. She felt a rush of warmth in that few seconds when Rebecca let her guard down. Somewhere hidden behind the mask of cool indifference, she sensed a mutual attraction and cursed the inability to pursue it. "So, tell me what got you into this business?"

Rebecca's husky laugh filled the air. "My dad actually."

"Really? One of those *my dad did it, so I've got to follow in his footsteps* things?"

"Actually, no." Rebecca shoved off the bridge. "Come on, let's walk. If you're going to force me to stand out in the cold, I need to keep moving."

Jordan fell into step alongside her. She took the opportunity to study Rebecca. When she looked closely, she saw light freckles splashed across her face, barely visible against her creamy skin. She was just as beautiful in profile as she was head on, despite the fact that Jordan couldn't see her green eyes, eyes that were quickly becoming hard to look into without getting lost. She stumbled over the uneven pavement and caught herself with a sheepish grin.

"Watch that first step. It's a doozie." They said it in unison and broke out in uncontained laughter. "*Groundhog Day!*"

Somewhere in between Jordan's misstep and laughing over their memories of the movie, Rebecca made the mistake of looking into Jordan's eyes. She felt herself being pulled into them, and rather than back away, she felt herself narrowing the distance. The warmth emanating from Jordan's body enveloped her and made her blood rush wildly in her veins. Her stomach fluttered pleasantly, and it wasn't until she felt the cold hit her moistened lips, that she remembered where she was, and she backed away shyly.

She heard her ragged breathing and could tell from Jordan's sudden silence, that she had affected her as much as Jordan had affected her. "I…I…where was I?"

Jordan stepped closer and brushed a red strand behind her ear with such gentleness that Rebecca thought her knees might fail her. The naked hunger staring back at her unnerved her even further, until she had no choice but to run for safety.

When Jordan finally caught up to her and put a hand on her arm to stop her, she shook it off with more force than she meant to. "Everything okay?"

"Yes." Rebecca forced herself to nod affirmatively. "I just needed to warm up." She knew that was a lie. If anything, she needed to cool off. She mentally willed her heartbeat to slow down.

"We can go back to the car." Jordan offered softly. Right now, if Rebecca had said she wanted to go to the moon, Jordan would have built her a spaceship to get there.

Rebecca shook her head. "No, let's just walk." She wasn't ready for the intimacy being alone in the car would give them. "So, what were we talking about?"

"You were telling me about your dad and how you decided to be a Detective."

"Oh yeah." Rebecca ran a tube of Chapstick over her lips, a move that almost pushed Jordan over the edge. If she knew the effect she was having on Jordan, she showed no sign of it. "Pop was a truck driver, but there was always something about law enforcement that intrigued him. He had watched every detective show that was ever on TV. I remember sitting on the couch watching *Cagney and Lacey* or *Magnum P.I.,* or whichever of the dozen shows that he lived by. He went on and on about how he had always wanted to be a cop, but just sort of fell into driving. I think he just talked about it so much when I was growing up, that it was the only thing I saw myself doing. They made it look a lot sexier on TV."

"I don't know, you make it look pretty sexy."

Rebecca met Jordan's eyes, and she saw the sparkle of laughter in them. She knew that, at least for now, even if she meant it, Jordan was taking mercy on her fragile soul by throwing some humor in the situation.

"You wear the gun pretty well."

"Thanks." Rebecca smiled, and her whole face lit up. "The funny thing is, I found out I was pretty damn good at it, and it makes the old man proud."

"I can't see how he couldn't be proud of you." Jordan's voice was so genuine that Rebecca knew she had finally found someone that believed she could actually be great at her job, despite the fact that she was a woman.

"Thanks." Rebecca felt herself blush and hoped Jordan didn't see it. She needn't worry, her cheeks were already pink from the cold. "So, what about you?"

"Well, my dad wasn't a cop, either." Jordan's voice was hard and sardonic. Rebecca could tell that there was no lost love between Jordan and her father. "As a matter of fact, I'm not really sure what the bastard was."

"What happened to him?"

"He left when I was just a kid. Mom didn't talk much about him, and when she did, it was only to curse the mess he left her with."

"Oh." Rebecca couldn't imagine a life without her father and hearing Jordan's admission made her heart break. She tried to lighten the mood. "So, which one did you have a crush on, Cagney or Lacey?"

Jordan laughed heartily. "Probably both. Actually, it was kind of by accident that I ended up where I am. When my sperm donor left, Mom had it pretty rough. She worked all the time trying to support us. I was your typical latch key kid. I spent most days after school and in the summer with no contact except the kids on the street. I was pretty messed up, by the time I hit sixteen."

"Wow." Rebecca watched the proverbial layers fall away, and she learned more and more about the strength of the woman beside her. "Troublemaker, huh?" She said with a mischievous smile.

"Pretty much." Jordan shrugged.

"So, what saved you from a life on the other side of the law?"

"Woz. Tony Wozniak." Jordan added quickly, as if supplying a full name would make him any more recognizable to Rebecca. "I was already into some pretty bad shit. We stole stuff, lifted cars, you name it. Life on the streets was pretty rough. I was this close to messing up for real when I walked past this gym. I saw a sign for boxing lessons. I figured I might as well sign up. That would give me a way to defend myself that wasn't a gun or a knife. Woz took me under his wing, and I've been following him ever since."

"Sounds like a good guy."

Jordan nodded. "He is. Kind of the father I never had. Woz is retired FBI, and I was lucky enough to mentor with him before he left. I learned everything I know from him."

"You probably knew a lot already, and some of it can't be learned. You just have it." Rebecca knew from her own job as a Detective that you could learn to investigate, shoot, all the tangible lessons, but the intangible ones, the visceral side of being a cop, you couldn't learn. The sixth sense, following a gut feeling, knowing what leads to follow, when to shoot, that was something a person was born with. You either had it or you didn't. She was pretty certain she had it, maybe not as sure of herself as Jordan was, but she was no slouch.

"Yeah, I'm sure some of it I picked up on the street, but a great deal of it I owe to Woz. You know you can learn a lot from boxing." Jordan's voice was suddenly serious, and her features became schooled with the look of someone about to divulge the secret to all life's questions. She was certain boxing had taught her enough to keep her alive.

"How so?" Rebecca asked, interested to see how Jordan would relate boxing to life, or the job.

"Reading people, their tells. You learn to see what side is someone's weak side. What punches they are going to throw. If they drop their chin or their shoulder a certain way. How they plant their feet. Where they hold their gloves. It's a game just like this whole thing is. It's all about seeing the signs. Woz taught me that."

"He may have helped you strengthen what you already had, but I still say, some things you can't teach, and that is one of them." Rebecca studied Jordan's face. She saw a hint of self—deprecation in her eyes and knew that years of knowing she had been abandoned had taken their toll. "You can't just admit you are that good, can you?"

"Oh, I can admit I'm that good." Jordan's face broke into a smile. She couldn't take talking about her childhood and growing up too long. If she did, the anger and betrayal of being left would come flooding back and hit her square in the stomach with a sickening punch.

"Sarcasm. Good defense." Rebecca smiled to soften her words. "You cover anything serious with humor to protect yourself. Do you ever allow yourself to be serious about anything but boxing?"

Jordan shrugged. "I try not to. Listen, it was hard enough growing up that way. I hate thinking about it, much less talking about it. This job, boxing, whatever else I choose to do, makes me forget the pain. My dad left, I pretty much raised myself, big deal. You can talk to a hundred people and more than half of them will have the same story. There's no point in rehashing that shit all the time."

"Maybe not. But it did make you who you are today, and I'll allow myself this small indulgence. To say that at least the little I know about you, it made you into a woman I admire and respect."

"And maybe you are attracted to…a little bit?" Jordan's eyes sparkled.

Rebecca shook her head. "Do you ever give up?"

"No." Jordan stopped and turned Rebecca towards her, paralyzing her with her gaze. "And something tells me you don't want me to give up."

Rebecca's response froze in her throat as she realized she wanted just that. Someone who matched her drive with the same intensity she had. She knew in that moment, beyond the shadow of a doubt, that whatever Jordan set her mind to, she would get.

Chapter 13

Jordan watched Rebecca walk to her car and drive off. She shook her head. Much as she didn't want to admit it, she was quickly starting to like this woman, and from past experience, that only meant trouble.

She didn't want a relationship. She had learned the hard way, people didn't stick around long, and she wasn't in the mood to put herself out there, just to get left. No, her mom had done that, and she wasn't a believer in repeating someone else's mistakes. It was a shame, though. Detective Foxx was someone she knew she would enjoy having sex with. *What a waste!*

When she walked back into the office, Matt pulled her aside quickly. "I got something I think you're going to want to see."

She followed him down to the lab. The display on the dual monitors was a pair of graphs that, at first glance, looked very similar. "Is this what I think it is?"

His eyes sparkled. "Yeah. And you're not going to believe who it matches."

"One guess." Jordan smirked. "And I'll get to tell Rebecca I was right."

Matt's smile vanished. "Rebecca? Sounds like a lot has happened with you working point on this."

Jordan smiled sheepishly. "Chill, Matty. It's nothing like what you're thinking. We simply learned how to get along." She turned away to hide the blush. If anything, things were starting to get interesting, and Matt didn't need to hear that the object of his crush didn't swing his way, or at least Jordan didn't believe she did. "So, tell me I'm right."

Matt watched her warily. He didn't know what to make of her explanation for being on a first-name basis, but he had known Jordan long enough to know that she had a way with women. "You're right...sort of."

Jordan quirked an eyebrow. "What do you mean *sort of?*"

"I had NDIS run a search of the Forensic Index against the Convicted Offender Index. I got a couple of hits on cold cases from 2007. Two unsolved rape cases. Same MO, and like Julie, the UNSUB was interrupted before he could kill them. Detectives couldn't put a face to the perp, so they shelved the cases."

"So, how does that make me right?" Jordan sounded exasperated, but in truth, she was intrigued. A tie to several unsolved cases might make this series of murders easier to solve.

"I'm getting to that." He pointed at the screen, and Jordan's eyes followed his finger to the DNA markers on the screen. "This is the UNSUB's DNA on the left. On the right is Richard Hudson's DNA from the NDIS. Both match the DNA sample left at the scene. They would never have gotten a hit on Richard Hudson. We only did because you asked me to check against the Convicted Offender Index."

"Son of a bitch." Jordan shook her head in disbelief. "That fucking bastard killed his own wife."

"CDD never would have made the connection. His DNA isn't in CODIS."

"Shit." Jordan slapped her leg. "She fell for his whole distraught husband routine and let him walk right out the fucking door. He's probably halfway to China by now."

A cryptic smile spread across his face. "If he's running, it's in a car."

Jordan regarded him quizzically. "What do you mean?"

"Let's just say when this popped up, I took the liberty of putting him on the no-fly list."

"Genius." Jordan slapped him on the back. "This is why you are the brains of the operation."

"And the looks, don't forget." Matt's smile grew broader. He tapped her phone. "Guess you better call *your friend* Rebecca and tell her the good news."

Jordan shot him a parting smile and winked. "Remind me, I owe you a steak."

"Just go. Get that bastard." Matt watched her back disappear down the hallway. He hadn't let on that he saw the blush or believed that there was anything between Jordan and Rebecca, but Matt was no fool. It only took one look in her face to know that Jordan was emotionally invested in the Detective, even if they hadn't slept together.

He should have been mad, but instead he felt worry in the pit of his stomach. If he read the look correctly, Jordan was interested in more than just sex, and she had no idea the rough road ahead. And that he didn't begrudge her that at all.

Jordan was halfway to Grand Central before she dialed Rebecca's number. She held her breath waiting for the voice she knew would make her stomach flutter. When Rebecca picked up, she wasn't disappointed. She smiled in spite of herself. "Hey, stranger."

Rebecca could hear the smile in her voice. "Hi, yourself."

"You ready for some interesting news?" Jordan asked cryptically.

"If by interesting, you mean good then yes, I do want some interesting news."

"I just left the lab. Matt ran the sample you gave us from Julie's attacker against the Forensic Index and the Convicted Offender Index in NDIS. He got a hit, well, two, actually."

Rebecca processed the information. "It's starting to get interesting. Continue."

"Two unsolved rapes from 2007. Same MO, and like Julie, the women got away before they were murdered. This is where it gets interesting. The DNA from those unsolved cases matches Richard Hudson."

Rebecca let out a loud sigh. It looked as though they had finally gotten a break in the case and were one step closer to catching what the press had dubbed *The Cradle Killer.* "Is this where I'm supposed to jump in and say you were right?"

"Normally, yes." Jordan said seriously. "But I think you and I both know, that more important than you admitting I'm right, is bringing this guy to justice."

"I'd say it's time to pay Richard Hudson another visit." Rebecca rubbed the bridge of her nose. A headache was starting just behind her eyes, and she could feel the blood pulsating behind her right eye. She grabbed a bottle of ibuprofen off her desk and fought with the cap. "Shit."

"Problem, Detective?"

"Nothing painkillers won't get rid of…if I can ever get this damn childproof cap off." She pushed up with her thumb, almost calling it quits when, at the last minute, it popped off and rolled to the floor. "Are you on your way?"

"Here."

Rebecca looked up startled. She put her phone down and stared at Jordan. "Don't you know it's a bad idea to scare a cop?"

Jordan eyed the full holster on her desk and smiled sheepishly. "Sorry. Traffic wasn't that bad for this late."

Rebecca tossed the pills into her mouth and chased them down with a swig of day old, cold coffee. "Ugh."

"You ready?"

"Yeah. Let me call it in. I am not meeting that guy without backup."

"What?" Jordan's feigned mock horror. "You don't trust me to keep you safe?"

"Given what we've seen him do to the victims, I am not taking any chances." Rebecca grabbed her coat off the chair. She was about to put it on when Jordan took it from her. She stood behind her and held it for her to slip her arms in then pulled it up over her shoulders. "Thanks."

Twenty minutes later, Jordan eased to a stop two houses down from Richard Hudson's house.

"Why are you stopping?" Rebecca pointed to the nondescript car sitting opposite the house. "Plain clothes are already here. Let's get this bastard."

"Doesn't this seem too easy?" Jordan rubbed her chin. "Julien said he was smart. This seems all wrong. Do you honestly think he would be dumb enough to give us a trail of bread crumbs? Leaving his DNA at the scene. He might as well have left his business card."

"I'm sure he didn't leave it on purpose. He got spooked. And you said yourself—he technically doesn't have a record. He would have no reason to believe the DNA would lead us to him."

Jordan shrugged. "Maybe you're right."

"Besides this is your guy. You called it."

"I guess so." Jordan opened the door, got out and nodded at the undercover officers. "How do you want to do this?"

"Just a conversation. I want to get this guy downtown. Have a little chat with him. I can't arrest him without a warrant, and I don't want to give him a reason to run."

"Works for me. You take the lead." Jordan followed Rebecca up the steps to his door, taking in her surroundings. In the dull glow of the porch light, she could just make out flowerbeds. Neat and tidy, despite the fact that the winter had killed all the plants, and there was only rock filling them. The house was impeccable and showed no visible signs of wear.

Meticulously cared for, some would say. Jordan's mind went to Julien's profile of the UNSUB. Meticulous would certainly describe him. He didn't leave but one loose end. She rapped on the door loudly and saw a faint light at the back of the house. She was carefully schooling her face to look as nonchalant as possible, which was a difficult task, given the fact that she knew how brutally he had treated those women.

What seemed like an eternity later, Richard Hudson finally answered the door. His clothes hung haphazardly, and his eyes were puffy and swollen. He held a half-empty bottle of tequila, and Jordan could tell this wasn't his first.

"Detective?" His voice slurred, and the word was almost lost in a mumble of incoherence. "Can I help you?"

Rebecca stepped forward, stopping just shy of the door. "Mr. Hudson, there's been some new developments in the case. We'd like to get you up to speed." She looked around, feigning suspicion. "In a more secure location, if possible."

His inebriated state erased the suspicion he might normally feel at their oddly timed arrival. In fact, if asked, Jordan could swear it appeared as though his eyes lit up. *God, he's good.*

"Sure. Right now?"

He started to pitch forward, and Rebecca caught him at the shoulders, righting him quickly. She felt the sinewy muscles beneath his sweater, and she could see where someone with his wiry, but strong build, would have no trouble subduing a woman, especially one in late-stage pregnancy. "Is an hour okay? I can have plain clothes bring you down…since you're in no condition to drive."

He flicked his eyes to the bottle and laughed sardonically. "Seems to be the only thing holding me together right now."

Rebecca stepped back, freeing up his personal space. She wasn't sure what to make of the man in front her. He didn't seem like a cold—hearted killer, but she was sure they hadn't contaminated the DNA. "We can wait until tomorrow, if you would prefer."

Jordan let out a quiet sigh. She wasn't sure what angle Rebecca was playing, but was pretty certain she would have approached it differently, for fear of giving him a chance to run. She bit her tongue to keep from talking.

"No." He stood up straighter, suddenly sober. "I'll come now."

Rebecca nodded her ascent and walked off the porch. She stopped at the dark sedan parked across the street. "Bring him down to Grand."

On the way back to the Precinct, Rebecca called the Assistant DA, pulling him away from dinner. She gave him the information she had on the case and requested a warrant for Richard Hudson's arrest.

She hung up the phone and turned to Jordan. "I just want to be ready."

"Good plan."

"Once he realizes what we have on him, he's going to run or lawyer up, and I'm not letting him slip through the cracks this time." Rebecca toyed with a piece of lint on her pants. "Thank you, by the way."

"For?" Jordan turned and studied her face.

"We wouldn't have caught him without you."

"Sure you would have. Just maybe not as fast." Jordan smiled sincerely. "With or without the FBI's help, you would have eventually tracked him down."

Rebecca shook her head. "I'm not so sure about that. He got away with at least two rapes and who knows what else."

Jordan captured Rebecca's hand in hers, and gave it a reassuring squeeze. The initial contact made her jump. Heat radiated from her palm straight to her stomach and a pleasant flutter started building within. She let go just as quickly, afraid her feelings would get the better of her. "Let's not split hairs. It doesn't matter who is responsible for catching him. Let's worry about taking him down. No mistakes."

"No mistakes." Rebecca repeated the words almost to herself. She rubbed her hand subconsciously. She couldn't remember a time when her body had reacted to another woman the way hers did with Jordan. A simple, harmless touch and she was ready to come unglued, and that was unacceptable. Rebecca Foxx didn't come unglued for anyone.

Chapter 14

Jordan watched Rebecca lead Richard Hudson into one of the precinct's three interrogation rooms. She offered him water, which he summarily refused. She watched his body for signs of guilt. Hands he couldn't still, eyes that looked around shiftily. There were none.

She wanted to sit with Rebecca while she interviewed him, but she had been refused, and now she was stuck on the opposite side of the glass listening to a tinny, second—rate version of the conversation.

"Mr. Hudson, I wanted to bring you down here so we could get a better idea of your wife's habits, find out if there was anyone that she fought with recently, something to help us build a timeline up to her death." She opened a folder. "Do you mind if I start with some questions?"

He shook his head. "No. I want to help. I want you to catch whoever did this to my wife."

She nodded and read several notes before continuing. "Give me a rundown of your wife's day. Does she work outside the home?"

"Yes." He winced with renewed pain. "Lizzie and I fought about that all the time."

Rebecca raised an eyebrow and regarded him suspiciously.

"We argued, okay? I didn't hurt my wife, if that's what you're thinking." His eyes softened. "Lizzie didn't need to work. I make enough. But that's the type of woman she is. She was a teacher at Northwest Middle School."

Rebecca scribbled on a notepad. "Did your wife enjoy her work? Had she had any *arguments* with anyone there?"

Richard shook his head. "No, everyone loved Lizzie."

"How was Mrs. Hudson lately? Was she depressed? How was she handling the pregnancy? Did you notice any behavioral changes in her?"

Jordan watched Rebecca, and the corners of her mouth quirked up in a slight smile. She was incredibly calm, given the circumstances. Anyone watching would have thought she was conducting the interview with every intention of catching the real killer and not actually sitting in the same room with him. Her focus jumped back to Richard Hudson as he answered, still searching for signs that he was guilty.

"No. In fact, I've never seen her happier. She loved being pregnant." His hands wrung together slowly. "We had a really hard time getting pregnant and when it finally took, she was ecstatic."

"When it finally took?"

His gaze leveled on Rebecca. "I…well…we had to use artificial insemination."

Rebecca's hand stilled. She felt a chill run down her spine and she willed herself not to let him know. This was the piece they were looking for. In spite of the DNA match, she needed motive and this was a pretty good start. "Why did your wife have trouble getting pregnant?"

Richard ran a hand through his bedraggled hair. "It was my fault." He gestured towards his crotch. "They don't work so well. That's why when Lizzie finally got pregnant, we were beside ourselves. It took three years and a lot of failed attempts. We had all but given up hope when the last one finally took."

"May I ask what agency you used?"

"Helping Hands…on Lake. Just past the river."

Jordan felt a brief flash of recognition, but she couldn't place it. Instead, she filed the information in the recesses of her mind for processing later.

"And how was that process? Was it stressful?"

"No, not at all." His mouth smiled slightly. "They made it incredibly easy. I guess that's what money gets you."

"How do you mean?"

"They charge almost double what other agencies do, but it was worth it."

Rebecca raised an eyebrow. Double what other agencies charged would put the total cost for each attempt to inseminate somewhere around twenty grand. Putting out that kind of money could make someone resentful, maybe even violent, especially if it wasn't something he wanted to do. "Forgive me for being a little dense, but what made Helping Hands that much better?"

"Everything, I think. The director handles each case personally, and they offer in house counseling. It's all extremely professional and very discreet."

"Did you and Mrs. Hudson take advantage of the counseling service?"

Jordan stifled a laugh. She was thorough. Stalling for time, but definitely thorough. She saw Richard visibly relax and knew it was Rebecca's demeanor that had facilitated that.

"Yes. I did, anyway."

"Can I ask you the nature of your conversations?

"Sure, I have nothing to hide." Richard's hands were intertwined lazily. "I was married before…"

Rebecca's pen slowed slightly. She couldn't believe it. He was giving them everything they needed.

"We had trouble getting pregnant. We used Helping Hands as well. I was somewhat daunted by repeating the whole process again, and I wanted to talk to someone about it. Anyone on the outside can't understand how painful it can be. Not being able to get your wife pregnant and having to rely on help for that. Add to that, the failed tries. It can be very depressing."

"How did that make you feel? Not being able to impregnate your wife?" Rebecca sounded every bit the concerned, caring person she knew she needed to be to elicit the responses she needed to make a conviction stick.

"Depressed. Emasculated. You name it. No man wants to think he can't fulfill his duties as a husband."

Jordan felt the corners of her mouth crook up. Rebecca was good. Richard Hudson was using all the keywords Julien had said the UNSUB exhibited.

"How did you deal with those feelings?"

His eyebrows furrowed in confusion. "Besides talking to the director?"

"Yes." Rebecca met his gaze, and her face softened. "I would imagine that would make you pretty angry. How did you deal with those feelings of rage?"

"Not well. I went through periods of depression. I withdrew from Lizzie, buried myself in my work."

"How was your relationship with Mrs. Hudson? Had your depression affected that?"

"Very much so. I had a hard time touching her. I was no longer open with her. Even after she got pregnant, I was still angry."

"Angry enough to lash out at her?"

A small vein on the side of his head started to pulse. "No! No way! I would never touch my wife."

"Calm down, Mr. Hudson. I'm just trying to get a picture of what things were like. If perhaps Mrs. Hudson was looking for comfort outside the home."

He shook his head. "No, not Lizzie. She loved me."

"But you didn't love her?"

"That's not what I meant. Don't put words in my mouth." The anger flashed in his eyes as realization dawn on him. "Is that what this is about? You think I killed my wife? I didn't kill Lizzie."

Rebecca opened her mouth to respond, but snapped it shut when her beeper buzzed. She checked the display. "If you'll excuse me a moment."

When she stepped outside the interrogation room, her eyes flicked to her Chief.

He waived a single sheet of paper in the air. "Wrap it up."

Rebecca took a deep breath and joined Richard Hudson again. She didn't need to see the paper to know it was her warrant. Now, she wanted a confession. "I'm sorry about that."

One glance told her he had calmed down. She half expected him to bolt any minute. "Mr. Hudson, let's talk about the night your wife was killed. You were at a hotel near O'Hare. Did you leave the hotel for any reason?"

"No." His started to wring his hands together again. "I got there about eight, ordered room service around 9:30 then watched TV and went to sleep around eleven."

Rebecca cocked an eyebrow. Eight p.m. gave him plenty of time to commit the murder.

"Did you talk to Mrs. Hudson that evening?"

"A couple of times. Lizzie was eight months pregnant. I wanted to make sure she was doing alright. I spoke to her right before I checked in. She was getting ready to go out."

Rebecca looked confused. "Where was she going so late?"

"She was meeting a friend for dinner."

"That's pretty late for dinner."

"Maggie, that's her friend, works retail. Her hours were pretty hectic."

"Do you know where they were meeting?" Rebecca was scrawling notes on a legal pad. She hoped she could make out her chicken scratch tomorrow.

"Yes. Catch Thirty—Five on Wacker."

That certainly put her close to the murder site. She mentally calculated the time it would take to get from O'Hare, kill Mrs. Hudson and drive back in time to order room service as an alibi. A little over an hour and a half. It would be tight, but doable. "When was the last time you saw your wife?"

"That morning. I left the house at six—thirty and didn't go back after work. I had my bag with me."

She fished through the folder once more and pulled out pictures of Elizabeth Hudson's crime scene photos. She slid them in front of him. He blanched immediately and looked away. "Why? Why are you showing me these?"

"This is how we found your wife's body, Mr. Hudson. As you can see, the murder was quite brutal. Someone very angry did this to her."

He looked down and bit his lip. He was visibly fighting back tears. "Please, please catch whoever did this."

"Tell me about your ex—wife, Sarah."

More color drained from his face. "What does she have to do with this?"

"I think you know. She filed a restraining order against you. What was that all about?"

He swallowed loudly. "I have…had some issues managing my emotions. I yelled at her a couple of times, but nothing more than that."

"She had you arrested for battery."

"That was a misunderstanding. It was cleared up."

"Then she filed for divorce and mysteriously ended up dead. Coincidentally, the exact same way Elizabeth died. That makes you either really unlucky, or…"

Richard knew immediately what she was hinting at by her pause. "So, now I'm a person of interest."

"No, Mr. Hudson, you're not interesting, you're just a suspect." Rebecca answered sarcastically.

"I didn't kill anyone." His hands balled into tight fists. "I know my rights, Detective. Unless you have something besides speculation to book me on, I'm leaving."

Rebecca turned to the glass and nodded. Within seconds, two men came into the room and pulled Richard Hudson from the chair. They wrenched his arms behind him and cuffed him roughly. She met his furious gaze. "Richard Hudson, you are under arrest for the murder of Elizabeth Hudson. You have the right to remain silent. Anything you say can and will be used against you in a court of law…"

"I want my lawyer."

One of the detectives eyed Rebecca. She shook her head. "Not yet. I want to show you what you took."

She pulled out photos from all the previous victims and threw them haphazardly in front of him. "Take a good, long look, Mr. Hudson. These are your victims. The women you murdered."

Richard Hudson shoved back from the table, visibly shaking. "I told you I didn't kill anyone."

"Sit down, Mr. Hudson." Rebecca's voice was calm, but firm. "Anger is a very, very compelling motive for murder."

He stopped shouting, realizing that her words were somewhat foreboding. He took several deep breaths, calming himself. Settling back into the chair, he lifted his chin defiantly. "I'm not guilty of anything. You have nothing on me."

She pulled out an evidence bag this time. "Someone interrupted you halfway through one of your attacks, and you left this behind."

He looked closely at the bag containing the condom found inside Julie Keppler. "That's not mine."

"Funny thing about DNA, isn't it, Mr. Hudson? It led us right to you. It also tied you to two unsolved rape cases."

His face registered horrified shock. "I've never raped or killed anyone. Especially not my wife. Now why don't you take the cuffs off me and figure out who really did this."

"You did this." Rebecca leaned back to meet his eyes. "This is what I figure happened. Guy like you gets married, figures he'll have a nice little family in the suburbs. A couple of kids, a dog, barbecues in the back yard. Only, you couldn't do that. Your wives wanted kids, and you couldn't get them pregnant. So, they decide to use sperm donors. That gets pretty costly for you, and it's not even your kid. That has to make you pretty mad. Mad enough to kill. But you can't just kill your wife because that's too obvious. So, you kill seven other people to cover the murder."

Richard Hudson shook his head from side—to—side, refusing to believe her, refusing to admit to her words.

"You almost got away with it too. It was a brilliant idea. But you forgot one thing. Even the smartest criminals are stupid, and they make mistakes. You made yours and now you're going to pay for every single life you took, *especially* your wives."

She glared at him with thinly veiled disgust. "Get him out of my sight."

Chapter 15

"Yeah, we got him. He's in custody now. Tell Julie it's over." Jordan hung up the phone after a brief and tearful conversation with Assistant Director Mitchell. She walked back into the bullpen and watched Rebecca typing in the last of the notes on The Cradle Killer case. The lines from stress had started to disappear, and Jordan had to admit that she was even more beautiful now than she was when they met. She decided to take a chance. That was what her life was about anyway, wasn't it? Chances. Isn't that what everyone's life came down to? Everyone had hopes and dreams, and they took chances to get them. Sometimes you failed, but more times than not, when the chances paid off, and you held your dreams in your hand, then you knew what happiness felt like. At this particular moment, Jordan wanted to jump at the chance, even a small one, that she could find happiness.

"Will you have dinner with me?" Jordan's voice caught, and she coughed to cover it. She had never had trouble asking a woman out, but Rebecca made her nervous, or the possibility of being rejected by Rebecca made her nervous.

Rebecca glanced up from her computer. "We can celebrate another time. I'm exhausted. I just want to take a hot bath and go to bed for the next two days."

"I'm good with both." Jordan waggled her eyebrows.

"Uh—uh, I'm not interested, Agent Gray." Rebecca's tone was firm, but the look of longing in her eyes gave her true feelings away.

"Agent?" Jordan stepped closer and ran a finger along her jaw. "You know I prefer Jordan."

Rebecca's eyes widened slightly, and Jordan saw the vein in her neck pulsing delicately. "Please don't. I prefer to keep our relationship professional." She pushed Jordan's hand away and stood up, hitting the enter key. "As a matter of fact, we are done here. The CDD appreciates all your help, Agent Gray, but we won't need the FBI anymore. We're all done here."

Jordan heard the words, but her eyes saw something behind them, and she acted without thinking. Closing the gap between them, she cupped Rebecca's neck and pulled her mouth towards hers with deadly accuracy. She heard the faintest whisper of protest before Rebecca's lips softened against hers, and her tongue slipped inside the inviting warmth that she had craved for so long.

Rebecca's heart hammered against her chest. Whatever dreams she had dreamed about Jordan paled in comparison to the real thing. Her lips were soft, and she tasted like innocence and promise. Rebecca poured herself into their kiss and when Jordan pulled away, after what seemed like an eternity, her breath came in ragged gasps.

Jordan caressed Rebecca's swollen lips with her thumb and stared into her soul, losing herself in the emerald-green depths. Her ragged breaths matched Rebecca's, and she struggled to pull herself away. Her sanity finally broke through, and she smiled sadly. "Now, we are done."

Rebecca watched her walk away, sucking in deep breaths and praying that her heart wouldn't pound out of her chest. Her fingers touched her lips. No one had kissed her like that in…well in ever, and she struggled to put the emotions she was feeling into a safe place where she could come back and sort through them. What she was surprised to discover was she didn't want to think right now. What she wanted was to feel and forget what it was like to think.

Ignoring the warning signals her brain was sending, she ran out of the station, looking for Jordan. She caught up to her as she was getting into her car. From somewhere deep inside, her hunger took over, and she grabbed Jordan's arm and pinned her against the car.

Had she given herself a moment to think, Rebecca would have realized the insanity of her actions, but a need to touch Jordan pulsed through her body. She reached up and pulled Jordan's mouth to hers and ravaged her with her tongue.

Jordan groaned into her mouth, her arms finding their way around Rebecca's soft and supple body. Their bodies melded together perfectly and within seconds, the need to touch had grown to an insatiable hunger that neither one could control.

Rebecca's hands clawed at Jordan's back as their tongues tangled together in a wild frenzy. Seconds turned into minutes, and Rebecca clawed at the last shreds of sanity and broke their kiss. She leaned against Jordan's body and met her eyes, her desire mirrored in the dark pools. "I was wrong. We aren't done. We've only just begun."

They barely made it to Jordan's house before Rebecca starting ripping her clothes off. The need to feel their bodies pressed tightly together overrode all other rational thought. She almost ripped the buttons off Jordan's shirt in her haste, and a hungry growl erupted from deep inside as she unsnapped the button holding her jeans together. She slid the zipper down, and the brief flash of Jordan's black briefs caused a sudden intake of breath.

The soft skin below her navel begged to be touched and Rebecca left a warm, wet stripe just above Jordan's briefs with her tongue. The responding groan and twitching in Jordan's muscles made her even hungrier. Ignoring Jordan's hands, Rebecca pulled her jeans open and inhaled deeply. The sweet, musky scent of her arousal hit her nostrils and a welcome wave of pleasure rolled through her stomach. "Mmm, you smell perfect."

Jordan's knees buckled with pleasure, and she edged towards the bed, trying to keep her balance. She pulled Rebecca up so quickly her weight caught Jordan off balance, and they tumbled backwards onto the bed. Jordan felt Rebecca's weight settle on top of her, and she gathered her against her body, feeling the welcome warmth tucked in all the right places. "Kiss me."

Rebecca heard the gentle plea and the urgency of earlier lessened until it was just a small fire burning within her core. She lowered her lips and captured Jordan's mouth against hers, and the fire that had simmered only seconds before, threatened to burn out of control once again. Their tongues met, and Rebecca's need for contact took control again. She wrenched her lips away and pulled her own top off. She started to undo her bra, but her hands were pushed away, and Jordan's hands skillfully unhooked the clasps. Her fingers slipped under the strap and slowly worked the material off her shoulders, her knuckles grazing the sensitive skin beneath them.

Rebecca's breasts broke free from her bra, and Jordan sucked in a breath. Her eyes caressed the creamy-white mounds. The skin was sprinkled with pale freckles, and her areolas were light brown and perfectly round. Her nipples were taut from her arousal. Jordan lifted her head and pulled the round bud into her mouth and rolled it gently against her tongue, lighting fires of arousal throughout their bodies.

Rebecca's moans of pleasure filled the room and when Jordan nipped the taut bud between her teeth, she nearly jumped off the bed. "God, you make me feel so good."

Jordan pulled her mouth away and smiled devilishly. "Just wait. I plan on showing you just how good it feels to have a woman worship your body."

Rebecca's eyes darkened in response to Jordan's promise, and she leaned over her until their naked breasts brushed together. The feeling was as close to perfection as Rebecca could remember. She felt desire rush through her body and pool at her aroused center.

Jordan captured Rebecca's bottom lip in hers and nipped it gently. She teased Rebecca's mouth open, slid her tongue inside and began a slow exploration with her tongue, teasing and tasting all that Rebecca had to offer. She felt a rush of wetness between her legs. She knew she needed to taste Rebecca now or die from wanting. She ran her hands down the length of Rebecca's back and slid them into her pants, cupping her bottom in her hands. She pulled Rebecca's body into her pelvis roughly and the pressure on her sensitive clit only served to heighten her need.

Rebecca could sense the change in Jordan's pace and when she felt Jordan adjust her weight and flipped Rebecca onto the bed and tucked her body beneath her weight, Rebecca responded by arching her hips into Jordan's pelvis with a wicked smile. "Show me. Show me how much you want me."

Jordan studied her face and saw desire mirrored in her eyes. She kissed her soundly, her right hand slipping inside Rebecca's panties and cupping her mound. She stroked her clit with a practiced finger, feeling it harden underneath her touch. She could feel Rebecca's body begin to dance beneath her fingers and knew she was close. "Can I?"

Rebecca nodded, and Jordan pulled her hand away and unbuttoned her pants. She leaned up on her knees and eased her pants over her hips and down her long legs. She tossed them into a pile on the chair and slid her body up Rebecca's and settled between her thighs, her eyes drinking in the pale red curls between her legs. She inhaled deeply, and a rush of wetness flooded her briefs anew.

She kissed her inner thigh and licked the sensitive skin at the apex of her legs, relishing the feeling of letting go of everything and being in the moment. She slid her tongue through the slick wet folds, and all rational thought escaped her. Her focus narrowed until the only thing she knew was the sweet taste of Rebecca, and the moans that her mouth was eliciting.

Jordan stroked deep within and devoured Rebecca's essence. Every nerve in her body tingled with raw pleasure. Somewhere in the haze, her mind registered Rebecca's hips arching to meet her mouth, and she slid her hands under her bottom and pulled her body upwards towards her waiting mouth.

Rebecca felt wildfires igniting and spreading throughout her body. "Fuck. Your tongue is dangerous. Please, Jordan, I need to come so bad." Her hips rolled in time with Jordan's tongue, driving her deeper and deeper inside.

Jordan felt Rebecca's body tense around her, and she knew she was close. She captured her clit in her mouth and stroked it roughly with her tongue, sending shivers of pleasure racing up her spine.

"Oh, fuck yes, just like that. Yeah, baby, you fuck me so good. You know how to eat my pussy." Rebecca's voice was raw, her words tinged with desire, and they burned through Jordan's body. No one had ever talked to her like that, and the words were almost enough to make her come. She sucked Rebecca's clit until it pulsed against her, and her legs shook.

Loud moans escaped Rebecca's mouth and filled the tiny room. She couldn't contain the need within her, and the pleasure built like a dormant volcano waiting to erupt. She clamped her knees around Jordan's head, her hands finding the sheets, desperately searching for something to contain the pleasure that rippled through her body. She couldn't think, couldn't function, could feel nothing except Jordan's tongue on her, and when the first waves of her orgasm exploded from deep within, she arched off the bed, her body more alive than she had ever known it.

Jordan pulled wave after wave of molten pleasure from her body, taking her to immense peaks and pulling her back again, only to stroke her higher once, twice, a third time. When the last wave crested and ebbed away, Rebecca's body fell back to the bed, exhaustion was her captor, and she was its willing slave. Every inch of her body was alive and tingled with aftershocks of pleasure.

When she finally stilled, Jordan moved her body up Rebecca's and slid her tongue along Rebecca's lips, letting her taste her own desire. "You taste so fucking perfect, Detective Foxx."

Rebecca shuddered with delight. She had tasted her own juices before, but now mingled with Jordan's tongue, she tasted sweeter than she remembered. Maybe that's what a proper fuck did, brought out previously undiscovered treasures. She licked her lips and grinned devilishly. "You make me feel so good."

Jordan kissed the tip of her nose and smiled. "That's just the start. Stick around and I'll show you the good stuff."

"That wasn't the good stuff?" Rebecca's eyes widened. "I'm not sure my body can handle any more. I can't move at all. You'll kill me."

"Only if pleasure kills." Jordan smirked. "Oh, I can promise you, it will be worth finding out."

Rebecca smiled, feeling stupidly giddy. "Something tells me you are worth the risk." She slid her hand inside Jordan's briefs and felt slick warmth. "What about you, baby? Got something we need to take care of?"

Jordan shook her head. "I'm okay. Taking care of you is all I need."

Rebecca slid two fingers along her slick folds and grinned. "That's not fair. I can't very well leave you in this state."

"Really." Jordan smiled. "You can barely move. I'll take care of it later."

"Take care of it now." Rebecca countered. "I want to watch you come."

Jordan's eyes darkened. Sure, she had taken care of things plenty of times before, but never in front of anyone. She searched Rebecca's eyes and saw nothing but honest intensity. "I don't know…"

"Please." Rebecca pleaded. "You're so wet. You don't have to wait."

The earnest please was all Rebecca had to say, and Jordan came undone. She slid her hands inside her briefs and felt just how wet she was. "Help me."

Rebecca's brow arched briefly before her hand covered Jordan's and forced her hand lower. Jordan slid her finger inside and felt her muscles contract instantaneously. She was close. It would only take her a few deft strokes before she came.

She held her hand still, forcing Rebecca to take control. Rebecca's hand pushed against hers, setting the pace and soon, Jordan felt her own clit harden against her palm. She slid her fingers deep inside then pulled them out and spread her juices on her clit. Rebecca's hand moved hers in circles and soon her clit jumped against her fingers. She arched her hips and increased the pace.

The orgasm hit her before she knew it, and her breath caught in her throat as the first waves of pleasure started deep and rolled through her body. Her eyes met Rebecca's gaze. She looked into rough seas of desire and felt herself pitch headlong into the second wave of pleasure. She felt Rebecca's hand press against hers, and she stroked every last bit of pleasure from her sensitive body. Moments later, when the aftershocks had finally died down, she felt Rebecca pull her into her arms and cover them both. Her last thought, before sleep took her away, was that Rebecca's sweet scent made her feel at home. As close as she could get to the perfect home she had always craved. Rather than scare her, she welcomed it, embraced it, and took it with her as she slipped into sweet oblivion.

Chapter 16

Two Months Later…

The voice is here again. Always, the voice in my ears. It starts as a low whisper and escalates to a cacophonous pounding in my head. I pull wildly at my ears as if separating them from my body will quiet the maddening cries.

It is time. That is what the voice tells me. *Time for atonement. She must pay for her sins.* Sometimes I wonder if she has paid enough, but the voice reminds me, there is no way she can pay until she dies. I spend nights like these searching for her, taking out her punishment on someone else equally as guilty.

"I want to have children."

I see the look in her eyes, as though she is suddenly ashamed of me because I can't give her the one thing she wants.

"There are other ways. We can see someone about it."

She shakes her head, not even open to my suggestion. "I don't want to go through all that. It may not work anyway."

This is a fight we have had many times before. She stayed so long out of obligation, or perhaps because she felt sorry for me, but never because she loved me. I have lost the fight before I have even been offered the chance to try. "You don't understand. It's not like it was years ago. Can't we at least try? Please say yes…for me."

That's all I need. One word. A simple yes to validate my feelings. Inadequacy has been my companion for too long and yet, here I am again, feeling its cold touch against me.

"I've made up my mind. I don't want to go through that. I don't want you."

The words are whispered so softly that I almost miss them. Now, years later, they wake me from the precious few hours of sleep I do get and taunt me.

I have seen the news. I know that someone else stands trial for my crimes. It is a small price to pay. His hands are as stained with sin as mine and then some. God exacts punishment for wavering from his word, just as she wavered.

Tonight, I must hunt again. To quiet the voice. It tires me and keeps me from sleep. I would give anything to have a moment's peace. I shiver involuntarily as I wait in the dark. The streets are deserted, save a few brave souls. Tonight they are lucky that it isn't them I am hunting. No, tonight she is my prey.

As with all of them, they do not know I have been watching them, waiting for the perfect moment. She is too far away, but I imagine I am inhaling her scent. The cold burns my nostrils and wakens the voice. One last chance to tell me what I am to do. But I know already. I cannot forget the words that are part of me now.

I tell it to be quiet and a wicked laugh is the only reply, as if I can tell the voice what to do. I press my fingers into my ears in a vain attempt to silence it. I push off the building where the dark has hidden me and make my way across the deserted streets. Even at this hour, the city has gone to sleep.

She walks about aimlessly, her hand rubbing her stomach without even thinking. I imagine I can see a smile tease at the corner of her mouth. Like any mother, she protects her cub. But not from me. Not from the hunter. The wolf. I quicken my pace, treading the ground with silent footfalls.

I close the distance and wait for the stiffening. The shudder of realization. There is none. She has not realized that tonight she will die. I walk ever closer, needing to feel her fear. Needing to smell the distinct scent of helplessness. To see the wild eyes of the prey begging for its life.

She hears the sound of my breathing, and her step falters. Now, I smell it. The fear mixed with the cold odors of the city. She doesn't turn around, thinking perhaps that she only imagined me, and if she keeps walking, she will find comfort in some safe place. She is completely surprised when my hand finds her shoulder, and I yank her body roughly into mine. "Can you feel me? Did you know tonight would be your last? Surely, you must have guessed I was coming for you."

She shakes her head and screams into my hand. The answer is always the same. They never know I am coming for them. She won't know until it is too late. *This is all for you, my sweet wife.* I tell her time and time again. I wonder if somewhere in the night, she senses the chill of evil and shivers without knowing why.

I pull her into the alley, my eyes and ears constantly on the alert. She is strong. She is fighting so bravely for the life I have not yet begun to take. I throw her roughly into a wall, and the blow to the head stuns her, and for a moment, she goes limp in my arms. This is all the opportunity I need to push her into the ground.

She is on her back now, her eyes wild with fear. She shakes her head from side-to-side, the unevenness of the concrete below cutting into her scalp. But she doesn't feel it. The only thing she feels now is the urge to fight. She knees me in the bottom and I pitch forward, teetering just above her. It is in this moment when our eyes meet, that she recognizes the hunter and confusion alters her features.

I smile evilly and push back up on my haunches. It is then that she sees the glint of steel in my right hand and perhaps feels how hard I am against her distended belly. A low, guttural laugh escapes my lips, and she realizes I am no human. I am a madman. She starts to claw at my body, trying to reach my face, but I capture her hands against her body and send her a look of warning. She stills immediately, perhaps finding somewhere in the recesses of her mind, some ill advice not to fight your attacker. Tonight is the night she should have fought.

I rip her pants away exposing the white flesh beneath and my erection dances wildly. She is still quiet, fearing what will happen to her. One last bit of fight awakens somewhere inside and she starts to writhe beneath me. This sudden movement against me evokes memories long laid to rest, and the faintest sound of laughter teases at my subconscious from far off. Visions of her body underneath mine, her legs wrapped around me, pulling me closer as I drive into her, bringing her to climax.

A blow to my head wakes me from the dream. I am momentarily dazed and not sure what I am doing. But the voice, the voice is there to remind me and with renewed fury, I loosen my own pants and release my aching hardness. There is no slowness tonight. All my moves are done with angry deliberation now. I shove myself inside her roughly, and she screams into my hand. There is no one around to hear, no one to save her.

I pause briefly and look into her wide eyes. It is time. She has to pay for her sins. I run the knife across her neck and as the first drops of blood mingle with the night air, I release a primal howl and punish the woman beneath me. It is over too quickly, and although a sense of calm has taken over, I feel empty. There is just one more thing to do. One small thing to ease the ache that her leaving has left.

She must pay the ultimate price. What God has given, let no man take away. I laugh at this simple, misguided adage. For God didn't give to me. No, he took away. He took everything, and now as my recompense, he has sent me to take her confession. To gather her sacrifice, her atonement for her sins.

I pull away from her and caress the mound beneath me. There is no movement, only hardness, and as I cut away the last of her gift, the anger subsides. I wait for the voice, but it doesn't come. I am alone in this part. I pull the life from within her and wrap it carefully in a small blanket. One less life lived in sin. I'm saving you, can't you see that?

He is too small to understand, though, and the corners of my mouth curve up slightly. It is done. I brush my hand over her eyes and close them mercifully. I wipe the knife on a cloth and pull my gloves off. I put them in an open dumpster and slip the small bundle under my coat. I leave the alley, altered in some fashion that I can't quite put my finger on yet.

A small grain of doubt has started to take seed somewhere in the deep recesses of my mind. I cannot put my finger on it exactly. It is enough to make me wonder when I will be called upon for my atonement. This time when I shiver, it has nothing to do with the cold and everything to do with the inevitability of my demise.

Chapter 17

Jordan rubbed her eyes and squinted against the morning sun peeking through her blinds. She felt a slight tingling in her arm and realized it was pinned against the bed. She smiled at the woman sleeping beside her. Amazing what a change two months brought on.

An arm was thrown haphazardly over her stomach, and a leg was draped over her thigh. The soft warmth felt wonderful against her body, and she tried not to move for fear of rousing her. She didn't need to worry, though, as the hand splayed over her stomach crept up slowly and teased her nipple.

"Good morning, Sunshine."

"Morning, babe." Jordan smiled at the emerald-green eyes peeking out from behind masses of wild red hair.

Rebecca snuggled closer and rested her head in the crook of Jordan's arm. "Have you been up long?"

Jordan shook her head. "Just a minute or so."

Rebecca's hand worked lazy circles around Jordan's breast and within seconds, her nipple hardened to a painful peak. "You should have gotten me up earlier."

"Why?" Jordan choked out, her body quickly becoming aroused. Rebecca could do that to her anytime she touched her. In the two months since they had gotten together, Jordan couldn't count the number of times a look or brief touch would send them scrambling to find a secret place where they could show each other just how much they meant to one another.

It happened rather by accident the first time. Jordan had asked Rebecca to dinner to celebrate their capture of Richard Hudson. The news was hailing the CDD as heroes for catching a cold-blooded killer, and Rebecca herself had been spotlighted as the lead investigator.

Rebecca resisted at first, a last attempt to keep her relationship with Jordan on a professional level. But then Jordan had done the one thing that broke down her defenses. She kissed her. One kiss and all the desire that Rebecca had tried to keep buried came rushing to the surface. In one moment, she went from cold and reserved to hot and bothered. Jordan took care of rest. And the rest, as Jordan liked to say, was history.

"I was hoping we would have time to shower together this morning." The sexy lilt of Rebecca's voice coupled with the hand that was moving down Jordan's stomach, and through the tight curls between her legs erased all possibility of rational thought.

Jordan stilled Rebecca's hand. "You sure? Jury selec…"

Rebecca slid her finger into Jordan's warm center, effectively shutting her up. "Believe me, I remember exactly what today is. But I would really like to forget about it for a minute before I have to face it."

Jordan arched her hips and met Rebecca's hand. "How could I say no to that face?" She caught Rebecca's chin between her thumb and forefinger and brought her face to hers. Jordan captured Rebecca's lips against hers and kissed her softly. "And since you ask so sweetly, I think we have time for both."

Rebecca grinned lasciviously. She moved her hand and slid her body onto Jordan's, settling her hips between Jordan's legs. Her stomach moved against Jordan's distended clit and Rebecca felt Jordan jump beneath her body. "A bit wound up are we? I think I need to take care of my baby."

Rebecca pulled Jordan's bottom lip into her mouth and sucked it softly, eliciting a small groan of approval. Her tongue delved inside, seeking Jordan's and when she felt it against hers, she moaned. Kissing Jordan always made her hot. Her own arousal was quickly becoming hard to ignore. She pulled away and licked Jordan's neck just below her jaw. She licked the small indention at the base of her neck, and Jordan jumped slightly.

Jordan was so sensitive there that Rebecca couldn't help but tease her until a slight chuckle escaped from her lips. "Babe, you're killing me."

"Sorry." Rebecca's eyes twinkled, and Jordan could tell she was anything but sorry. Rebecca winked and moved lower, capturing Jordan's nipple in her mouth. She teased it with her tongue and when it was taut, she caught it between her teeth.

Jordan arched off the bed. Rebecca knew her body, as well as she did her own now. Her nipples were very sensitive and so connected to her clit that she had gotten off just from Rebecca's playful teasing. "You're killing me."

Rebecca didn't respond with words, but the next place her mouth touched made Jordan jump off the bed. Her tongue brushed over Jordan's aching clit and sent her body soaring. As worked up as she was, Rebecca knew it wouldn't take long to bring Jordan to climax. She circled the tightened bud and then slid lower, delving into Jordan's slick folds, relishing the sweet flavor of her arousal.

Jordan's hips moved against Rebecca's face and within moments, she felt the muscles around Rebecca's tongue start to contract. She arched higher. "Oh fuck, yes. It feels so good."

Rebecca smiled and pulled Jordan's pulsating clit into her mouth. She felt it dance against her tongue, and she deftly stroked her until Jordan's body started to convulse, the orgasm overtaking her.

Jordan gripped the sheets, her hips arching off the bed. She writhed underneath Rebecca's mouth as wave after wave of her orgasm ebbed through her body. When the rolling pleasure finally returned her body to her, Jordan sank back into the bed, sated. She felt Rebecca's tongue sliding through her slick folds, and her heart clenched at the thought of this woman drinking up every bit of her.

She grabbed Rebecca's arm softly and pulled her up over her body. She smiled tenderly and kissed Rebecca, tasting herself on her lips. "As soon as I can move, how about that shower, you promised me?"

Rebecca returned her smile. "I'll start the water."

Somehow Jordan managed to rouse herself and joined Rebecca in the bathroom several moments later. She could see through the glass that Rebecca was starting without her. One hand was pulling at her nipple, and the other was working lazy circles around her clit. Jordan pulled the door open and pretended to frown. "Hey, that's my job."

Rebecca pulled Jordan into the shower and kissed her longingly. She backed up until she was against the wall and wrapped a leg around Jordan's hip. She grabbed Jordan's hand and slid it over her body and pushed her fingers into her throbbing core. "It's time to go to work, darling."

Jordan grinned mischievously and pulled her fingers out only to slide them in again. "What's the matter, babe? You all worked up this morning? Need me to take care of you?"

Rebecca nodded. She could feel Jordan's fingers poised against her warm center. She wrapped her arms around Jordan and pulled their bodies together. She bit her collarbone gently and whispered against her ear. "Please fuck me."

The three words were all Jordan needed to break her bravado. She wrapped her free arm around Rebecca's body and pulled her onto her fingers. A moan escaped from Rebecca's mouth, and Jordan swallowed it with a passionate kiss. Normally, Jordan preferred to take her time, but as they had discovered rather soon after getting together, sometimes quick and hot was all they had time for.

Jordan's fingers plunged inside Rebecca's body, and her thumb stroked Rebecca's clit deftly. She could feel Rebecca move with her, drawing her further inside her body. It was only a matter of minutes before Rebecca threw back her head. "Yes. Fuck, yes. I'm coming."

Jordan smirked and increased the pace. That was the other thing that she had discovered rather quickly about Rebecca. She was quite loud in bed and as the screams of her orgasm filled the tiny bathroom, Jordan knew she had found the woman that she would do anything to keep.

A half an hour later, Rebecca watched Jordan rub gel through her wild hair. She ran her fingertip over her jaw line and smiled. "Have I mentioned how much I enjoy watching you get ready in the morning?"

Jordan cocked an eyebrow and smiled. "Only about a hundred times, but tell me again."

Rebecca stepped closer, and her naked breasts brushed against Jordan's arm. "I. Love. Watching. You. Get. Ready. In. The. Morning." She punctuated each word with a quick kiss.

Jordan grabbed Rebecca and pulled her body flush against hers. "Keep that up and you will be watching me get ready again."

Rebecca grinned mischievously and pulled away. She waggled her finger in Jordan's face. "Uh-uh. Not today."

Jordan watched her walk saucily out of the bathroom and into her closet, her naked bottom inviting a prolonged gaze. She forced her eyes back to the mirror and took a deep breath. "I think I should say I'm the lucky one when it comes to watching someone get ready."

"What?" Rebecca's muffled response got lost in the closet, and Jordan just shook her head. Rebecca seemed to do everything in the nude. She had told Jordan early on that she was in clothes, and uncomfortable ones at that, so much that when she was home, she didn't want to be dressed. Jordan didn't see a problem with that at all. Menial chores had unexpectedly taken on new life when she was with Rebecca, and food suddenly tasted better than it ever had before when prepared by a naked Rebecca.

"Hey, you want to ride in together?" They were going to the Federal Courthouse this morning for the jury selection in Richard Hudson's trial. The judge moved the trial date up as quickly as possible. He was up for re-election, and a conviction in the Cradle Killer case would certainly sew up the election.

When no reply came, Jordan stuck her head out of the bathroom. Rebecca was standing with her pants halfway on, her eyes fixed on the television.

"We have breaking news in the case against alleged murderer Richard Hudson. In a very unexpected turn of events, Mr. Hudson has been released from jail, and all charges have been dropped."

"What the fuck?" Jordan grabbed the remote and turned the volume up.

"In light of the new developments in the Cradle Killer case, Judge Thomas has dropped all the charges and released Richard Hudson. The CDD won't comment on exactly what that new evidence is, but a source close to the CDD did confirm that Richard Hudson is no longer a suspect in the murders. Stay tuned to WXIN for further details as we will be following this developing story."

Rebecca's face was pale. "Son of a fucking bitch." She grabbed her phone off the nightstand and checked the display. Twenty-one missed calls and at least one new voice message. She swore loudly. She had turned the ringer off last night at the movies and forgotten to turn it back on, and she had finally given up her antiquated pager last month.

She punched in her code and waited as the messages played. Jordan watched the emotions play across her face. She couldn't imagine what had happened that would make the judge dismiss the case. A DNA mix up? It was possible, but not likely. She checked her own phone and was surprised to see that Matt had called several times. No message though, which was odd, except that they had not been on the best of terms since she had gotten the girl.

"God damn it!" Rebecca threw the phone onto the bed and ran her hand through her hair. "How is that possible?"

"What happened?" Jordan crossed the room, but stopped short of Rebecca, recognizing her need for space.

"Another murder last night."

"A copycat?"

Rebecca shook her head. "Not unless they got a hold of Richard Hudson's dick and left his sperm at the scene."

"What do you mean?"

"Apparently, the DNA left at the scene, almost too conveniently I might add, matched Richard Hudson's."

"How is that possible?" Jordan was getting more and more confused by the minute.

"Now how the fuck do you think I would know that?" Rebecca snapped testily.

Jordan winced at Rebecca's harsh words. She took a step back and tried not to bristle at the anger in her eyes. It wasn't directed at her. "I didn't mean that. I was just thinking out loud."

Rebecca started storming around the room, throwing clothes on. "See, this is why I don't get involved. It makes things complicated, and it throws me off my game."

Jordan grabbed her arms softly and forced Rebecca to look at her. "You couldn't have done anything differently than what you did. No one could have suspected it wasn't Richard Hudson."

Rebecca wrenched her arms away and glared at her. "I could have if I wasn't distracted." She sat down on the bed and tied her shoes silently. "Listen, this case just went from bad to worse. I can't afford to be distracted. I think we need to cool it."

"Do you really mean that?" Jordan was unprepared for the clench in her chest. She thoroughly enjoyed Rebecca's company, in and out of bed, but she wasn't emotionally involved, or at least she thought she wasn't, so the tug in her heart surprised her. "You can't think that you missed something because of us."

"I function better alone, without all the shit that comes with a relationship. I need to make sure my head's in the game this time. I messed up, and another woman is dead."

"This isn't your fault. You followed the evidence, and it led us to Richard Hudson."

Rebecca shook her head. "I need to follow my gut, and right now you make it impossible to think clearly. I can't do this anymore. From this point on, we're going back to Detective and Agent. Nothing can get in the way of figuring out who the real killer is and how Richard Hudson ties into all of this."

Jordan studied her face and knew that she couldn't convince Rebecca otherwise. No matter how good they were, Rebecca was all about the job. She was the job. A wave of pain hit her square in the gut, and Jordan pushed it away. "Guess that answers my question about riding in together."

Chapter 18

Jordan slipped under the yellow caution tape and while she flashed a small smile in Rick's direction, she merely nodded curtly to Rebecca. The change between them was imperceptible to anyone around them, but the energy that hummed between them was palpable. Hours earlier, they had showered together, totally sated from their lovemaking, but now there was an intangible distance between them.

She surveyed the scene, not at all surprised that the M.E. had already removed the body. They were here to study the crime scene and find whatever evidence may eventually lead them to the killer.

Jordan stepped around the outline of the body and stopped near Rebecca and Rick. "Find anything?"

"Nothing." Rebecca sounded the same as she always did, but there was a coolness to her tone that shook Jordan. "CSI swept the area already." She pointed to several yellow markers. "Same as always. Not much to go on."

"You said they found DNA."

Rick nodded. "Same as the last one. Condom left inside the victim. He's mocking us now. Knows he is getting away with it while someone else sits in jail."

"Any idea how he got Richard Hudson's DNA?" Jordan's gaze fell on Rebecca, and had she not been studying her as closely as she was, she would have missed her swallow before she spoke. At least, Rebecca was having as hard a time as she was being so close.

"No, but I think it's time we revisit the sperm bank. So far, that's the only tie we have to all the victims."

Jordan nodded towards the chalk outline. "This one too?"

"Yes." Rebecca said with a nod. "Uniforms confirmed it with the husband this morning."

"Want me to drive?" Jordan asked with no hint of an ulterior motive.

"No." Rebecca pulled a gloved hand out of her pocket and checked her watch. "Why don't you see if Special Agent Riley can meet us there? I think we could use his help on this one."

Jordan nodded. Rebecca wasn't going to give an inch on this one, no matter how much her eyes said she wanted to. "Fine."

"Oh, and Agent Gray?" Rebecca's tone held a warning note. "Don't go in without us."

Jordan rolled her eyes and walked away. *Damn infuriating woman.* She stalked off to her car and called Matt. "You busy?"

"Nah." His voice was low. Their friendship had been somewhat strained since he found out that Jordan and Rebecca were dating. His interest in Rebecca had been very real, and his pride and maybe his heart had been wounded a little in the process. "What do you have?"

"I guess you heard the news already."

"I saw it briefly this morning. I called you."

"Yeah, I know. I'm sorry I didn't hear it ring."

"It's no big deal." Matt paused. "I know you're *busy.*" Before Rebecca, that had been a joke that they shared. Jordan loved women, and it hadn't escaped her partner's notice that she was with a different one all the time. Now, it was almost as though he was censuring her for her choice in women.

It wasn't her fault that both of them had fallen for Rebecca's charms. Nor was it her fault that Rebecca had chosen her. It just happened that way, and right now, Matt was sorting through that. Eventually, he would get over it, and they would get back to normal, but for now, she let him rake her over the coals.

"Detective Foxx wants us both in on this. We are going back to the sperm bank. She thinks it all ties back to that somehow."

"And why do you need me?" The question was asked innocently enough, but Jordan could hear the second part of the inquiry loud and clear. *You seem to be handling it just fine on your own.*

"Guess she wants your expertise. Besides, I think she could use a buffer." Jordan admitted quietly.

"Oh yeah, piss her off already?" Matt's tone hinted at a smile, and Jordan could almost recognize her old partner.

"Something like that." Jordan started her car and listened as the engine revved loudly. "You in or not?"

"Yeah, yeah. I'm at the office."

"Be there in ten." Jordan ended the call and looked up briefly, catching Rebecca's emerald-green eyes. She could see regret in them and something else. She wasn't sure what Rebecca was thinking, but she winced inwardly. Nothing like being someone's morning-after remorse.

She shifted into first and shot Rebecca an apologetic smile as she started to drive away. If she had any hope of rectifying the problem, behaving like an asshole wasn't going to be the route she took.

The ride from the office to the Helping Hands Fertilization Clinic was made in relative silence. Matt still wasn't up to idle chitchat and rather than push the envelope of awkward silence any further, Jordan cranked up the radio and let the soulful voice of Serena Ryder fill the void.

When Rebecca pulled up, Jordan slid out of the car and stretched herself out. The unconventional choices for sex had her body totally out of whack. A person couldn't make love in a 370Z without some pain and stiffness the next morning, and she was feeling it.

Matt studied the two of them and chuckled softly. "Well, this should be a fun morning."

Jordan glared in his direction. "Just pay attention to the case."

"Like you did?" Matt asked sarcastically.

Jordan swore under her breath. It was going to be a long day.

"Agents." Rebecca's tone was the same as she had used the first day they met, and much to their disliking, she still dropped the *Special.* Jordan rolled her eyes for the sake of rolling them. Their relationship aside, the least Rebecca could do was acknowledge their accomplishment in the FBI's rank.

"Detective Jones. Detective Foxx. A pleasure to see you again, although I wish it was under different circumstances." Matt, always the gentleman. Nice to a fault, but not missing the opportunity to throw it in Jordan's face that he did not win the girl. Rebecca didn't catch the underlying meaning. She shot Matt a forced smile.

"So do I. When I woke up this morning, I pictured the day going somewhat differently."

Jordan didn't miss the pained look that flashed across her features. The selfish side of her was glad this wasn't any easier for Rebecca than it was for her. The rational side hoped that they both could put this behind them and concentrate on the case.

"Agent Riley, given your background in psychology, I'd like you to talk to as many of the employees here. See what you can find out. Maybe you can pick up on something we missed." She met Rick's questioning eyes. "Jonesy, see if you can't get someone to open up. See if there is something that we missed the first time.

They nodded, and Rick saluted her with mock humility. "Sure thing, boss."

"Agent Gray. You'll be with me. I think it's time to interview the director again."

Jordan followed Rebecca into the building, a safe distance between them. She watched Rebecca flash her badge to a mousy looking receptionist and, for a moment, she thought she saw genuine fear in her eyes. But she masked it just as quickly.

"I'm Detective Foxx with the CDD, and these are Agents Riley and Gray with the FBI. We would like to talk to Dr. Stein, if he's in."

Ruth Dawson, according to the nametag on her desk, paled visibly. "Dr. Stein is no longer employed here. Our new Director is Dr. Mercer. However, the schedule is quite full today."

If Rebecca was surprised by the news, she didn't show it. Jordan, however, wondered what had happened to the former director and what was making Ruth Dawson so agitated.

"Let Dr. Mercer know we would like a moment of his time." Rebecca's tone suggested that whatever the Director had going on at this particular moment, it was going to take a back seat to their investigation.

Ruth nodded and picked up the phone. Her hand shook slightly as she dialed, and she pulled it into her lap the second she pressed the last number. Her voice, which matched her face in its sallowness, trembled somewhat. "Dr. Mercer. There's a Detective here to see you."

She paused then answered an unheard question. "No. The FBI is here also." Ruth's voice trembled again.

A loud gulp preceded Ruth's next statement. "I tried to tell them you were busy."

"Yes. Right away."

Ruth hung up the phone. Her cheeks were tinged pink. Whoever the Director was, it was obvious that Ruth wasn't a particularly big fan of him. "You can go in now."

Rebecca and Jordan followed her finger to a set of double doors to their right. The plaque beside the door read Director-in-Charge, Dr. M. Mercer.

As they walked away, Matt slid into a chair and smiled at Ruth. Jordan saw her relax visibly. Maybe Rebecca's idea to pull him in wasn't such a bad one after all.

Rebecca pushed the door open and walked into a large, well-appointed office overlooking the Chicago River. Situated opposite the door was a huge mahogany desk that was at least eight feet wide. A large wingback chair sat empty behind it. She looked around the room, searching for its occupant.

To their left was a small unmarked door and beside it, a large leather sofa. In addition to the sofa was a small coffee table with copies of the latest baby magazines displayed tastefully. To the right was a wall of built-ins filled with medical journals. The walls were covered with evenly spaced pictures, each marking a different phase of pregnancy.

Jordan stole glances of Rebecca's face as she scanned the empty room, and at the sound of running water from behind the door, jumped slightly. When the door opened, Jordan's jaw dropped.

Mistaking the look of shock for their obvious assumption that Dr. Mercer was a man, Rebecca flashed her badge again. "Dr. Mercer. Detective Foxx. CDD."

"Yes, Detective, I remember you." Dr. Mercer smiled. "You've been on this investigation a long time." Her eyes met Jordan's, and a look of recognition flashed in her eyes before she carefully schooled her features to nonchalance. "You are?"

Jordan fumbled for her badge. "Special Agent Gray. FBI."

Dr. Mercer smirked slightly. Her eyes raked over Jordan's body lasciviously, and for a moment, her mind flashed back to their brief encounter. "Dr. *Meghan* Mercer. A pleasure to see you again, Agent."

Jordan swallowed nervously. She was looking into the bemused eyes of the woman she had met at the gym and traded blows and much more than that with. She reddened slightly as she remembered what had happened between them. Suddenly, things had gotten complicated. "Ahh, you too."

Meghan gave her another once-over and turned her attention back to Rebecca, who was watching the exchange between the two women with renewed interest. She reminded herself to ask Jordan what the hell that look was all about later. "Sorry about that. You see Agent Gray and I are previously acquainted."

Rebecca's gaze fell on Jordan, and her eyes asked for an explanation. Preferably, one that didn't make her involvement in the case an issue.

"We, uhh, met at the gym. Megh…Dr. Mercer and I sparred together a couple of times."

Meghan quirked an eyebrow at the politically-correct explanation that Jordan offered Detective Foxx regarding their past. She picked up on the energy between the two women and wondered at their connection. She chuckled at the confused look on Rebecca's face. "Boxing. Agent Gray was kind enough to box with me one evening."

If Rebecca thought anything happened beyond that, she didn't show it. "I'm sorry to have to bother you again. We've had another murder, and it seems that the only connection between the victims is their tie to the sperm bank."

Meghan dismissed her apology with a wave. "I'm happy to help out anyway I can. I'll let my employees know that their full cooperation with the CDD is expected. Please have a seat. Can I get you anything?"

Rebecca and Jordan took the offered chairs and declined her other offer.

"Thank you, Dr. Mercer." Rebecca pulled a small recorder from her pocket. She waived it in the air. "Do you mind?"

"Not at all."

Rebecca pushed the record button. She settled back in the chair. "Do you mind stating your name, for the record?"

"Dr. Meghan Mercer. Director of the Helping Hands Fertilization Clinic." She met Rebecca's inquisitive glance. "Sorry, second time around. I seem to have the questions down to a science now."

Rebecca laughed and studied Meghan. There was a distant look in her eyes, as though she was distracted. "I know you're busy. We won't take much of your time."

Meghan smiled slightly, but it stopped at her eyes. "It's fine."

"Congratulations on your promotion."

"Thank you. It came as a bit of a surprise."

"Oh? What happened to Dr. Stein?" Rebecca checked to make sure the tape was moving.

"Retired. Rather abruptly I might add." Meghan's eyes bounced between Rebecca and Jordan. She still couldn't quite make out the underlying connection between them. It was almost as if they were sleeping together, but she didn't think that was the case. Her eyes met Jordan's, and she toyed with the idea of once again bedding her. She was exceedingly handsome, and she wondered what it would be like to have Jordan fuck her for real this time.

Jordan must have sensed where her thoughts were going because her face reddened again, and she coughed nervously.

"Are you okay? Sure I can't get you anything?" Meghan asked innocently enough, but Jordan heard the underlying meaning, and she shook her head quickly.

Rebecca watched Jordan's reaction to Meghan, and she felt a pang of jealousy. She shook her head, berating her foolishness. They boxed with each other, not slept together. She dismissed her doubts as quickly as they arose.

"If you don't mind me asking, what were the circumstances of his retirement?"

"Not at all. I've nothing to hide." Meghan was just as willing to help this time as she had been before. Almost too helpful, Rebecca thought, like she couldn't wait to give us information. She hadn't recognized the name at first, but once Dr. Mercer had mentioned knowing her, she was starting to put the pieces together. They had interviewed so many people regarding the murders, and if her memory served her correctly, Rick had handled Dr. Mercer's interviews. "Dr. Stein was caught substituting donor samples."

"I'm afraid I don't understand." Rebecca's brow furrowed with confusion.

"Let me give you a quick summation. Most of our clients are married women whose husbands can't impregnate them, whether the reason is physical or psychological. We use artificial insemination or assisted reproductive technology to help them conceive. A woman's cycle is followed and when she is ovulating, sperm is inserted into her uterus. It can be either sperm collected from her husband or donor sperm. In any case, the sperm is inserted into the woman in hopes of conception."

"And Dr. Stein was in charge of the procedure?"

Meghan shook her head. "If he didn't do it personally, he at least oversaw the procedure. What he was doing was substituting his own sperm in place of the sperm that was supposed to be used."

"How did they find out?"

"He got caught." Meghan leaned forward and laced her fingers together. "This is a multi-million dollar business, Detective. Aside from that, the women who use artificial insemination aren't in an emotional state to deal with this kind of surprise. We take the process very seriously, and when a technician alerted me that he suspected Dr. Stein of deception, I can assure you, that is not looked upon lightly."

"What made the technician suspect him?" Rebecca wouldn't accept something as simple as Dr. Stein getting caught. No, she needed more. She was building a case again him and she needed to know his behavior leading up to and during the murders.

"I'm not sure." Meghan replied quickly.

Rebecca's brow furrowed. "It seems rather careless to accuse a man of wrongdoing based on a guess."

Meghan frowned and let out a loud sigh. She was tiring of Detective Foxx and her questions. "I'm sure it would be difficult to explain given that you have no knowledge of the insemination process."

Rebecca felt her face get hot and she bit her lip to keep from saying what she really wanted to say to the bitch sitting across from her. What she didn't need in the middle of this investigation was Dr. Mercer playing high and mighty. Several deep breaths later, she met Meghan's eyes. "Give me the sperm donor for dummies version then."

The slight eye roll at Rebecca's request was not lost on anyone in the room, least of all Rebecca. "The insemination process is such a tightly controlled process that even the slightest deviation raises some eyebrows. Dr. Stein had started rejecting vials of sperm as unusable. He would then request vials that were not marked according to our normal coding system. This happened several times before the technician brought it to my attention. We investigated further and found missing vials of sperm that Dr. Stein could not explain. When he was questioned about it, he couldn't offer an explanation and in the end, confessed to switching the vials before doing the insemination procedure."

"If things are so tightly controlled and monitored, why weren't the missing vials or coding errors found earlier?"

Meghan's eyes narrowed slightly. Being questioned about Dr. Stein was one thing, being questioned about the clinic was entirely different. When she spoke, her tone had a decidedly chilling edge to it. "The technician was fairly new to the clinic and as such, was not aware of inconsistencies in our processes."

"And after all of the *inconsistencies* were discovered, that's when Dr. Stein was forced to retire?" Rebecca asked.

"The board wanted him gone. The chance for a lawsuit against the clinic outweighed any tenure that Dr. Stein might have had, not to mention the moral issues his actions brought up. Once he was gone, they named me the interim director and I have been here ever since."

Jordan rubbed her chin. "What was Dr. Stein's personality like?"

Meghan smiled. "He was God, or so he thought. His position here went to his head. It was almost as if he believed he was the one that was getting each woman pregnant. His last few months here, his behavior was very erratic. He never got over his wife leaving and, eventually, he took it personally when a woman wouldn't conceive."

Rebecca scribbled on her notepad. "Did he ever act out physically that you know of?"

Meghan shook her head. "Never physically. But there were times I would see him, and he looked like he wasn't here."

"What do you mean?"

"Like he was somewhere else. I could tell by his eyes, and he would mutter under his breath all the time. Always about his wife leaving him. He looked crazy and then something would happen and just as quickly, the old Dr. Stein was back."

Jordan leaned forward. "Sounds like the guy was delusional, maybe even suffering from some dissociative identity disorder."

"Multiple personalities?" Meghan asked. "It's plausible. Like I said, there were times when it was clearly not Dr. Stein in the room, but some out—to—dinner version of him. Look, all I know is someone who misuses his power the way he did is dangerous."

"Dangerous enough to kill?" Rebecca sat up quickly. They had interviewed him before and had not found a reason to suspect him, but the new information was painting him in a completely different light.

"Perhaps. He was volatile, but the day the board let him go, he was furious."

"Did he threaten the board? What about you? As the interim Director and the person responsible for getting him fired, he had to be particularly resentful towards you."

Meghan chuckled. "I won't say he didn't threaten me once or twice, but I dismissed it as idle threats made by a desperate man."

"And you've had no trouble since then?"

Meghan shook her head. "None. I haven't heard from him since."

"So you wouldn't know where we can find Dr. Stein, do you?"

"I'm sorry. That I don't know. You might try calling our attorney. As part of the deal we made with him, he was required to provide us with a forwarding address, in case we were sued by any of the clients that were treated by him."

"And have you been contacted by any?"

"Thankfully, no. I can't imagine the backlash a scandal like that would have on this business."

"If you hear from him, I'd appreciate it if you let us know immediately."

"Of course." Meghan stood up, a clear signal that she was putting an end to this interview.

Jordan's mind was working overtime. Suddenly, it seemed as though they had hit on something. "Was Dr. Stein married?"

"No, divorced actually." Meghan leaned back again. "Dr. Stein's wife left him for another man. He confided in me that it was their inability to conceive that had driven them apart. He never remarried. Instead, he buried himself in his work here, and in the end, I think it drove him mad."

A knowing look passed between Rebecca and Jordan. Was it that simple? Had the murderer been under their noses the whole time? Was it as easy as tracking him down?

Rebecca stood up, thanked Meghan for her time and shut off the recorder. She picked up a frame off the desk and smiled at the young faces in it. "Yours?"

"No." Meghan's face clouded over then she smiled just as quickly. "My nieces. This means I get to spoil them rotten."

"They are adorable." Rebecca put the frame back down and started for the door then stopped. "One more thing. Does Dr. Stein have any connection to Richard Hudson? Would he have any reason to go after him?"

Meghan walked around the desk and stopped in front of them. Her carefully schooled features showed no recognition. "Not that I know of. Mr. Hudson was a client here?"

"Yes." Rebecca was surprised that she didn't realize that. Given the extensive time that each client received, at least according to Richard Hudson, that alone should have at least warranted her remembering his name. "His wife was one of the women who was murdered."

"Oh." Meghan tried to look surprised. "I guess I didn't make the connection."

"Odd." Rebecca added to herself. "Mr. Hudson led us to believe that the reason he chose Helping Hands, despite the cost, was the personal service. He actually came here with his ex-wife as well. He mentioned the in—house counseling, as well. I would have thought as exclusive as the clinic is, you would make it a priority to know your clients."

Meghan reddened slightly. "I'm sure you can understand we maintain a large client base. I can't possibly get to know each one on a personal level."

"No, I suppose not." Rebecca opened the door. "If you don't mind, we'll come back and interview everyone again. I'd like to see if anyone else knew of a reason that Richard Hudson might have been a target, and get more information on Dr. Stein."

"Certainly." Meghan shut the door behind them and hit her fist into her palm. *"No, I suppose not."* Detective Foxx's words rang in her ears. What did that uppity detective know anyway? She was suddenly furious. She couldn't risk the negative publicity it would bring to the clinic if the word got out that its former Director was involved in the killings. "Fuck!"

She yanked open the bathroom door and rolled her old Ever flex sparring partner into her office. She pulled gloves on and cinched them tightly. When her first punch landed, she felt her anger start to subside. Twenty minutes later, she sank to the floor exhausted. "Oh, Dr. Stein, still managing to fuck this place over, aren't you?"

Chapter 19

Rebecca unlocked the doors to her sedan and glared at Jordan over the hood.

"What?" Jordan's irritation at the morning's turn of events was still boiling just beneath the surface.

"Is there something you want to tell me?" There was no mistaking the warning in Rebecca's tone. "Something that will jeopardize my investigation?"

"No." Jordan pulled her eyes away, flinching under Rebecca's penetrating gaze. She wasn't sure, but she thought she might have heard Matt snort underneath his breath. She resisted the urge to tell him to fuck off. She was in no mood to put up with his shit, especially after this morning, and running into Meghan was not helping any.

Rebecca didn't let it drop. "I saw the bullshit look that she was giving you. What I don't want is some past indiscretion to give me any problems."

"I told you, there is nothing to worry about." Jordan's tone was hard. It wouldn't matter anyway. Meghan ran the clinic and there was no guarantee the killings were tied to that anyway.

Rick cupped her elbow in his palm and shot Jordan a smile. "Listen, Agent Gray, don't pay her any attention. She gets this way anytime we work a big case. Day after it's over, you'll be best friends again."

Jordan snorted loudly. The likelihood of that happening was about as possible as her getting eaten by a shark in the middle of Lake Michigan. She caught Rick's wink, and knew without a doubt, he knew about their relationship outside of the case. She felt her cheeks color and dropped her eyes, unable to keep his gaze.

"Maybe this will make you feel better." Rick leaned against the car and crossed his arms over his chests, his face breaking into a knowing grin. "Agent Riley here managed to make friends with our receptionist, and I don't think it had anything to do with his dimples."

"Whatever, Rick." Matt protested. "I saw you making eyes at her. I don't think she even realized I was alive."

Rick waved his hand in the air, dismissing the idea. "Found out she's a little coo—coo." He made circles in the air near his ear with his forefinger. "Lady is nutso to have a baby, and let's just say the new director Dr. Mercer, isn't so high on her list of people she likes."

Rebecca's gaze narrowed. "What do you mean?"

"Guess she and the former director, Dr. Stein, had an arrangement. She and her husband weren't able to get pregnant and couldn't afford to go through in vitro, so the good old doctor said he would help her out at no charge, but he was fired before they could do the procedure."

"So, how does that help us?" Rebecca asked impatiently.

Rick sighed loudly as if completely annoyed that she couldn't put two and two together. "How it helps us is that when she approached Dr. Mercer for the same favor, she pretty much kicked her out on her ass. Even threatened to can her if she brought it up again."

Rebecca circled her finger in the air, a sign for him to explain what she was missing.

"Ruth Dawson is privy to almost everything that happens in that place, and with a little encouragement, I think she may open up about what goes on behind closed doors."

Realization dawned on Rebecca. In a business like that, it paid to keep your mouth shut. She wouldn't be at all surprised if the interviews from the previous investigation were full of half—truths and cover—ups. Ruth Dawson may prove to be invaluable, if they could get her to open up. "Nice work, Jonesy. I think we need to talk to her again."

She opened her door and shot him a look. "And we need to find Dr. Stein again. Something tells me he might be guilty of more than just fraud."

Rick pushed off the car and stepped towards Matt. "How about we follow up with Mrs. Dawson? I don't think she's too keen on you anyway. You and Agent Gray need to see if you can talk to Richard Hudson again and find out if there is a reason Dr. Stein would be targeting him."

Rebecca opened her mouth to protest, but quieted when she saw the look Rick was giving her. Had it been anyone else, she would have told him to fuck off as rudely as possible, but this was her partner, and she trusted his judgment.

Rick held his hand up, and she threw the keys over the car begrudgingly. "Agent Gray, can you make sure our little Foxx makes it home safe and sound?"

Jordan's lip curled up. She would almost bet Rick was throwing them together on purpose. She shot him a grateful smile and could swear she saw him smirk knowingly.

Jordan tossed her keys up and down loudly, mocking Rebecca and her misfortune at being forced to ride with her. She pivoted and headed toward her car without a word. She was just starting the car when Rebecca opened the door and flopped down on the passenger seat.

Rebecca watched Jordan slide the shifter into first gear with practiced skill, her long fingers almost caressing the knob. She felt a shudder run through her body, and she had to force away images of Jordan stroking her until she came out of her mind. She let out a loud sigh. "This doesn't mean anything."

"What would it mean?" Jordan cocked an eyebrow questioningly. "We're investigating a lead. Nothing more."

Rebecca let out a disappointed sigh. She wasn't sure what she wanted Jordan to do or say. All day, a quiet nagging pulled at her from somewhere in the recesses of her mind. She had acted irrationally this morning, and in her haste, lashed out at

Jordan for no reason. Despite her feelings of guilt, she wasn't sure exactly how to smooth things over. Saying she was sorry seemed inadequate.

She studied Jordan's jaw in the late-afternoon sun and marveled at how handsome she was. The muscles in her jaw clenched reflexively, and Rebecca knew she was still pissed. She had every right to be. She had practically dumped her this morning, accused her of sleeping with Dr. Mercer. No wonder she was angry with her.

Rebecca watched her closely, waiting for Jordan to feel her gaze and turn and meet her eyes. It never happened, and the miles burned away in uncomfortable silence. Finally, unable to take the distance she had put between them, she laid her hand on Jordan's thigh. She felt the tight muscles ripple beneath her palm and half—expected her to push her away. "Remember that night?"

Jordan didn't answer right away. Of course she remembered that night. Her body still ached from sex in the close confines of her car. At the time, they hadn't been able to keep their hands off of each other. Looking back, anywhere but the car would probably have felt better. Unable to stop herself, she chuckled. "Yeah, I remember." After what seemed an indeterminate wait, Jordan's hand came off the gearshift and covered Rebecca's.

It wasn't a perfect way to fix things, and Rebecca knew she would still have some amends to make, but it was a start. More than she would have allowed herself with any woman before and when her chest clenched tightly, Rebecca knew that she would spend a lifetime making amends if she needed too.

Jordan brought the car to stop in front of Richard Hudson's house, and she squeezed Rebecca's hand reassuringly. Maybe it was her way of saying we are okay for now, or offering her strength for what they were about to do. It didn't matter which, for Rebecca felt like with Jordan at her side, she would be able to face anything.

They knocked on Richard Hudson's door and waited, hoping he would at least agree to talk to them. The past couple of months had been hell on him. Falsely arrested and accused of his wife's murder, as well as the other victims at the hand of the Chicago Detective Division would put Rebecca pretty far down on the list of people he would be willing to talk to. She only hoped that his desire to catch his wife's killer would help outweigh his outrage.

When he finally answered the door, the hatred was evident on his face, and Rebecca expected him to order them off his porch. He looked much more haggard than he had two months ago. His skin was sunken and sallow, and his eyes looked empty. He looked to be thirty pounds lighter than he was when they first met, and she thought emaciated was a good word to describe him. "Talk to my lawyer."

Rebecca worried that he might play that card. What they needed right now wasn't him lawyering up, although she understood. "Mr. Hudson, please. Tell us about Dr. Stein."

The door stopped closing, and he met her with a searing glare. Maybe, he could hear the desperation in her voice. Perhaps it matched his own. More than likely, she was right, and Dr. Stein had more to do with the murders than he let on. "What?"

"Elizabeth's killer is still out there. We need help finding him." Her voice held an almost desperate tone, which she hoped he would pick up on and agree to at least talk to them. "We just want to ask you a few questions about Dr. Phillip Stein."

Richard Hudson rubbed his eyes with his thumb and forefinger. He dropped his head wearily and opened the door, letting them in.

Jordan followed Rebecca in. He motioned toward the couch and flopped down opposite of them in a large recliner. Jordan eyed the half-empty bottle of whiskey on the coffee table. From the looks of it, he was subsisting on alcohol only and eating very little. "Mr. Hudson, we appreciate you letting us in. We're hoping you can give us some information on Dr. Stein."

The look of anger that had previously mellowed into mild disdain came back full force. "I'll help anyway I can. I told you that before. My only concern is catching Lizzie's killer and bringing him to justice." He downed the glass and refilled it before he continued. "At least this time, you aren't concentrating on the wrong man."

Rebecca winced. It wasn't often that the forensic evidence pointed to the wrong person and truth be told, she felt like shit for imprisoning the wrong person and allowing one more woman to die. "We're very sorry, Mr. Hudson. I can't make up for that, but I can promise to do whatever is in my power to catch the real killer. Your wife...and you deserve that."

"Thank you for that. No one ever tells you they are sorry. Just some shit about how the forensic evidence isn't always a hundred percent, no skin off your back. Stuff like that." He downed another shot and refilled it again. His hands shook unsteadily, and drops of whiskey hit the table and splashed almost silently. "What do you need to know about that bastard?"

Rebecca's eyebrows shot up, and she threw Jordan a look. It would seem that not everyone was a fan of Dr. Stein, and they were about to find out why. "What can you tell us about Dr. Stein?"

"Besides the fact that the guy is a royal fucker, not much." He leaned back in his chair and closed his eyes. He was silent for several moments, and Jordan could almost sense that he was replaying some past meeting. "The guy is supposed to be some miracle worker, giving unlucky women the gift of children, and he was nothing more than a wolf in sheep's clothing. That bastard hit on my wife."

Rebecca's sixth sense suddenly went wild. Things were suddenly starting to fall into place. "What happened?"

"What do you mean, what happened?" Richard leaned forward again, eyes flashing. "I put him in his place. Never messed with her again."

Jordan leaned forward, meeting his eyes. "Was the clinic aware of the problem?"

"Hell yes, they were. I spoke to his assistant, Dr. Mercer. I requested that Dr. Stein no longer handle Lizzie's procedures.

She assured me that the proper disciplinary action would be taken."

, and she could see a look of confusion pass across Jordan's face before she buried it just as quickly. Why had Dr. Mercer lie? Was she covering for him? And, if so, why? "How did Dr. Stein react to being caught?"

"He had the nerve to threaten me. He said he would take me to court. His last words to me were you will pay."

Rebecca smothered a smile. That pretty much cinched it. Means, motive and opportunity. Dr. Stein had all three. Getting caught, and subsequently disciplined, would be the perfect motive to frame Richard Hudson for murder. The pieces were finally starting to line up. "Have you seen Dr. Stein since then? Has he tried to contact you?"

"No. You have to understand, Detective Foxx, I made it very clear to Dr. Stein that if he gave us any trouble or tried to back up his threat, I would make things extremely difficult for him." He leaned forward again, and the glaze in his eyes disappeared. "Why are you asking me all these questions about Dr. Stein?"

Rebecca decided it was time to level with him. She owed him that much at least. "We have reason to believe he may be involved in the killings and is trying to frame you for the murders."

"That fucking son of a bitch!" Richard slammed his fist on the coffee table. "I'm going to kill him."

"Please, Mr. Hudson." Rebecca's eyes pleaded with him. "Let us do our jobs. Killing him isn't going to bring Lizzie back. I know it's asking a lot, but can you promise me you won't go after him? Please let the CDD do our job."

"Like you did it when you arrested me?" His voice was a sneering growl. "He killed my wife, and the bastard is going to pay."

Rebecca leaned across the table and clasped his hand tightly, trying to make him listen to reason. "Lizzie wouldn't want that. She wouldn't want you to give up your life trying to find misguided justice. Don't let her die in vain. If there is justice to be had, let us get that for you."

His nostrils were still flaring, but he didn't respond. His eyes started to well up, and Rebecca hoped, no prayed that somewhere deep inside, the voice of reason would prevail. She didn't want to have to throw the guy in jail twice. "I can promise you this, Mr. Hudson. I won't rest until he is serving a life sentence with no hope of parole."

He didn't reply, merely pulled his hand away and nodded at the door. He was already raising the bottle of whiskey to his lips when Rebecca and Jordan slipped out the door.

"Guy's a mess." Jordan said softly. "I can't imagine what it must be like to lose one wife, much less two."

"I wasn't blowing smoke in there." Rebecca punched the unlock button. "I'll see to it that bastard rots in jail."

She started the car and headed back to District Five. Rick and Matt were already there, faces buried in what looked like day-old donuts. "Hey, boss. Find out anything good?"

A cryptic smile spread across her face. "It's something so good that if I were straight, I'd kiss your ugly mug."

Matt busted out laughing, and Rick shot him a glare that said to knock it off. "Oh yeah? Well, me and Matt may have struck pay dirt as well."

Rebecca pulled up a chair in front of the whiteboard and straddled it hooking her arms over the back. "Don't tease, Jonesy. Tell us what you got."

Jordan swiped a donut and perched on the corner of the nearest desk. She wasn't sure what to expect, but what Rick relayed to them was the furthest thing from her mind. "Apparently, Ruth Dawson and Dr. Stein were closer than what they originally led on. They had an affair about five years ago."

Rebecca leaned forward, waiting for the link. Rick saw the impatient look in her eyes and paused just to piss her off. "It was short—lived, and nothing came of it. But Mrs. Dawson said while they were sleeping together, she helped him take frozen, uhh, samples to his house. She didn't say anything because of their arrangement."

Jordan shook her head and dusted off her pants. "Bastard paid her to keep her mouth shut."

Rebecca concurred. "It would have been nice if she would have told us that the first go round."

Rick nodded. "Said she was too scared to. Dr. Stein had a temper, and he threatened to fire her if she opened her mouth. She needed the income since her husband worked construction and it was seasonal."

"She say why she was coming forward now?" Rebecca stood up and added a new section to the whiteboard with the words Ruth Dawson and affair writtten next to Dr. Stein's name.

"Said she didn't feel right someone else paying for his crimes…if he was truly guilty. My guess is she will feel safer with him in prison than out on the streets. And get this?" A Cheshire grin broke out on Rick's face. "Tell 'em what you found out, Matt."

Matt smirked. "Jimmy Dawson, Ruth's husband, apparently didn't know about the affair or his wife's arrangement with Dr. Stein. He's got a history of beating women up and wouldn't have taken too kindly to his wife's stepping out. But he did tell us that he had his own little arrangement with Dr. Stein. Guy hired Jimmy in the offseason to do odds and ends around his house…including digging some pretty decent size holes out in the back yard. Dr. Stein said it was for compost or something. Apparently, Dr. Stein is into the green thing."

"Apparently." Jordan said sarcastically. "Recycled his own boys a few times."

The reference to substituting sperm brought a chuckle out of the room.

Jordan continued. "Five—to—one, we find something besides old fruits and veggies buried in his backyard."

Rebecca was adding new lines as they spoke. "Okay, so let's get this straight. Around the time the murders began, Ruth Dawson was helping Dr. Stein smuggle frozen samples out of the office. He starts killing women from the clinic. A few years pass and he gets ticked off at Richard Hudson and starts leaving his DNA at the scene. He figures no one will doubt forensic evidence, and Richard will go down for it."

"Except…" Jordan took the marker and drew a line to the last victim. "He can't control his urges and kills another woman while Richard is getting ready to stand trial, effectively ruling Richard Hudson out as the perp." She capped the pen and tapped her chin with it. "What I'm confused about is why those particular women? What ties them all together?"

Rick grabbed another donut and bit into it. "The clinic. What else would there be besides opportunity?"

"That's just it. He had opportunity. But there would have been lots of clients in a clinic that size. Why pick those particular women?" Jordan bit her lip in deep thought.

"I'm following you." Rebecca sat back down on the edge of the desk and studied the board. "What made them so special?"

The room was silent until Jordan jumped up and snapped her fingers. "I got it." She pointed at each one of the victims. "They remind him of someone. Look at how much they all look alike. Long, dark hair, blue eyes. Perfect porcelain skin. They have to look like his ex—wife."

"Except…" Matt pointed at two of the women. "They're blond."

"Not naturally." Jordan pointed at their eyebrows, which were dark in contrast to their lighter hair. "Hundred bucks says they aren't natural blonds."

Rebecca pointed at Rick's computer. "Find a picture of Stein's ex—wife. I want to see her."

Rick's fingers flew over the keyboard, and within in minutes, an image popped up on the large monitor in front of them. "Driver's license okay? It's all I can pull up on her."

No one needed to state the obvious. The likeness was uncanny. The hair, the eyes, way too similar to be coincidence.

"I think we have our killer." Rebecca circled Dr. Stein's name and snapped the lid back on the pen loudly. "What do you say we get a warrant and arrest this bastard?"

"I don't know, boss." Rick cautioned. "What we've got is circumstantial at best."

"Why you busting my balls, Jonesy?" Rebecca countered. "We've got enough to at least bring him in."

"I'm busting your balls 'cause the judge is going to bust your balls. You know I can't call him up and ask any favors right now. Give me something concrete."

"What about the Dawsons?" Jordan ran a hand through her hair. "Think we can get them to issue an official statement? She can corroborate his access to the sperm samples and taking them off clinic property."

"True." Rebecca agreed. "We need them both to give a statement. I want to search the yard too."

Rick shook his head. "That guy ain't doing anything out of the kindness of his heart. It's going to take a favor."

"Money?" Rebecca cocked an eyebrow.

"Uh—uh." Rick pulled up his record. "We're gonna have to wipe this."

Rebecca eyed the miscellaneous rap sheet. A couple of misdemeanors for public disorder, one prior for beating the shit out of his wife. "Do it. Just make sure he understands if he touches her again, I'll fucking castrate him myself."

Rick nodded.

"Jonesy, whatever we need to do, get me that warrant." Rebecca was still tossing the pen, clearly worked up. She hated being this close and staring at a wall. What they needed to do was figure out a way to get around the wall. "Until then, I want you two on Stein. I want to know where he is at all times, what he's doing, if he stops to take a piss, I want to know if he puts the seat back down."

"Sure thing, boss." Rick nudged Matt on the arm. "Good old-fashioned stake out. Bet you ain't done one of those in a while."

Rebecca watched them walk away then met Jordan's questioning gaze. "Go home. Get some rest. Tomorrow we're going to find out why Dr. Mercer lied to us."

Jordan looked crestfallen. For the past month, they hadn't spent a night apart. Tonight, despite the fact that Rebecca had moved past her doubts, Jordan was getting banished to a night alone. "Fine. See ya tomorrow, boss."

Rebecca's heart went out to Jordan. It wasn't her fault Rebecca was having trouble looking past the obvious connection with Dr. Mercer. She just didn't trust the woman and was having a hard time believing nothing had happened. Tonight, she needed some space. She needed to re-evaluate where their relationship was going. What she needed most was a clear head to focus on the case.

She watched Jordan leave and wondered again if she had made the right choice, and if she would ever be able to let go of the job enough to let herself love without reserve.

Chapter 20

Jordan punched the bag angrily, taking her mounting frustration out on the vinyl and stuffing. She felt sweat start to bead on her brow and run down the side of her face. Good, she thought. Maybe I can sweat the hurt out. Every punch landed with a thud, and she punched until there was nothing left inside to let go of.

She saw Rebecca's flaming red hair and brilliant emerald eyes looking longingly at her. She could almost taste her creamy-white skin, and an involuntary shudder coursed through her veins. She couldn't fault Rebecca for her choice to push her away. Jordan had been mostly honest with her sexual history, and she knew she came across as a player. Maybe it was Rebecca's one last attempt to protect herself from getting hurt, but maybe it was just what Rebecca had told her. She needed space to think.

There was some truth to that. Love had a way of being distracting, and even though they hadn't gotten to that point yet, lust was just as bad sometimes, maybe worse. Jordan was probably just as distracted, but she hadn't had to face it…until that night. The night when they knew that Richard Hudson wasn't the killer. Still, even with acknowledging there was some truth to Rebecca's request, it didn't make it hurt any less.

"Hey, kiddo, you keep attacking that poor soul like that, there ain't gonna be a bag left for the next guy."

Jordan looked up and found Tony grinning at her. "Hey, Woz. Long day and an even longer couple of months."

"Yeah, I heard somewhere you might be working that Cradle Killer case on the side." There was no doubt Tony had heard it straight from a source at the FBI. He may have been retired, but he was still as connected as he had been twenty years ago. "Hell of a mix up with that Hudson fellow."

Jordan growled at the mention of his name. "Damn waste of manpower and money and the SOB responsible is still on the street."

"You getting any closer to catching the real guy?" Tony nearly missed her eyebrow cock slightly, and he smiled. "So you are, eh? That's good."

"I didn't say that." She walked by and punched him in the arm. "Buy me a drink and I'll give you some what if's."

Tony chuckled loudly. He still believed he was one of the guys, and Jordan knew that anything she shared with him would stay between them. "Shower first, would ya? I can't have the boys at the bar thinking I'm losing my touch with the ladies. I walk in with you smelling like that, and they'll have my balls in a jar."

"Yeah, yeah." Jordan's voice trailed off as she rounded the corner and out of sight.

Tony walked up to the bag and rubbed his calloused hands along the shiny vinyl. He smiled and shook his head. A lot of hours had been spent in this gym working on cases, getting rid of stress. Apparently, the apple didn't fall far from the tree with Jordan. He may not have been her real father, but he had more influence on who she was today than that sorry son—of—a— bitch that was half of her DNA.

He took a step back and made a fist, tapping the bag lightly with a satisfying thud. He heard the chain rattle and he grabbed the bag and steadied it once more. He pivoted and started to walk away before stopping and executing a perfect roundhouse kick to the middle of the bag. His pleased chuckle echoed off the walls. "Still got it."

"Talking to yourself again, old man?" Jordan teased. "Let's get out of here before someone hears you and has you committed."

Ten minutes later, they were seated at a small table in the back corner at Frank's. Jordan had caught the pool table out of the corner of her eye, and her mind flashed back to the night she had played Rebecca the first time. She hadn't realized it at the time, but Rebecca was feeling just as much sexual tension as she had.

Since that night, they had been back several times, and it never failed. The competition between them fueled their sexual tension, but now when it was almost too much, Jordan had only to give Rebecca a look, and they would be in bed minutes later making love. Not tonight. She breathed a loud sigh that wasn't lost on Tony.

"What's up, kiddo?" His eyes had lost the teasing sparkle that normally took up residence there, and he looked genuinely concerned. "More than the job I'd say."

Jordan took a long swig of her Corona and leaned back in her chair, her face breaking into a weary smile. "How come you never settled down?"

An uncomfortable laugh answered her question. "Well, I can honestly say I wasn't expecting that question. What's got you wondering that?"

"Women." Jordan blew out an exasperated breath.

"Women...or *woman?*"

Jordan pulled at the label on her beer. "Woman, I guess."

'That's why I never settled down."

"I don't get it." Jordan's brow furrowed. "What's why you didn't settle down?"

Tony leaned over the table, his chin resting on his laced fingers. "Look at yourself. A mess over some chick. I never wanted to be that way. Man, it's easier to keep it simple."

"Didn't you ever want more?" Jordan pressed.

He shrugged, but Jordan saw a cloud pass over his face before his happy—go—lucky smile replaced it. "Nah, not really."

"You lying sack of shit. What's her name?" Jordan grinned widely, already chomping at the bit. In all the years she had known Tony, he hadn't seen the same woman more than once or twice and usually had more than one at a time.

Tony rubbed his meaty hands over his face and sighed loudly. "You know what, kid, you really know how to get to the old man, don't ya?"

Jordan smiled ruefully. "You're the closest thing I've ever had to a father. I just wondered why you never got married."

"I was in love once." He confessed. "Back before I met you. We were running point on a big art theft ring that was hitting the art museum, and the mastermind behind it was a woman who actually worked at the museum. It was my job to know everything about her. You can't get that close to someone and not learn a little bit about them in the process."

"You fell for an art thief?" Jordan asked incredulously.

Tony smiled ruefully. "Can't help who you fall in love with. It took three years to get enough on them to take them down. By the time that it was all said and done, I had long since fallen for her."

"How on earth does that happen?" Jordan's voice reverberated with disbelief.

Tony shrugged. "I was undercover. I probably took the case a little too personally. I ended up asking her out. Figured that was the only way to get close enough to find out how she was setting up the thefts."

"She fell for your cover?"

"Fell for it and fell for me. In the end, my boss was worried I got too close. The only way to prove my loyalty was to take her down myself. Hardest thing I've ever had to do."

"Unbelievable." Jordan shook her head. "You could have disappeared with her."

"And done what?" Tony searched Jordan's eyes. "As regimented as it was, this was the only life I had ever known, the only city I had ever lived in. I didn't see myself hiding out in some remote island in the Caribbean for the rest of my life. I like people too much."

"Wow." Jordan downed her beer. "You never cease to amaze me. So, how did it end?"

He shook his head as his voice trailed off, a faraway look in his eyes. "She got fifteen years in a federal penitentiary, and I got a lifetime of memories. I poured myself into my work, and a couple of years later, I met the only person I ever loved more than myself."

He didn't say who it was, but Jordan could tell from the softening of his eyes and the fatherly smile he bestowed on her that she was that someone.

"I suddenly had someone to focus my energy on, someone who needed my undivided attention."

"Hey!" Jordan took a playful swipe at his arm. "I wasn't that bad."

"Kiddo, when I found you, you were one arrest shy of juvie. I saved your ass, and you know it." He patted her hand. "In a way, you saved mine. You stopped me from going off the deep end."

He nodded at her empty bottle. "You want another?"

She shook her head. "Yeah, got more I need to talk to you about. Let's call this a night of fatherly advice."

Tony stood up with a chuckle. "Maybe I better get us a couple of shots too. Sounds like this could be a long night."

When he returned, Jordan thanked him with her eyes. They tapped glasses and downed shots of half-decent tequila. She felt the heat go all the way down to her stomach and light a pleasant tingling from deep within. She met his questioning gaze and wrung her hands nervously.

"Come on, kiddo, spit it out. Whatever it is, it can't be that bad." Tony smiled the same warm smile she had seen a hundred times before. "Lay it on your old man."

"I'm in love with Rebecca." Jordan almost spit the words out for fear she wouldn't have the courage to say them after all. "The red—headed bird, right?" Tony rubbed his chin thoughtfully. "She's a looker alright. So, what's the problem?" "Well, as of this morning, she may not even like me." The pain etched in Jordan's features was evident, even to Tony. Somewhere between walking into Rebecca's office and waking up with her this morning, Jordan had fallen in love with her. She couldn't pinpoint the exact moment, but now, before she had even had a chance to tell Rebecca how she felt, she was seeing the end of their relationship.

"What's not to like?" Tony wrinkled his brow in confusion. "You got a great job, stellar personality, and if I do say so myself, good looks like your old man. That broad is crazy if she isn't half in love with you already."

"Thanks, Woz." Jordan smiled. "I wish it were that easy. The crazy thing is I didn't even do anything to mess it up. She says I distract her. That she needs space. She can't concentrate enough to do her job."

Tony chuckled softly. "You distract her? Well, kiddo, that's sign enough that she loves you. She wouldn't have any trouble working if you meant nothing to her."

A hint of a smile worked its way onto Jordan's face. "You think so?"

"I know so." Tony smiled cryptically. "I know, because that's what nearly blew it for me. Love almost messed my life up, and at the time, I would have let it. Hell, looking back, there are times I think I made the wrong choice. However, you, you're different. I always knew you were meant for more."

"What do you mean?"

He pointed at her chest. "'Cause that's too big."

"My boob is too big?" Jordan laughed. "Woz, I don't know if you need glasses or not, but 34A isn't exactly big."

Tony reddened slightly. "I meant your heart, kiddo. People like you need love. You long for it." He saw her open her mouth to protest. "Oh I know, you have spent your life running because you thought love was bad, but all you really wanted was to find it."

"And now that I have found it, I'm about to lose it." Jordan's head hung low. The effect of the alcohol was making her totally bummed out and feeling sorry for herself. "Now do you see why I avoided it like the plague? I was right all those years. Love does suck."

Tony shook his head. He recognized the despondency he had seen in his own eyes all those years ago. He grabbed her chin in between his thumb and forefinger, and forced her eyes up to meet his. "Don't go getting all girly on me. Don't let that broad flip you inside out. That kind of thinking isn't going to do you a damn bit of good. You need to find a way to remind her why she fell in love with you in the first place. Odds are she's going to realize not being with you is more distracting than loving you ever could be."

Jordan swallowed her beer and gave his words some silent thought. "You think so?"

"I know so. You want to do something good for yourself? Do whatever it takes to show this girl you love her. If you need to, be an ass. Show her how distracting you can be when it matters. I gave up on my chance, and this is what you get, a man who barely learns a broad's name before I sleep with her. In this case, don't try to follow in your old man's footsteps. It's a long, lonely road."

Jordan searched his eyes. "Who knew? Somewhere inside your devil-may-care exterior, is a heart."

Tony growled softly. "Don't you dare let that out. I got a rep to protect."

Jordan laughed. "So, you think she'll fall for it?"

"If you're anything like me, she won't be able to forget you." Tony wriggled his eyebrows. "One night with The Woz and the ladies always beg for more."

"Did you seriously just call yourself The Woz?" Jordan punched Tony in the arm. "I don't know why I thought I could get sane advice from you." Her tone was light, and she knew her teasing would only egg him on. If anyone had an ego bigger than hers, it was Tony, and he thought he was God's gift to women. No amount of razzing from Jordan was going to change that. "Best advice you're gonna get." His smiling eyes turned serious. "Take it for what it's worth, kiddo. Don't fuck it up like me. Even a man with a warm body in his bed every night gets lonely."

Jordan nodded. Unfortunately, the ache in her chest was telling her that the words he spoke were true, and if she didn't do something to change it, she was going to end up walking down the same road he had walked before her.

Chapter 21

"What we're interested in, Dr. Mercer, is why you chose to lie to us about the altercation between Dr. Stein and Richard Hudson?" Rebecca's gaze bore into Meghan, daring her to lie again.

Meghan pulled her glasses off and set them on her desk. She didn't like this line of questioning. She didn't like that Detective Foxx was sitting in her office grilling her again. She felt anger well up inside her. She had been the director for three years now, ever since Dr. Stein had been forcibly retired, and it seemed like she was still cleaning up his messes. "It wasn't an altercation per se, and I didn't feel that it had a bearing on the case. It was Richard Hudson that was wronged, not Dr. Stein."

"I'm confused, Dr. Mercer." Rebecca leaned forward pinning her with her emerald-green eyes. "When we ask you if you knew of any issues between Dr. Stein and Richard Hudson, one would assume that this altercation, or whatever you want to call it, would have warranted at least a mention."

"I'm sure you can understand that given the nature of the issue, it would not have crossed my mind that Dr. Stein would have held a grudge against Richard Hudson. As a matter of fact, it makes more sense that the opposite would be true."

Rebecca sighed loudly. She was getting nowhere with Dr. Mercer. She glanced at Jordan, wondering why she was choosing to remain as quiet as she was. Normally, she would have jumped in and said something. Instead, she was staying tight—lipped, which gave more weight to her suspicions that she and Dr. Mercer were previously acquainted, and not in a professional manner.

Finally, she rolled her eyes and turned her attention back to Meghan. "Fine. Whatever your reasoning, can we put that aside? Tell me your side of the issue."

Meghan shrugged. "Matters like this are always difficult to handle, Detective Foxx. It's a case of he said, well he said/he said in this instance. Richard Hudson complained to me that Dr. Stein made unwanted and unwelcome advances toward his wife. He asked that I remove Dr. Stein from his wife's procedures. Of course, I obliged. It's the clinic's stance that the patient is always right, and we take complaints against our staff very seriously. We do whatever we can to ensure that the patient has the best possible experience. Dr. Stein jeopardized that relationship, and it was my responsibility to deal with the matter in the best interests of the patient. However, I did not feel like the matter warranted police attention, nor had anything to do with Dr. Stein's alleged criminal activity."

Rebecca watched her face as she spoke, still watching for something that didn't match the cool, calm exterior. She wasn't sure if it was just her suspicion of Jordan's history with her or something else, but she didn't like her. "How did Dr. Stein react?"

"As you can imagine, Dr. Stein was quite upset with the allegations. He seemed genuinely distraught that his actions could have been misconstrued in such a manner. Despite his missteps, Dr. Stein was an excellent doctor and performed many successful procedures. At no time, did I feel like this particular complaint against him warranted further investigation by the board, or the police, for that matter. It was handled as requested by the patient."

"Did Dr. Stein happen to mention that Richard Hudson had threatened him?" Rebecca went into attack mode. "That seems like a perfect motive for Dr. Stein to have a personal vendetta against him."

"I was not aware of that." Meghan was caught off guard, and she didn't like it. Nor did she like the predatory look in Detective Foxx's eyes. If she didn't know any better, she could have sworn it was directed towards her on behalf of Jordan. And that was another reason she didn't do relationships anymore. One disastrous relationship for her was enough. Whatever fucked-up mess they were in the middle of, she wanted no part of it. "Dr. Stein kept to himself, especially after his ex—wife left him. I'm sure whatever went on between him and Richard Hudson didn't alarm him enough to mention it."

Rebecca narrowed her eyes. Meghan hadn't done anything other than lie to them, or sin by omission. However she chose to look at it. Nevertheless, there was something she didn't trust about her. "Did Dr. Stein ever have trouble with any of the other patients?"

Meghan didn't miss the suspicious look that seemed ever present on Rebecca's face. "Not to my knowledge. As I mentioned before, previous to Dr. Stein's mental breakdown, he was a good doctor. He treated everyone with respect, and that included the patients."

"All the patients, except Elizabeth Hudson, you mean." Rebecca corrected her in a stern voice.

Meghan hated being corrected. "Yes. I'm sorry I didn't mention it earlier, Detective Foxx. At the time, I firmly believed that the incident had nothing to do with Dr. Stein and his vendetta against Richard Hudson. I just assumed he was the unlucky victim of a mad man. By the time he was forced to resign, Dr. Stein was an entirely different man than the one that hired me. He took the divorce harder than most, and it changed him."

"Explain to me again how he was different." Rebecca didn't need to know Meghan's opinion. It didn't matter anyway. She firmly believed that Dr. Stein was their perp. She was merely enjoying making her uncomfortable, and it seemed the longer she questioned her, the more uncomfortable she got.

Meghan closed her eyes and counted to ten. She was on to Rebecca's game now, and she was out of the cooperating mood. "How do you mean?"

"What she means is what was Dr. Stein's personality like before he was fired?" Jordan finally leaned forward and spoke. She could see the anger flaring in Meghan's eyes, and she suddenly felt the need to stick up for her girlfriend. No, her ex—girlfriend, at least until she figured out a way to fix things with Rebecca.

Meghan rolled her eyes. "I understand that perfectly, Agent Gray. My confusion comes from the fact that we've discussed this several times already."

"Why don't you repeat it for my benefit?" The edge in Jordan's voice was unmistakable. She could be pushed only so far before the fangs came out. "Pretend like you haven't told me."

Meghan sighed loudly. "Fine. He was sporadic, moody, volatile, and angry. Everything set him off. I saw him threaten techs, other doctors. It wasn't unlike him to come to work drunk. He was angry and hurt, and he took it out on everyone around him."

Rebecca opened her mouth before Jordan could ask any more questions. "I know we discussed this before, but tell me again. Do you have any reason to believe that Dr. Stein would be angry enough to kill?"

Meghan was silent as she contemplated her next words. "Given how angry he was, it is entirely believable that he could kill someone."

"See how easy that was." Rebecca said sarcastically. "I ask questions. You answer them."

Meghan stood up and stretched her lanky body to its full height in an obvious attempt to intimidate Rebecca. It didn't work. "If we're done here, I think it's time you and Agent Gray left. I've answered your questions and now, if you'll excuse me, I've got a business to run, which thankfully, is still here despite the CDD's efforts to the contrary."

"What's that supposed to mean?" Rebecca's eyes blazed.

Meghan shrugged nonchalantly. "You figure it out, Detective. You have dragged the clinic's name through the mud with your investigation. One, I might add, that hasn't produced a viable arrest. I've managed to keep things running smoothly, no thanks to you. I just think if you spent time actually investigating instead of harassing me, you might have already caught the right guy."

"Why you little…"

Jordan grabbed Rebecca's arm and shook her head. She shot Meghan an apologetic smile. "Thank you for your time, Dr. Mercer."

The angry snarl disappeared from Meghan's face, and she shot Jordan a coy smile. "It was my pleasure, Agent Gray." The words dripped off her tongue, and Jordan groaned inwardly.

Whatever suspicions Rebecca may have had were pretty much confirmed with one sentence. Jordan cupped Rebecca's elbow and directed her towards the door. "Let's go, Rebecca. She's not worth it."

The words were spoken no louder than a whisper, but they reverberated across the room, and Meghan winced. Only one woman she had ever bedded said she wasn't worth it. She watched them walk out then slammed her fist against the desk. "Fuck you, Jordan! I'll show you who's worth it."

Chapter 22

Rebecca slammed the file on her desk. Their interview with Dr. Mercer still had her on edge. She had to remain professional when she really wanted to punch the smug look off her face. The look that Dr. Mercer gave Jordan confirmed her suspicions that they had past history beyond boxing. She pushed Jordan for an answer and hearing her say it pissed her off even more.

Jordan tried to tell her that it had no bearing on the case. That it was a long time ago. That it meant nothing. But it mattered to Rebecca. As of right now, she had to look that bitch in the eye with the knowledge that she was laughing at her behind her back. It may not jeopardize the case, but right now, it was seriously jeopardizing her sanity.

"Hey, boss, I got it!" Rick walked into the bull pen waving several sheets of paper. He handed them to her and waited as she read them.

She read each one and muttered under her breath. "House, yard, car. Strong work, Jonesy. Let's get this guy."

"You want me to call it in?" Rick picked up the phone and started dialing.

"No." Rebecca stopped him midway. "We go in alone. I don't want to scare him off with a bunch of blue and whites showing up in front of his house."

Rick hesitated. "Boss?"

"What is it, Jonesy?" Rebecca looped her badge around her neck and stuck her firearm in its holster.

"Riley and Gray?" Rick stammered. "It's their case too. They should be there."

"Damn it, Jonesy! It's our case, not the FBI's." Rebecca's eyes blazed and Rick took a step back, somewhat confused at her reaction. She saw him wince and immediately felt bad. "I'm sorry. It's just that…"

"Don't worry about it." Rick raised a dismissive hand. "I know the score."

"What's that supposed to mean?" Rebecca was irritated enough, and she wasn't in the mood for his shit.

"Nothing, boss. Forget I said anything."

He started to walk out, and Rebecca grabbed his arm and spun him around. "No, tell me what you mean. Enlighten me, 'cause right now I'm not so sure what is going on."

Rick met her steely gaze and held it firmly. "I know you got a thing for the Agent. I'm not sure what is going on with you two, but I've never seen you put your feelings before our safety in any case. I don't know about you, but I'm pretty fond of living right now, and if having them glued to my hip keeps me alive, I'm all for it. For once, think about someone besides yourself."

Rebecca's heart dropped. "You really think that? That I put myself first. I give my life to this place. Never ask for anything in return. My life is about putting others first."

Rick sighed. "You're right, you live the job. Nobody can refute that. But sometimes all you think about is yourself. I know you want this bastard, maybe more than anybody else but don't do it like this. Don't be a hero."

"Jonesy, I would never…" Rebecca stopped and let his words sink in. Was he right? Had it always been about her? She did have a temper, and that got the better of her sometimes. She could be rash. But she thought she put that aside when it mattered. She felt him studying her. Rick was the only person she would ever let accuse her of being selfish. Probably, because he had a point and more so because he was her partner and would do anything for her. She frowned.

"I didn't mean to upset you. I think you get so wrapped up in the job, you forget you're not the only one around...Jordan included."

She could have asked him to explain what he meant, but she didn't need him too. She knew. She didn't think about Jordan's feelings when she went off on her, just how she felt. How she hurt. And hadn't every relationship ended the same way? By her choice. Because it didn't work for her anymore. It wasn't convenient. And now with Rick, she was ready to storm into a madman's house by themselves. Putting both their lives at risk. "I...I didn't realize..."

Rick squeezed her hand gently. "You're a great cop, and you've always been there for me. I just want you to be there with me. We're partners, remember?"

"I know."

"And whether you want to accept it or not, Jordan cares about you. Maybe it's time to stop being so goddamn self—centered. Take it from me, it gets damn lonely."

"Oh." Rick's words hit her, and she felt her chest clench tightly. She knew he wasn't married. Hell, he hadn't dated anyone in months. The job made it hard to have a social life, much less find someone that could love you despite the crazy hours. She just figured that was his choice, and here he was pretty much admitting he hated his single life and telling her to get over herself. "I don't know what to say."

Rick smiled. "Hell, Boss, I didn't mean to ream you out. It's just that..."

"No, I know." Rebecca shrugged her shoulders. "I'm an asshole."

Rick's laughter filled the bullpen. "Well, that's one way to say it."

Rebecca smiled despite herself, and for the first time, she looked at Rick differently. She realized she loved him like a brother and knew she would die to protect him, just as he would for her. More importantly, she realized she was capable of opening herself up, and that thought frightened her. She shook it off and punched Rick in the shoulder. "Well, what the fuck are we waiting for? Let's get Riley and Gray and take this bastard down."

They agreed to go in silent. No lights, no sirens. There was something in the element of surprise after all. Matt's sedan slid to a quiet stop behind Rebecca's unmarked car, catty corner to Dr. Stein's house. The dim street lights afforded them more cover than they had expected and within moments, Rebecca and Rick were walking up to the door, eyes peeled, taking in everything. Neither one wanted any surprises. Jordan and Matt were already positioned around the back of the house, in case he decided to run.

Rebecca stepped up on the porch and lifted her hand to knock when a chill ran down her spine. The door was cracked slightly. She tensed and gave Rick a look. He stepped up and put himself between her and the door, neither knowing what they would find.

Rick raised his gun and put it in front of his lips, signaling for Rebecca to remain quiet. He pushed the door open with his foot and leaned his head in the crack. "Phillip Stein. Chicago PD."

They waited, breaths held for some response. None came. Rick toed the door open all the way and stepped into the entryway. He shouted again. "Hello! Dr. Stein, are you here? Chicago PD."

Still nothing. Rebecca stepped in behind him. Something wasn't right. The open door wasn't right. It felt all wrong.

Rick slid his hand across the wall and flipped a light switch illuminating the dark room. They surveyed the room. A sofa table lay upended, and an empty glass lay on the carpet with a wet stain spreading around it. He shot Rebecca another look, this time letting her know that whatever was going on wasn't what they expected.

She could feel a chill in the room and couldn't tell if it was the open door or the evil she knew lived here. They walked around the sofa, careful not to touch anything. "Dr. Stein. Chicago PD." Rick's voice was louder this time.

They heard a slight shuffle from the room next to the living room. Pulling a small flashlight out of his pocket, he led them into the kitchen. Both of their guns were ready, not sure if Phillip Stein would try to attack them. He obviously saw them pull up, and he was frantically trying to avoid being caught. He was a man with everything to lose. Rick fumbled for the light switch and flipped it on, ready to shoot if necessary.

"God damn it!" Rebecca pulled her gun back. "What are you doing in here?"

Jordan waived her gun at the door. "It was open."

"And you couldn't give us a head's up?" Rebecca was glaring at her. Her heart was pounding, her nerves a frenzied mess.

"I wasn't sure if he was waiting to ambush you, and I didn't want to alert him if he was."

Matt came out a door to her right. "All clear."

"Basement?"

"Yeah." Matt slid his gun into the holster. "I don't think he's here."

"You're probably right. Let's check the rest of the house." Rebecca walked in front of Rick and repeated the same slow thorough sweep of the house. Phillip Stein wasn't home and from the looks of it, had left in a hurry.

"Fuck." Rebecca swore softly. "Put out an APB. I don't want him getting far. Send his plate info out to anyone in a two—hundred mile perimeter. He's not getting away."

Rick pulled out his cell and made a call. "It's done.

"What now?" Jordan said with a loud sigh.

"Get CSI out here. I want every inch of the property searched. We are going to go back and figure out where he's going. I want his phone records. Find out who he is talking to. Run his credit cards. Let's pull his bank accounts too. If he's running, he's going to need cash."

She met Jordan's questioning look. "See if you can get a hold of Ruth Dawson. Find out if they had any friends who would help. Maybe she knows something. It's obvious someone tipped him off, and my gut is telling me it's her."

Jordan nodded, thankful for the distraction. She still had a hard time looking at Rebecca without her heart clenching tightly. She sucked in a breath. "For her sake, I hope she didn't."

Back in the bullpen, Rick pulled up all his records. "Nothing unusual on his cards. No ATM withdrawals, at least nothing big." He scanned the cell records. "Wait a sec."

"What?" Rebecca nodded towards the monitor on the wall where all of Phillip Stein's personal info was popping up.

"There's a number on here. Called at least twenty times in the last couple of days."

"Run it." Rebecca crossed her arms over her chest and started chewing her bottom lip.

Rick punched the keys loudly. "Son—of—a—bitch."

"What?"

"It's Richard Hudson's number."

"What the hell?" Rebecca narrowed her eyes. "I told him to let us handle it."

"Last call was an hour before we got there." Rick clicked another couple of buttons. "It's his cell."

Rebecca spun around. "Find him. He's just crazy enough to try something stupid."

Rick pulled up another program and started searching for the tracking devise in Richard Hudson's phone, triangulating it against the map. Within minutes, a small red blip showed up on the monitor. "Got it."

"Let's go get him." She nodded towards the laptop.

Rick studied the laptop as they drove. The dot hadn't moved. It was a steady flash somewhere in Navy Pier. Not so strange for the middle of the day, but for late at night, it was strange. Even stranger because it was Richard Hudson, and he had called Phillip Stein more than twenty times in the last two days.

Rebecca had the lights and sirens on this time. Cars moved slowly out of the way as she maneuvered her way through the dense downtown Chicago traffic. She pulled into Navy Pier and crept along the road, waiting for Rick to signal they were close.

"There." Rick stopped them at a point on the back edge of the pier, closest to the Grand Ballroom. There was a dark sedan parked haphazardly. From the looks of it, the occupant had fled the car quickly. The driver's side door was thrown open, and the engine had been left running.

They got out and started walking towards the end of the pier. They passed the twin spires of the domed ballroom barely visible against the murky sky. Their guns were drawn, and both had flashlights trained on unseen spots in the dark.

"You son—of—a—bitch. You took everything from me."

Rebecca felt Rick tense next to her and without a word, they began running towards the sound. Their flashlights bouncing around wildly as they ran towards the voice.

"Please, I didn't do anything."

The sound of desperation filled the air, and Rebecca knew what they would see before they even spotted Richard Hudson.

"Richard. Chicago PD." Her flashlight finally found them at the edge of the pier. Richard had Phillip Stein on his knees, a gun leveled at the back of his head, ready to shoot him execution style. "Put the gun down now!"

Richard turned and the beam of her light hit his eyes. They glowed eerily, and she knew immediately that he had snapped. The look of crazy desperation penetrated the night. "Don't come any closer, Detective. He deserves to die."

"Put the gun down. He's not worth it. Let the law decide his punishment. This won't bring Lizzie back." Rebecca's voice carried softly across the air. She could tell that Phillip was already bleeding, and his face showed signs of bruising.

Rick saw him hesitate and used the opportunity to shut his flashlight off and back away from Rebecca. He knew immediately what he was going to try to do. If he could come around from behind Richard and surprise him, he just might be able to stop him before he hurt someone.

"He stole my life." Richard screamed. His voice was full of raw anguish.

Phillip craned his head, and Rebecca could make out the look of sheer fear in his eyes. "Please help me."

Richard pulled his hand back and slammed the gun into the side of Phillip's head, eliciting a painful howl.

"Richard." Rebecca moved closer, her gun still trained on Richard. "Think about what you're doing. Are you willing to give up your life for revenge? Is that what Lizzie would want for you? Ask yourself what Lizzie would want."

Richard's arm dropped slightly. He looked as though her words might have penetrated his brain and latched onto some shred of sanity.

Phillip tried to pull away, and Richard yanked his collar angrily. "Don't move. Tonight you will die."

Rebecca tensed. She could see in his demeanor that he was close to shooting. She couldn't make out Rick's position in the dark, but hoped he had been able to circle close to Richard. She just needed to keep him occupied for a couple of seconds longer. "Richard. Please. Think about Lizzie."

Richard heard her steps and whipped the gun around on her. "Don't come any closer to me, Detective. Don't make me shoot you too."

A chill ran through Rick's blood. Richard was completely out of control, and Rebecca was in his line of fire. He quickened his step. He had to completely back away from them and circle outside his line of vision, and having to be quiet was taking way too much time. He prayed Rebecca could keep his attention just a few seconds longer.

"I'm not your enemy, Richard. This isn't the way to deal with this." She was ten feet away now, close enough to see the whites in his eyes. She could shine the light directly in them, but worried that in his wild reaction. he would shoot her. "Put the gun down, Richard."

"Stop!" His voice was menacing. She had taken his mind off of Phillip and put it on her, a dangerous move.

He saw her move towards him. He loosed his grip of Phillip's collar and leveled the gun on her. Time suddenly stopped. Rebecca's eyes widened. She heard the gun fire and felt the bullet hit her. As she fell, her flashlight dropped from her hands and rolled towards Richard. She didn't see his body hit the concrete seconds behind hers, his blank eyes staring into the night sky.

Rick leveled his gun on Phillip. "Don't move! Don't you fucking move!" He knelt down next to Rebecca, panic racing through his veins. He shined his light on her body, searching for the wound. He saw blood on her right side, and he ripped her shirt away. "Stay with me, Rebecca."

Her eyes met his, and he saw the fear in them. She looked like a wounded animal. He pressed his hand to the wound and pulled his phone from his pocket. "Officer down! Repeat Officer down! The southeast corner of Navy Pier."

Rebecca's body was starting to shake. The cold, shock and blood loss making her tremble uncontrollably. "Jones…Jonesy, I'm s…sorry. I fu…fucked up."

"Shh, shh, it's okay, honey." He stroked her brow. "It's gonna be okay."

He heard sirens in the distance, and knew help was close. Beyond the distant sirens, he heard something new. A small, shuffling sound. Whipping around, he saw Phillip pushing off the ground. He whipped around, his hand grabbing his gun. "Get down! Get down! Don't make me fucking shoot you, you sick fuck."

Phillip hit the ground with a loud thud and raised his hands above his head. "Don't shoot. Don't shoot. I'll stay down."

Rick watched him a second longer and knew he wouldn't move. He turned his attention back to Rebecca. "It's okay, Boss. We're gonna get you taken care of."

Rebecca smiled weakly. "I ne…need J…Jordan. P…please."

He squeezed her hand reassuringly. "I'll get her."
Rebecca's eyes fluttered close.
"She'll be there when you wake up."

Chapter 23

Jordan listened to Rebecca's slow, even breathing. When Rick called her and told her they were taking her to Mercy for a gunshot wound to the abdomen, she had nearly lost it. She had grilled him for hours before finally calming down. Fortunately, the bullet had gone straight through her abdomen and missed all her organs.

Richard Hudson was dead. A single gunshot to the head. Once Rick realized that he was going to shoot Rebecca, he had fired without even thinking. It was only the dark and Richard's poor aim that had kept the bullet from penetrating her heart or some other organ and possibly killing her. Jordan was furious at them for following a lead without them.

Her anger had turned to concern when she saw Rebecca. Her face was incredibly pale, and even in repose, Jordan could tell she was in pain. Jordan hadn't left the room except to shower for the three days that Rebecca had been there, needing to be there when she woke up.

She was exhausted and not even sure if Rebecca would be happy to see her when she woke up. She wasn't certain where they stood anymore. Rebecca had told her she couldn't do the relationship thing. She was too distracting. Then she had held her hand and Jordan thought everything was okay. But then after their disastrous meeting with Meghan Mercer, things had gone south again.

Confusion was the order of the day, and Jordan had had three full helpings. Even when she woke up, they probably wouldn't be discussing the subject anyway. That is if Rebecca didn't kick her out of the room when she saw her.

"Hey kid, how's she doing?"

Rick's soft voice broke through the silence, and Jordan shot him a weary smile. "Same as earlier."

Rick squeezed her shoulder. "She's going to be okay, you know?"

"Yeah, I know." Jordan rolled her shoulders. She was tired and sore from being curled up in that chair for seventy—two hours.

"Listen, why don't you take a break? I'll keep an eye on her." Rick nodded towards the door. "Besides, there is someone outside that wants to talk to you."

Jordan's brow knitted in confusion. "Who would be here?"

"Matt." Rick bent over her. "I don't think he feels comfortable coming in here, but he wanted to come by and check on Rebecca. Make sure she was okay, and I think check on you."

"Oh." Jordan swallowed. Things between her partner and her still weren't great. His feelings for Rebecca were stronger than Jordan had known, and the fact that she had started a relationship with Rebecca stung his ego a little bit. It would take a while, but she knew in time, things would get back to normal. For now, she would just tread lightly.

She ran a hand through her unruly hair and pushed herself out of the chair, sighing loudly.

Rick cupped her elbow. "Don't worry too much. Pretty soon this will all just be a bad memory. The important thing is we finally got the right guy."

Jordan nodded, her eyes flicking to Rebecca and resting on her face. "But at what cost?"

Rick opened his mouth to reply, but Jordan stopped him. "I know, I know."

Matt turned at the sound of Jordan's footfalls, a tentative smile breaking out on his face. "Hey, Jordie."

Jordan shot him a grateful smile. "Hey, yourself."

Matt shuffled nervously. "How is she?"

"Oh, you know." Jordan shrugged. "Still unconscious but stable."

"Rick said she got lucky." Matt met Jordan's gaze. "How are you holding up?"

Jordan's breath caught in her throat. No matter what, Matt was like a brother to her, and when things got tough, he genuinely cared about her well—being. "I'm alright. Anxious and worried."

"I figured." Matt nodded towards the door. "Let's get some coffee. You look like you could use it."

"You saying I look tired?" Jordan asked.

"Nah." Matt smirked. "I'm saying you look like shit."

Jordan punched him in the arm. "Thanks, dude. Way to kick me when I'm down."

Matt chuckled softly. "You can take it."

"Probably." Jordan fell in step with Matt, and they walked to the waiting room and stopped at the vending machine.

He slid a dollar into the machine and punched several buttons. He waited while the machine dispensed a Styrofoam cup, filled it with hot liquid and opened the door for retrieval. He handed Jordan the first cup and bought a second for himself.

"Thanks." Jordan blew on her cup and took a tentative first drink. "So, did you talk to Mitchell?"

"Yeah." Matt sat in one of the chairs, and Jordan sank down beside him. "Until Stein is convicted and put away, she's still worried. Especially after catching the wrong guy."

"I'm sure she's just worried about Julie. That somehow he'll try to come after her."

"Hell, can you blame her?" Matt stared at his cup. "I don't think Mitchell's let her out of the house for months without being attached at the hip."

"Maybe now they can finally get back to normal."

"She said she is going to push for a quick trial and conviction."

"What Mitchell wants, Mitchell gets." Jordan said softly. "In this case, I think she deserves it."

"She's not going to let anyone mess up the investigation or the trial." Matt nodded down the hall. "Rick says he's handling it, but Mitchell wants us on his ass twenty—four, seven. She doesn't want any mistakes."

Jordan nodded. "No, I know. I just need to make sure Rebecca's okay. Maybe you could play detective with Rick for a while. I know that's asking a lot, but I'm not there right now." She tapped her temple. "In here, until I know she's out of the woods, I can't focus on anything else."

"Yeah, I'm on it." Matt crumpled his empty cup and stood up with a groan. "And whatever is going on with you guys, fix it. She's good for you."

"You think?" Jordan stretched her arms over her head and looked up at Matt. "So, are we good?"

Matt met her gaze and held it, obviously thinking over her question. He was quiet for so long that Jordan worried what he might say. Finally, a smile broke out on his face. "Yeah, yeah, we'll be okay."

Jordan watched him walk out of the waiting room and smiled at his retreating form.

She knew that whatever happened, they were good and Matty would always have her back.

"Jordan." Rick's voice broke through the silence. "She's awake."

Jordan shot out of the chair and practically ran to Rebecca's room. She took a tentative step into the room and felt Rebecca's emerald green gaze boring through her. She stood paralyzed, trying to find her voice.

Sensing her insecurity, Rick pulled her towards Rebecca's bedside and stepped back behind her. He pointed to Jordan and mouthed so only Rebecca could see. *"Talk to her."*

He left the room silently, and Jordan laughed nervously. "Hi."

Rebecca swallowed, and when she spoke, her voice was weak and raspy. "Hi."

"How are you?" Jordan couldn't hold her gaze, and she stared at her feet. "I mean, do you hurt? Can I get you anything?"

"Jordan." Rebecca's voice penetrated Jordan's tough exterior and coursed through her veins like healing balm. "Sit down."

Jordan slid into the chair silently and took her hand, caressing her palm with her thumb. Her eyes drank in Rebecca's face hungrily. Despite her pallor, Jordan thought she was the most beautiful woman she had ever seen. "I'm sorry."

"For?" Rebecca's eyebrows knitted in confusion.

"For not telling you about Meghan, for not being there to save you." Jordan smiled ruefully. "I fucked up royally, and I messed us up."

"That doesn't matter anymore. It's the past." Rebecca shook her head. "And it's my fault. I didn't call in backup."

"Why?" Jordan narrowed her eyes questioningly.

Rebecca shrugged. "I'm stubborn and selfish. At least, that's what Jonesy calls it. Apparently, I have a habit of doing what's right for me and not considering anyone else's feelings. It's that way with work. In my relationships. That's why I pushed you away. I push everyone away. I don't want to do that anymore. I don't want to push you away. I need you in my life. You ground me. I was wrong. When I'm with you, I'm not distracted. It's when I'm away from you that I can't think. I can't function."

"Stop." Jordan put a finger to Rebecca's lips. "You're being too hard…on the woman I love."

Rebecca's eyes locked onto Jordan's, and she smiled shyly. "You love me?"

Jordan nodded. "I'm sorry to just throw it out there, but I do. Somewhere along the way, you got inside me."

Rebecca felt her chest clench tightly. It wasn't hearing the words or seeing the look on her face. It was a feeling. Somewhere deep inside. A sense that everything would be all right because this woman loved her. And with that knowledge came the realization that her heart belonged to Jordan. There would be no pushing her away again.

Chapter 24

Jordan grabbed the phone on the last ring. "Gray."

Rick's gravelly voice came through the phone. "It's Detective Jones." He paused a second. "We got a problem."

Jordan's blood froze. "What? Rebecca?"

"No." She could hear muted voices in the background, and she knew he must be at the precinct. "We got a call this morning. They found another body."

The color drained from Jordan's face. The nightmare was repeating itself. "Where?"

"Alley near Adams off Michigan."

"Give me twenty." Jordan grabbed her keys.

"We got a small break this time. We've got video of the alley. Hopefully, we can get something to identify this bastard."

Jordan sighed. "I hope so. We can't afford to be wrong again."

"Well, you know what they say. Third times a charm."

Jordan ended the call as Rick's nervous laughter faded into the background. She pulled her coat on and ran to the garage. Within minutes, she had called Matt, picked him up and was pulling latex gloves on searching for Rebecca's red hair among the crowd gathered around the body. She knew she would find her at the crime scene despite being shot only ten days before. She had one thing right about herself. She was as stubborn as they came.

She stopped next to Rebecca and lowered her voice. "What are you doing here?"

Rebecca flicked her eyes to the yellow tape. "It's my case."

"That's not what I meant." Jordan's voice lowered to a warning tone. "I mean, why are you here? You shouldn't be here after you know."

"Jordan, I'm fine. Really."

"Detective."

Rebecca pulled her gaze away from Jordan's face. "What do you have?"

"I think you will want to see this."

Jordan pulled the crime-scene tape up and she and Rebecca stopped over the body. The M.E. pulled back the victim's hair. A large bruise discolored the right side of her face from her forehead to her jaw. "This one got the shit beat out of her. These wounds are perimortem. She sustained them right before she died."

Rebecca leaned over and tried to hide the wince of pain in her abdomen. She hadn't had the stitches removed yet and pulling against them hurt. "Damn."

"And look at this." The M.E. lifted her hand and held out her fingernails. "We've got skin and blood under the nails. Probably the perp's."

Rebecca studied her hands. "Bag 'em. I don't want to do anything to compromise the evidence. In case you didn't notice, the CDD is pretty much the laughing stock of Chicago. Fucking this one up again isn't an option."

The M.E. nodded. Rebecca tried to stand up, but the pain stopped her and her breath caught in her throat. Jordan slipped her hands under her arms and pulled her up before anyone else noticed she was struggling. "Thanks."

Jordan looked at her askance. "This is why you don't need to be out here. You're not ready."

Rebecca's eyes flashed, and she opened her mouth then shut it just as quickly when Jordan shot her a look. "I'm sorry, babe. I had to be here."

"You know Rick can handle it." Jordan cupped her elbow and held the tape up, so she could walk under it. "And there isn't anything that you will see here that you can't see in the crime scene photos."

Rebecca wanted to object, but she couldn't. Jordan was right. In one last attempt to show her independence, she rolled her eyes. "Take me back to the precinct. Let's see if there is anything on the video that can identify this guy."

Rick and Matt were watching the video by the time they walked into the bullpen surrounded by boxes of donuts and coffee.

"Anything yet?" Jordan passed the box around then grabbed a donut for herself. She had eaten more donuts in the past three months than in her whole life.

Rick pushed a couple of buttons and paused it on a woman walking across from the Institute. He advanced it several more scenes and stopped again. "That's him."

The footage was grainy, but Rebecca could see him in the dim lights of the jewelry store. His head was turned and he was obviously watching her. "Roll it forward slowly. I want to see if we can make out his face."

Rick advanced it frame by frame with no luck. He had a dark hat pulled low over his face, and the collar of his coat pulled up over the lower half of his face. The description was dead on though. Tall and lanky, and from what they had witnessed on the previous victims, he was incredibly strong.

They watched in horror as each frame played out the scene they had just left. He caught up to her and when he grabbed her, she whipped around and swiped at his face. His hand flew to his cheek, and in the same breath, he stepped back on his right foot and dropped his right shoulder. His fist flew into her face with such force that they wouldn't be surprised if there were shattered bones beneath the bruising.

"Roll it back."

Rick stopped and rewound the tape slowly.

"There." Jordan pointed at the screen. They watched her swipe at his face again and then saw her reel backwards from the crushing blow. Somewhere in the back of her mind, she felt a slight nagging, but couldn't place it. Something in that few seconds bothered her. "Again."

Rick obliged again, and they watched it a third time in slow motion.

"What do you see?" Rebecca stepped closer to the TV.

Jordan shook her head. "I'm not sure." She pointed at the paused video. "Here. See this. That's a boxer's move. The drop in the shoulder. I've seen it before. I just can't remember where."

Matt shrugged. "Probably on TV. We watch fights all the time."

Jordan nodded. He was right. They got together all the time at Frank's. "Yeah, you're probably right." She looked over her shoulder at Rick. "I'm sorry, you can start it up again."

Rick started the playback again. In slow motion, they watched him wrestle her to the ground, slit her throat and sexually assault her. The last few minutes of the attack were almost too much, but they forced themselves to watch. They watched as he brutally ripped the last vestiges of her clothing away and stole from her the very life that she had nurtured and died protecting.

They couldn't ignore the change in his demeanor as he wrapped the fetus in a small cloth and tucked it inside his coat. He was gentle, where only moments before he had brutally taken a life. He turned, and on the way out of the alley, pulled his hat down lower and pulled his coat tightly around his prize.

"God." Rebecca breathed quietly. "It's almost eerie to watch. Julien was dead on with his take on the murders. This man is exacting revenge on women, but the babies are precious. Who is this guy? What happened to mess him up this way?"

Jordan tapped her temple. "Guy's a fucking nut job, but you won't know it to look at him. I feel like we are back to square one."

Rick nodded. "Every lead has turned into a dead end."

Matt snapped his fingers. "The Dawsons. He had a rap sheet, and wifey lost her chance to get a kid when Stein got fired. That chick is one brick shy of a load. What's to say she didn't orchestrate the whole thing?"

"No, timing's off." Rick pointed at the first victim. "He started killing before Stein was canned. It can't be him."

"Why not?' Jordan met Matt's eyes. "I think I'm following you. She works there and sees couple after couple come in and get pregnant, and she's still barren. That would make a woman who wanted kids pretty upset. She gets her husband to start killing the women. In some sick, twisted way, she feels she has leveled the playing field. She can't have a baby, why should they?"

"Nah." Rick shook his head. "It's no good. When she makes the deal with Stein, there should have been a break in the killings."

"Not necessarily." Rebecca pulled her picture off the whiteboard. "Even with the deal, as long as she doesn't get pregnant, she is still not getting her way. I agree. It makes perfect sense. I'd say it's time we bring them in for questioning."

"Rebecca and I will take the Mrs. You guys take him. I don't want her anywhere near a guy who could blow at the drop of a hat."

"I can handle myself." Rebecca rolled her eyes, but she felt the heat rise in her cheeks. She wasn't used to someone caring about her like Jordan did or returning the feelings. It was still new and made her feel totally protected. "I made it to thirty—one alive, you know."

"Just stay close, alright." Jordan pulled Rebecca's coat off the chair and held it out for her. "I think we should drop in unannounced. Perhaps a little surprise will give us an edge over Ruth Dawson and right now, we need every advantage we can get."

Chapter 25

Jordan watched Ruth Dawson's face as they approached, looking for any sign of guilt. If she was surprised to see them, she didn't show it. She schooled her features into a look of thinly veiled tolerance. "Detective Foxx. What a pleasure to see you again. And Agent Gray. Where are the other two guys?"

Bingo. Rebecca thought quickly. She was right on about Ruth Dawson. She was just the type that would be interested in two good—looking guys in uniform. Guys who weren't her husband, and she hadn't been abused by. Perhaps they would be able to get her to open up and maybe confess. "Ruth, we have a couple more questions about Dr. Stein. We wondered if you would be kind enough to come down to the station."

Ruth swallowed audibly. "I don't…don't think that's a good idea. Dr. Mercer is out, and I can't leave the office unattended."

"We can wait until she comes back."

"She won't be back for several days." Ruth answered defensively. "She's going to a conference in New York."

"Can you call her? Let her know you're going to be gone for a while?" Rebecca studied Ruth's features. She really was unremarkable. Plain, the fade into the wall type. She did not like the attention that the two women were paying her.

"I don't think so. Before she left, she had a personal appointment." Her eyes flicked nervously between the two women. "It's really impossible for me to leave the office."

"Where's her appointment?" Jordan leaned over the desk, her gaze boring into Ruth's eyes. "This is important enough to interrupt."

Fear flashed in her eyes. "I don't think that's a good idea. Dr. Mercer doesn't like to be bothered."

Jordan leaned over further, invading her space. "Let me try to be perfectly clear, Mrs. Dawson. It's imperative that you cooperate. I'd hate to slap cuffs on you for impeding an investigation."

She shook slightly. "I…I don't know where she is."

Rebecca decided to add to her fear. "Don't lie to us, Mrs. Dawson. Lying to a federal agent is a felony. It comes with jail time. You don't look like the prison type." She didn't add that if she was the one that had orchestrated the murders, she would be facing life behind bars, if not the death penalty. "If you have knowledge of Dr. Mercer's whereabouts, I suggest you divulge them."

"No, no. I don't want to go to prison." She pulled her calendar up and typed for several minutes before she spun the screen around. "This is her private schedule. She doesn't know I have access to it. She's making a house call."

Jordan took one look at the screen. Julie Keppler's name screamed at her from the monitor. She stood up quickly. "Why would she make a house call? Why wouldn't she just schedule an appointment? Has she done this before?"

"No." Ruth shook her head. "Never. This is the first time."

A thought so foreign to Jordan invaded the recesses of her mind like a black fog rolling through her, and she forced herself to give credence to its absurdity. When she accepted it for truth, she froze. "What time did she leave?"

Ruth saw the panic in her eyes, and she withered. "A half an hour ago, forty—five minutes tops."

Rebecca saw the color drain from her face. She put her hand on her arm. "What's wrong?"

"We need to leave now. Julie's in danger." The panic was evident.

Rebecca didn't question the sudden snap. She just went with it. She had known Jordan long enough to know that if she had a feeling, it was usually right.

Jordan was already sprinting to the car. She started it with one hand and dialed her phone with the other. Seconds later, she slammed her palm against the wheel. "Shit! She isn't answering." She dialed another number. "Come on! Come on!" Again, there was no answer. She swore loudly.

"What's going on, Jordan?" Rebecca hadn't put two and two together, and Jordan's erratic behavior was starting to make her nervous.

"It's Dr. Mercer." Jordan punched numbers on her phone. "Matt? It's Dr. Mercer. The killer is Meghan Mercer. Just trust me. She's going after Julie." A pause. "We have to get to their house now! Susan isn't answering. Call in backup. God damn it, Matty, we have to get there. She's in danger."

"Jordan, what is going on?" Rebecca's tone snapped through Jordan's haze.

"The video from the alley. Something kept bothering me about it. The way the guy stepped back and dropped his shoulder before the punch. It clicked when I heard that Dr. Mercer was making a special house call. She's a fighter, and she's used the move on me before."

"You're sure?" Rebecca's brow furrowed. "You're saying that the perp that everyone thought was a man is actually a woman. How's she doing it?"

"I don't know." Jordan slid through a red light, her eyes flicking to the oncoming traffic. A horn blared to their right, and Jordan gunned it. "I haven't got that part figured out. But I know I'm right. I can feel it." She dialed the phone again, hoping against hope, she was wrong, but her gut told her she wasn't, and as time slipped away, she felt her hope slipping away.

"It's going to be okay. She's FBI. I'm sure she can protect herself." Rebecca tried to sound reassuring, but her voice sounded unconvincing even to herself.

Jordan's phone rang. "Gray."

"It's Matt. Rick has five blue and whites on the way. ETA is five minutes. We're still fifteen minutes away."

"Okay, good." Jordan's hand was white where she gripped the phone. "We're almost there." She ended the call, and as if feeling danger, inched the speedometer towards the red.

Minutes later, Jordan screeched to a halt behind a black Range Rover. There were no other cars. Rick's backup hadn't arrived yet, and Jordan prayed they were close. The vanity plate said it all. BBYMKR. Jordan's instincts had been right, and now she hoped it wasn't too late. Why hadn't she seen it before? She knew it was because of their night together. It meant nothing, but acknowledging that Meghan was a killer would eventually make her have to question her judgment.

She leapt out of the car and pulled out her Glock. Rebecca was on her heels before she could even say anything. The front door was ajar. Jordan motioned for Rebecca to stand to the side, and she pushed the door open with her gun. She waited. Nothing. She leaned her head around the doorjamb and looked through the living room into the large kitchen. She saw nothing. Heard nothing. At least she didn't see anyone lying on the floor.

She put her finger up to her lips, signaling Rebecca to stay silent. They crept inside wordlessly, guns poised and ready. The hall was dark and Jordan made out a light creeping underneath a door at the back of the house. She waived Rebecca down the hall.

The wood floor creaked, and they froze. Waiting. In their silence, Jordan heard soft murmurs coming from behind the door at the end of the hall. Her eyes narrowed. She recognized the deep voice and froze at the words she heard.

"You left me and now you deserve to die."

Jordan jumped, her legs covering the last fifteen feet in less than a second. She flung the door open. Her eyes met Meghan's, and she knew that whoever was behind those wild eyes was not the cool, collected doctor whom they had met before. Her eyes flashed madly. "You!"

Jordan couldn't move. Meghan had Julie's hair in her grasp, and a large knife pressed against her neck. Fear and something else flashed in her eyes. Something akin to resignation. Jordan's jaw clenched tightly. This could only end one way.

Susan was duct—taped to a chair, blood seeping from her leg. Her fingers curled around the arms of the chair. Her mouth was taped. Where Julie had all but given up, fury flashed in Susan's eyes, and Jordan knew if she got a hold of Meghan, she would kill her.

She leveled her gun on Meghan. "Put the knife down. All I need is you to give me a reason, and I'll blow your head off."

Meghan cackled. She spied Rebecca standing behind Jordan, and her face broke into an evil smile. "Mmm, you little bitch. How is it fucking Jordan? She's good, isn't she?"

"Meghan, stop." Jordan's voice was a low, menacing tone.

Meghan shrugged it off as though she was just having a conversation with a girlfriend. "She tastes good, doesn't she? Did she tell you I fucked her too?"

Rebecca tensed, her temper and fear getting the best of her. "Fuck you."

"Fuck me?" Meghan laughed cynically. "That's what my whole life has been. People fucking me and walking away." She cinched Julie's hair tighter. She leaned close to Julie's ear and bared her teeth. "That's why you have to die, Christine."

Suddenly, it made sense. Christine was the woman who had left Meghan and put into motion a series of events that had left too many women dead and the fear of one more.

Susan tried to yell through the tape, and it came out as a desperate groan.

Meghan's head snapped up. She leveled her gaze on Susan. "I'm saving you. She'll just fuck you and leave you."

Jordan took a step closer. "Meghan, please. Don't do this. It's not Christine. It's not too late. You can put the knife down and walk away. We can get you a plea bargain. You need help."

Meghan dug the knife into Julie's neck, breaking the skin and sending the first droplets of blood sliding down her neck.

Meghan sniffed the air like a hunter picking up on the blood of its wounded prey. "Yes."

Jordan stepped closer again. She wanted to close the gap in the moments that Meghan slipped out of consciousness. One step. Another step and Meghan's eyes snapped to hers. "Get back, or I'll kill her now." Meghan's sneer was menacing, and Jordan took a step back. She couldn't risk pushing Meghan off the very narrow precipice that she now occupied. There was a very visible line that separated Julie from life and death and Jordan was holding it in her hand.

"Stop, Meghan. It's not Christine. She's not here." Jordan's voice was calm. She needed to distract her. Keep her occupied just a little longer. "Meghan, tell me about Christine. Tell me how you met." She silently prayed that Rebecca's men were close.

Meghan paused. Her eyes regarded Jordan quizzically as if wondering why she would ask that question. Then suddenly as if a switch had been flipped, a smile broke across her face. "College. We met in college. I was in pre—med. She was going to school for music history. One day I was walking across the campus, and there she was." Meghan's voice was almost sing—song.

"Was it love at first sight?" Jordan moved almost imperceptibly. She needed to get herself close enough to get the knife away without hurting Julie. She couldn't risk taking a shot. It was too dangerous. Her eyes flicked to Julie's, and she tried to reassure her that it would be okay. *Just hang in there, Julie. I promise I'll get you out alive.*

"For me it was. Maybe for her too. We were young and crazy and everything new seems like love." The lilt in Meghan's voice was a stark juxtaposition to the crazed look in her eyes.

Jordan studied her closely. Her grip loosened on the knife. She inched closer, her eyes never leaving Meghan's face. The silence in the room crackled around them with such intensity it threatened to suffocate them. The room had closed in and there was only her and Julie and Meghan. She sucked in a breath.

Keep her talking. "Tell me about your first date. Where did you take her?"

"A Beethoven concert. In the park." Jordan moved another inch.

"We sat there under the stars, and I saw the way the music went through her. It made her come alive."

Meghan's eyes closed, and Jordan inched closer.

"I wanted to make her feel that way."

Two inches. Jordan could almost touch her. She put her hand up to block any immediate moves, keeping her gun trained on Meghan. As if sensing the movement, Meghan's eyes flew open. Her eyes widened like an animal caught in a snare, and in one last attempt to keep her freedom, she pulled the knife away from Julie and slashed at Jordan wildly.

Jordan tried to sidestep the sharp blade, but it caught her in the arm. She howled and in her pain, dropped her gun a fraction of an inch. Meghan saw her opening and lunged towards her.

Rebecca, who had been quiet, up until now, raised her gun, watching for an opening. She needed one good shot, but Jordan was standing between them. She couldn't risk hitting Jordan. She opened her mouth to signal Jordan, needing her to move, but her breath left her.

The next seconds it seemed as though time stood still, the glint of the blade flashed in her eyes, and Jordan threw her hand up, hoping to block the majority of the blow.

The second Meghan pulled back to strike with the knife, Rebecca pulled the trigger. The sound rocketed through the room. The bullet hit with such force that it slammed Meghan into the wall behind her, the knife flying from her hand. She screamed loudly and covered the wound with her hand, blood already seeping around her fingers.

Jordan bent over her and grabbed Meghan by the arm, her gun leveled at her face. "Get up!" She hauled her to her feet roughly. Her head cocked at the sound of distant sirens. She put the gun up to Meghan's face. "Walk...now!" Her next stop was the back seat of a blue and white.

Confident that Jordan was okay, Rebecca started to pull the tape off Susan's mouth. Susan's eyes glistened with tears of pain and thankfulness. Her gaze found Julie's face. "Baby, are you alright?"

Julie stared ahead, the shock hitting her.

"Hurry up, please." Susan's eyes met Rebecca's, and she begged her to hurry. The pain was something she could forget, but she needed to get to Julie and make sure she was alright.

Rebecca freed her right hand, and before she could move to the left, Susan had already grabbed for it. She fumbled with the tape on her ankles before Susan pulled it off herself. She practically pushed Rebecca out of the way in her haste to get to her wife. She pulled Julie into her arms, cradling her against her chest. "It's okay. I've got you know. She will never hurt you again."

Rebecca watched the private moment a second longer then let them have a moment's peace. God knew, the next few days would be hell for them.

She left them and found Rick cuffing Meghan roughly. It was finally over. She met Jordan's eyes and silently asked if she were okay. Jordan nodded slightly and winked. The cut was a small price to pay. They had finally caught the Cradle Killer. Jordan stepped closer to Rebecca, feeling her warmth. Rick's voice wandered in and out of her head.

"...will be used against you in a court of law."

Chapter 26

Rebecca set her case file down and settled into the chair across from Meghan. She was handling the interrogation alone. It was the general consensus that she was the least threatening. Jordan was too close to the case, and Rick would be seen as a threat. Rebecca flicked her eyes across the table, meeting Meghan's gaze. "I just want to remind you that you do have a right to have an attorney present."

Meghan shrugged, her face cryptically nonchalant. Not the reaction that Rebecca expected from a woman who was certain to go to prison for multiple homicides.

Okay, Rebecca thought. *That's how you want to play this.* "Meghan, why don't you tell us why you killed all these women?"

Rebecca set pictures of all the victims in front of Meghan. She waited for her to react. Nothing. She didn't even blink. Rebecca narrowed her eyes. Time to play hardball. "What about Christine? Why did you want to kill her?"

Finally, a twitch. Meghan shifted in her chair. "If, and I do emphasize if, I wanted to kill her, she deserved it."

"Why did she deserve it?" Rebecca looped her hands together.

"That bitch left me." There was the twitch again. Christine was the only thing that seemed to faze Meghan. "Married for twelve years and she leaves me for a man. I gave her everything."

"Why did she leave?"

Meghan's eyes glazed over, and Rebecca knew that she was talking to the killer now. Her voice dropped to menacing low and Rebecca could see where she could have been confused for a man. "We wanted children. We tried the non-conventional methods, but nothing took. With my job, I could have done it, but she didn't want to mix our home life with my work."

Rebecca flicked her eyes to the two-way mirror where she knew the interrogation was being watched. This was the story they were looking for, and it was her job to stretch it into a confession. "That must have frustrated you. Especially knowing that you had the power to get your wife pregnant."

Meghan's eyes shifted, and Rebecca thought she lost her again, but just as quick the sneer returned. "She knew how good I was. I told her that this wouldn't fail. It was our only chance. But she wouldn't listen to me."

"How did that make you feel?" Rebecca gave the line another tug, just a little bit more, and she had her right where she wanted her.

The muscle in the side of Meghan's temple started to pulse, a steady but noticeable tempo. "Angry. I was so angry. I begged Christine to let me help. But she wouldn't. She pushed me away."

"How did you handle that?"

Silence. Meghan took several deep breaths. "I snapped."

Yes. Rebecca thought. *This is it. Come on, baby. I just need you to confess to one murder.* "Snapped how?"

"It consumed me. I had the power to fix everything, and she wouldn't let me. I went off the deep end trying to convince her. My job suffered. Everything suffered. But she kept refusing. Said that she wasn't going to allow me to foster my God complex with our child. If she did that, all that child would be in her mind was something grown in a petri dish."

"That must have hurt. Obviously, she knew you wanted children as badly as she did."

Meghan slammed her hand on the table, causing Rebecca to jump back. "It killed me. She was being unreasonable. The more

I pushed, the more she pulled away. Before she left, she could barely look at me. All those years together meant nothing."

"And she threw all that away and walked out of your marriage?" Rebecca tugged again. Ever so slightly, just enough to remind Meghan that she wouldn't get away.

Anger. Fury. Meghan's eyes flashed darkly. "She left me for a man. Some piece of shit with a dick because she wanted a baby and sleeping with him was less deplorable than just letting me do my fucking job."

Rebecca smothered a smile. She was so close. "What did you do when she left?"

Meghan calmed down slightly. She was a roller coaster of emotions, reliving the years that drove her to kill. "I tried to get her back for a while. She made it clear that it was over and there was nothing I could do or say that would change that. She eventually filed a restraining order. I turned to the only thing I could to dull the pain."

"What was that?"

"I drank. Did coke." Meghan swiped her finger across her nose subconsciously. "Started skipping work. The only thing I cared about was forgetting Christine. After a while, Dr. Stein had enough. He pulled me aside and pretty much told me if I didn't straighten up, he would have the board kick me to the curb."

And there's the reason you wanted us to focus on him. "Did you clean up after that?"

Meghan shrugged. "Enough to fool him. Stupid fuck. He couldn't fire me anyway. He needed me. I ran that place while he sat on his ass and used it to pick up women."

Bring it back to Christine. "Did you ever see Christine again after all that?"

Meghan nodded slightly. "Once. She was shopping downtown."

Her face dropped. "She was pregnant." She stated it so matter—of—fact that Rebecca almost believed that she had accepted it with nothing but stoic resignation, but she knew better. "That must have really hurt your feelings."

"I died that day."

"Was that when you started killing the other women?"

Meghan jumped. Her eyes cleared up. "Uh—uh, Detective. Did you really think I would fall for that?"

Rebecca leaned forward, her gaze locking in on Meghan's face. "Just for argument's sake, let me tell you what I think happened."

Meghan smirked, but nodded and gave her the go ahead, as if she was just listening to some funny anecdote.

"Here's what I think." Meghan pulled out the picture of the first victim. "I think you saw Christine pregnant, and you went ballistic. All these women coming into the clinic looking to you for help to get pregnant, and the one woman you wanted to help most, leaves you. The only way to get back at Christine is to take punishment out on innocent women. So you start picking women from the clinic, follow them, assault them and kill them. Every time you slice a woman's throat, it's Christine that dies."

"Interesting theory, Detective." Except for the vein in her temple pounding furiously, Meghan looked almost bored.

"But it's not enough to just kill them. You had to rape them to get back at Christine for fucking you over. But you don't stop there. You take her baby."

A ghost of a smile broke out on Meghan's face, but she said nothing.

"You robbed her of the one thing she wanted more than anything." Rebecca took the next picture out and slammed it on the table. And another one until she was done. She was angry, and she trembled. "You killed every single one of these women."

Meghan glanced at the pictures again. Still no reaction.

"Eight women and none of them was Christine." Rebecca pulled out the last photo and set it on the table silently.

Meghan's eyes dropped to Julie's photo. She picked it up wordlessly, her jaw tightening. She studied it a moment longer then flung it on the table.

Rebecca picked up the photo and showed Meghan the back where Julie's name had been written. "See that? Julie Keppler. Not Christine." She flipped it around and shoved it in Meghan's face.

Meghan flinched. No, this wasn't Julie. This was her Christine. She belonged to her, and she had left. She left and had a baby with someone else. She felt a dull pounding at her temple, and she massaged it with her fingers. *You let her get away.* Just like that, the voice was back, taunting her for her failure. "Shut up!"

She spoke not so much to Rebecca, but to the voice that never went away. Never let her have a moment's peace. She wanted it gone. "Get out of my head!"

Rebecca tensed. An odd transformation was happening. Meghan was fighting with something or someone. She watched the change and almost flinched at the look of pure hatred that flashed in Meghan's eyes. Realization slowly dawned on her. This was the Meghan that had committed the murders. "Meghan? Are you still with me?"

Evil glinted in Meghan's eyes. "Of course I am, you fucking bitch." She said it with as even a tone as someone talking about the weather, but the look in her eyes sent chills down Rebecca's spine. "Do you know why you're here?"

"Of course I do." A sneer. She picked up Julie's picture. Meghan rubbed the tip of her finger over Julie's mouth. "Sweet Christine. This is all your fault. You made me do it."

"What's all Christine's fault?" Rebecca asked quickly. She needed to get her to confess. She could deal with the details of insanity later.

"She left me and she had to die." Meghan stated angrily.

"Why all of them, Meghan?" Rebecca slid the photos closer, hoping to trigger another burst of anger.

An evil smirk broke out on Meghan's face. This time she looked at the photos with a sneer of satisfaction. "Every one of them wanted something she couldn't have. Just like every other woman in the world. All these stupid bitches begged me to play

God for them. Every single one of them wanted to be pregnant. I had to look at their faces when they told me how much they wanted a child and how grateful they were that I could give it to them. All of them had what should have been mine."

"What should have been yours, Meghan?"

"The baby. Every single baby should have been mine. That should have been Christine there, but I wasn't good enough."

"Is that why you took the babies?"

"I gave them that life."

Meghan stated it without ire, and Rebecca wondered if she had lost contact with the crazy Meghan. "So the baby was yours to do with as you pleased?"

"Yes, you stupid cunt." Meghan sneered.

"So, because Christine couldn't let you play God, you had to punish all of them?"

"You're so smart Detective. You've got this whole thing worked out, don't you?"

Rebecca shrugged nonchalantly. "Maybe. Some of the details are a bit foggy."

Meghan toyed with the edge of Julie's photo. "Oh, I think you've got it all figured out."

Rebecca held her gaze. "Tell me why you tried to frame Richard Hudson?"

Meghan chuckled evilly. "He was perfect."

"What do you mean?"

"Surely, you know that Richard's first wife was murdered, and the case is still unsolved."

Rebecca's brow furrowed. "How do you know about that?"

"Detective Foxx." Meghan said condescendingly. "As I told you before, the clinic offers mandatory counseling for all its clients. Richard's sessions proved very enlightening. His colored past made it all too easy to frame him."

"So, you took his loss and punished him for it?"

"Richard Hudson was a bastard. I did the world a favor by taking him out of the picture."

"And were you doing Elizabeth a favor by killing her and taking her baby?"

Meghan waggled her finger at Rebecca. "Tsk, tsk Detective." The word Detective dripped with disdain. "What the world didn't need was his spawn."

"And that was your choice to make?"

Meghan slammed her fist down. "Of course it was my choice. I'm the only reason she was pregnant in the first place."

"How did you kill them?"

Meghan studied her for a second, measuring her up. "The case files tell you all of that, I'm sure."

"Yes, they do." Rebecca nodded. "But as I said before, we weren't quite sure of some of the details."

"It was quite easy actually." Meghan studied her fingernails. "Women are so trusting these days. They don't sense danger. It made killing them rather simple."

"And raping them and leaving DNA at the scene? Kind of hard for a woman?"

"Not really." Meghan smug smile returned. "You're a lesbian, Detective. I'm sure you know that there are tools out there. A strap—on and a condom full of semen. It's not that hard to figure out."

"And taking the baby? How about that, Meghan? Was that easy too?" Rebecca's tone bordered on contempt.

Meghan's eyes softened slightly. The only sign that she cared about life at all. "They were my children. I was saving them, Detective. Can't you see that?"

"I don't understand."

"I couldn't let them grow up in a world where love and vows mean nothing. I couldn't let them be in a world where people like Christine could steal everything from them."

Rebecca's stomach turned. Meghan honestly believed she had done some magnanimous turn by killing them all. She swallowed as Meghan looked on expectantly. It was almost as though she took joy in what she had done.

Rebecca clasped her hands on the table. "What about Phillip Stein? Why him?"

Meghan looked at her askance. "Detective, everyone knows the perfect murder is the one you commit without being caught."

"So, you steered us to him?"

"Giving you Phillip was as easy as leading a pig to the slaughter. You had already fucked up and caught the wrong guy once. You needed to break the case. All I needed to do was put the suggestion out there and you would find a way to fit the pieces into the puzzle." The ghost of a smile formed in the corner of Meghan's mouth. Her eyes looked almost triumphant.

Another wave of nausea. "Nine people are dead because of you. Doesn't that bother you?"

Meghan sneered again. "They all died because of Christine. She still needs to die." She leaned forward, put her finger on Julie's picture and slid it in front of Rebecca. Their eyes locked. "She will die too."

Rebecca felt a cold chill slide down her spine. "No one else will die. I promise you this. You will rot in jail."

"Ahh, Detective." Meghan smiled eerily. "As I said before, that's the thing about the perfect murder…not getting caught. You have nothing on me. No way to tie me to any of them. At the most, you have assault and battery on a federal agent. But as you already know…" She rolled her finger in a circle near her temple. "…I'm crazy. I'll do a little time in a cozy institution somewhere for a year or so."

This time it was Rebecca's turn to smirk. "The funny thing about evidence is you never know where it will pop up." She looked over her shoulder and nodded.

The smile disappeared from Meghan's face as the door opened and two officers deposited several bags of evidence on the table containing items that she immediately recognized.

Rebecca picked up a bag containing specimen cups. Meghan's face blanched. "They've already been tested. Richard Hudson and Phillip Stein."

Meghan swallowed. "Where did you get that?"

Rebecca picked up the next item. "I'm pretty sure that if we test the epithelial cells found on this strap—on with yours, they will be a match."

"All that proves is I'm into penetration." Meghan crossed her arms defensively.

Rebecca pulled the case folder out that the officers had just dropped off. She pulled several pictures of perfectly preserved fetuses out and lined them up in front of Meghan, who jerked away quickly. She cocked her head. "How am I doing so far?"

"You've got nothing, Detective." Meghan said stoically, but her disdainful hubris was gone. "None of this ties me to the murders."

Rebecca leaned back and smiled cryptically. "The funny thing about the perfect murder is there is no perfect murder. You made a mistake. You thought you had committed the perfect murder. That's the problem with thinking you're smarter than everyone else."

There was a flash of panic in Meghan's eyes before it was replaced with cold fury. "You're just trying to trip me up."

"Not necessary." Rebecca leaned forward. "You did that on your own."

Meghan eyed her skeptically. "How so?"

"It's funny how people will talk, isn't it?" Rebecca smiled condescendingly. "You thought you had everything sewn up perfectly. Frame the perfect person. Leave behind nothing that really ties you to the case. This was all found at the clinic. It would be easy to fit it to Phillip Stein, just like you wanted. You figured it would be enough to convict someone else."

"You're fishing." Meghan said flatly.

"Am I?" Rebecca countered with barely veiled civility. This was the moment she had been working up to. The coup de grace. The finishing stroke. "What you didn't figure into the equation was human emotion."

Meghan stared at her blankly.

"You see when you got Phillip Stein fired, you took away Ruth Dawson's chance to get pregnant. She was perfectly happy to start talking once we asked the right questions."

Meghan blanched. She couldn't have known about that, could she? *Stupid cunt!*

As if on cue, the door to the interrogation room opened with an ominous creak. This time it was Jordan, who came into the room carrying a manila folder. "Here you go."

The air in the room crackled around them. Jordan handed the folder to Rebecca, nodded at her and shot Meghan a murderous look.

Meghan saw the smug look of satisfaction of Rebecca's face, and her breath caught. She knew what the folder contained. She was now the hunted. She was the prey. She balled her hands at her side angrily. "I want my lawyer."

"Believe me, you're going to need more than that." Rebecca shot her a cold smile, the feeling of having finally caught the killer filling her with a sense of pride. To drive the nail further into the coffin, Rebecca pulled a specimen bag out and smiled smugly. "You got too cocky, Meghan. Your last victim fought back. The scratches on your face, we know how you got them, and I'm pretty sure the cells found under the victim's fingernails are going to point to you."

Meghan shifted and touched the raw skin subconsciously. She could no longer hide the fear. Her world was unraveling right before her eyes and the stupid bitch in front of her was the reason.

Rebecca opened the folder and pulled out six pictures. She slid them across the table silently. Pictures of every victim besides Julie stared back at Meghan. She began to rock back and forth, the instinct to flee overwhelming. "I'm not saying anything else."

"You don't have to." Rebecca stood up. "I'm sure that the jury will just love the fact that you took pictures of your victims, and that each one of those pictures was found in a hidden access panel that only your fingerprint would open. And as far as your crazy plea goes, I hope you do a much better job acting for the jury."

Meghan stared back at her, unmasked fury in her eyes. "You won't get away with this. I'm coming after you too." Meghan shoved her chair back and lunged at Rebecca. No sooner than she jumped, her face was slammed into the table, and her arms were twisted behind her.

Rebecca leaned over the table almost in Meghan's face and sneered. "No, my dear…" Rebecca said softly. "I've already gotten away with it."

She watched them drag Meghan from the room then slumped against the wall. It was over.

Chapter 27

Rebecca grabbed Jordan's coat and held it out for her to step into. "Here."

"I can do it myself." Jordan shrugged herself into the arms and winced when it hit her wounded arm. The cut from Meghan's knife was healing slowly, but the muscle still ached at even the lightest contact.

"Are you always going to be this stubborn?" Rebecca pulled Jordan's coat around her and kissed her softly. "'Cause last time I checked, you are my girlfriend, and we help each other with stuff like that."

Jordan smiled ruefully. "I'm learning slowly. I'm a work in progress, remember?"

Rebecca stood on her tiptoes and wrapped her arms around Jordan's neck, pressing her lips tightly against hers. She pulled away and murmured against her lips. "Yes, I know. I figure I might as well stick around long enough to see how you turn out."

Jordan chuckled throatily, her eyes dancing mischievously. "I like the sound of that. You sticking around I mean. Maybe I'll just slow down my progress and keep you around a bit longer."

Rebecca reached down and smacked her bottom playfully. "You are incorrigible."

"That's why you love me." Jordan teased and pulled Rebecca into her for a long kiss. She felt the heat in her neck rise and a pull in her loins. Begrudgingly, she broke the kiss, but not before it left them both breathless. "We should get going."

Rebecca swallowed. "Umm, yeah. I'm thinking that is a good idea." She followed Jordan to the front door, grabbing her purse on the way. "Taking your car?"

"Only if you drive." Four months ago, Jordan would never have dreamed of saying that. Her 370Z was her baby, but she was still nursing a wounded arm and driving a stick was cumbersome if not painful.

Rebecca smiled. "Deal." She had never been a car person, but driving Jordan's 370Z was like sex with a lover. The hum of the engine underneath you, fingers skillfully coaxing it to higher levels of pleasure. The feel of pure adrenaline when you relax and let go.

The ride to the courthouse was quiet. It couldn't be helped. Meghan Mercer would stand trial today for the cold—blooded murders of nine people. Neither woman had a doubt that she would go away for a very long time, but the case had been too close to home for both of them and reliving it was going to be hell.

Rebecca slid the car into a spot and turned the car off. She turned to Jordan. "You ready?"

"More than." Jordan unconsciously rubbed her arm.

They weaved their way through a throng of media, dodging questions the entire way with firm "no comments" thrown to random faces. The doors shut behind them, and Rebecca breathed a sigh of relief. "God, I'm ready for this to be over. The press was ready to vilify us for messing up. Now we are the heroes. I just want this done, so we can move on with our lives."

Jordan squeezed her hand reassuringly and pushed the door to the courtroom open. They sat down behind the prosecutor's table. The room was oddly empty. The judge had ordered a closed trial, and the room was devoid of the normal volume of media and spectators.

The bailiff led Meghan in minutes later. She was dressed in orange scrubs that categorized her as a maximum-security prisoner. The letters D.O.C. emblazoned the front of her v—neck shirt. Her hands and feet were cuffed and chained together. The chain rattled quietly as she shuffled past them. Her gaze flicked to Rebecca, and her steps paused. She sneered menacingly and licked her lips as if she were an animal tasting the blood of her prey after the kill.

Rebecca shivered. Not from fear, but from the cold chill of pure evil. She felt Jordan's strong hand on hers, and she could breathe again.

Meghan pulled her eyes from Rebecca with a smirk. She slid into an empty seat next to her attorney, her face now devoid of any expression.

The judge entered from his chambers, and the bailiff's voice broke through the quiet. "All rise for the Honorable Judge Maddux."

The next few moments were a blur. Rebecca saw a lot of things in her time as a Detective. Things she never wanted to see again. She wanted to close her eyes and take them out of here. She wanted not to relive the horrors she still saw every night. She glanced sideways and saw Jordan's jaw clenched. She was her strength. Jordan was the person that made everything all right again.

For a second, it was just the two of them once more, and Rebecca knew no matter what happened during the trial, no matter what she would face in the future, she could face all of that with Jordan by her side. She squeezed her hand once again and when she looked forward, it wasn't the courtroom she saw anymore. It was her life. Her future. Her forever with the woman she loved.

Syd Parker was born in California and resides in Indiana. She loves golfing, biking and spoiling her ten nieces and nephews. She loves to travel and anywhere on the water feels like home. She spends her days toiling away at her day job until she figures out a way to drop the last fifteen strokes to make it on the LPGA tour, although she's totally mastered Tiger Woods Golf on the Wii.

Most days when she's not writing, you will find her on the trails or riding her road bike and praying she doesn't end up in another ditch.

She loves to read a good love story and thoroughly enjoys writing them as well. "It isn't just about writing a story, it's about creating a world and having the reader climb into it, experiencing it in first person. That's my goal...that's why I write."

Check out Syd Parker and Syd Parker Books on Facebook, or online at www.sydparkerbooks.com.

Other titles by Syd Parker:

Immediate Possession - Regan Sloan has had her share of bad luck in her relationships. She isn't sure she is even willing to give it another shot. But all bets are off when she "runs into" Darcy Grey. Darcy leaves more than just an impression. She gets inside Regan like no other woman has. That should have been just fine with Regan…except Darcy isn't exactly single and she isn't exactly a lesbian. Can the two women get past the hurdles and accept their love is bigger than the hurdles they face.

Secrets of the Heart – When Chase Berkley learns that her best friend was killed, she decides to finally visit the B & B they co-owned. At the funeral she finds out that Avery was carrying a huge secret that she is left to deal with. Avery's attorney, Jude Stafford, doesn't plan on making her stay any easier. As a matter of fact, Chase quickly learns, her life is about to get turned upside down…again.

Love's Abiding Spirit – Soren Lockhart knows heartbreak. Unable to get past her wife leaving and taking their daughter, she runs away so she doesn't have to face the pain. She buys a rundown house and hires contractor Merritt Tanner to do the renovations, unaware that they are waking up a ghost who is intent on telling her love story and pushing Soren toward the love of her life.

Just Tonight – At forty-five, Adrienne Thomas thought she was done being a mom, but when her son and daughter-in-law die and she inherits her granddaughter, and her partner of fifteen years subsequently leaves, she feels like she is right back at the beginning. Putting the heartache behind, she moves back home to collect herself. Nothing she experienced before could have prepared her for Dylan Montgomery, a loner who makes Adrienne's blood boil. Can Adrienne figure out a way to be a mother again and win Dylan's heart?

Twist of Fate – Storm chaser Remy Tate doesn't mess around when it comes to storms or women. She knows what she wants and goes after it. A chance encounter with fellow chaser, Sarah Phillips, has lingered in her mind for years and when they run into each other again, she puts everything on the line to prove to Sarah that she is interested in more than just a one night stand.

Printed in Great Britain
by Amazon.co.uk, Ltd.,
Marston Gate.